Trade winds to Meluhha

Novel set in Ancient Mesopotamia & Indus Valley

VASANT DAVÉ

ISBN-13: 978-81-922506-4-9

DEDICATION

To my father Purushottam Magan Davé
who - when he was just out of the teens -
sailed over 3,300 Kilometres on the high sea,
seeking destiny like the hero of this narrative.

CONTENTS

	ACKNOWLEDGMENTS	i
	PREFACE	iii
	MAP OF SAMASIN'S VOYAGE	iv
	CAST OF CHARACTERS	v
1	KING SHULGI'S REWARD	1
2	SAM'S TRIAL	7
3	'CELESTIAL IRE' ON BABILI	18
4	ON THE RUN	28
5	STOWAWAY	34
6	VELLI'S DILEMMA	41
7	GIRL FROM SUTANTORU	48
8	DRUNKEN SAM DROPS HINT	55
9	QUEST IN LOTHAL	64
10	VISITOR FOR SIWA	69
11	DACOITS OF NAL FOREST	74
12	SIGNS OF TROUBLE	79
13	MAD KUTTI'S CODE	85
14	'*HARSAG ZALAZALAG*'	91
15	DEMON OF GANGEVELL	101
16	SUMÉRIAN WOMAN IN MELUHHA	108

17	NIGHTMARE IN MUENDURU CEMETERY	116
18	MYSTERY OF THE FISH-HOOK	123
19	VELLI GETS WILD	130
20	OUTRAGEOUS PROPOSAL	135
21	BONDAGE OF DESIRE	142
22	ATTACK ON SIWA	151
23	EVENTS FALL INTO PLACE	165
24	PLOT ON THE SHIP	171
25	ABDUCTION IN URIM	177
26	DIAMOND FOR KING GUDEA	184
27	VELLI CALLS ON THE FOX	188
28	SMALLER CROCODILE GETS HIS DUE	195
29	KING SHULGI'S LAW AND THE FOX	203
30	THE FINALE	214
	Place names in the narrative	220
	Glossary of Sumérian & Tamil words	222
	About the Author	223

ACKNOWLEDGMENTS

I would like to thank the following for their help:

Dr. Shereen Ratnagar who offered valuable comments on veracity and plausibility of the past situation as constructed in the novel;
Website Harappa dot com which facilitated discussing various points with experts on Indus Valley Civilization;
Dr. Michael C. Anderson who addressed queries about Mesopotamia;
Darryl Bordeleau, Cynthia Sally Haggard, Dr. Mahendra J. Davé, Nilesh Oak, Sujata Shukla, Chris Ward and Jenny Kruschke who read the manuscript and offered helpful suggestions;
Ms. H. C. Davies, A. Bullock and Bhailal C. Patel, my school teachers in Mombasa-Kenya during 1962-66, who taught me English;
My family members – Bharti, Swati, Sachin and Nitasha – who encouraged me to pursue my dream of writing a novel.

PREFACE

Inspired by Thor Heyerdahl's expedition in a reed ship across the Persian Gulf and the Arabian Sea, *Trade winds to Meluhha* narrates one man's dogged pursuit to end an evil trade wrecking many a young Mesopotamian's life.

Trade winds to Meluhha is set in Mesopotamia and Indus Valley civilizations of the Bronze Age. The story starts in the year 2138 B.C., the year in which two unique astronomical events happened in Babylon as recorded in clay tablets discovered at the archaeological site there.

We possess good knowledge about Mesopotamia from thousands of such excavated tablets, and the success achieved in deciphering the Cuneiform script etched on them. On the other hand, artefacts carrying Indus Valley script are miniscule in number and therefore its decipherment is still a matter of conjecture.

As a result, contradictory viewpoints prevail on the location of the land which the Mesopotamians called 'Meluhha', the sudden disappearance of Indus Valley culture, the language in use there, its relation to ancient Hindu literature and the existence of river Saraswati and that of the horses. I have selected one of the possibilities in each case and moved on to create the plot. Some of my assumptions could be wrong. As far as possible I have followed archaeological evidence to recreate the life in the two ancient civilizations.

I have taken literary liberty on two aspects. The laws which I have cited are from the later period of Hammurabi and not of Shulgi, who reigned over Babylon during the period considered in the novel. Shulgi's Code of Ur-Nammu, the earliest legal text in existence, instituted non-violent punishment for physical harm and did not suite me as a writer of fiction. For the same reason, although my suggestion about the possibility of human trafficking was dismissed by all three experts who I consulted, I have included it in the narrative.

I hope you enjoy reading it.

Vasant Davé

SAMASIN'S VOYAGE

2138-37 BC

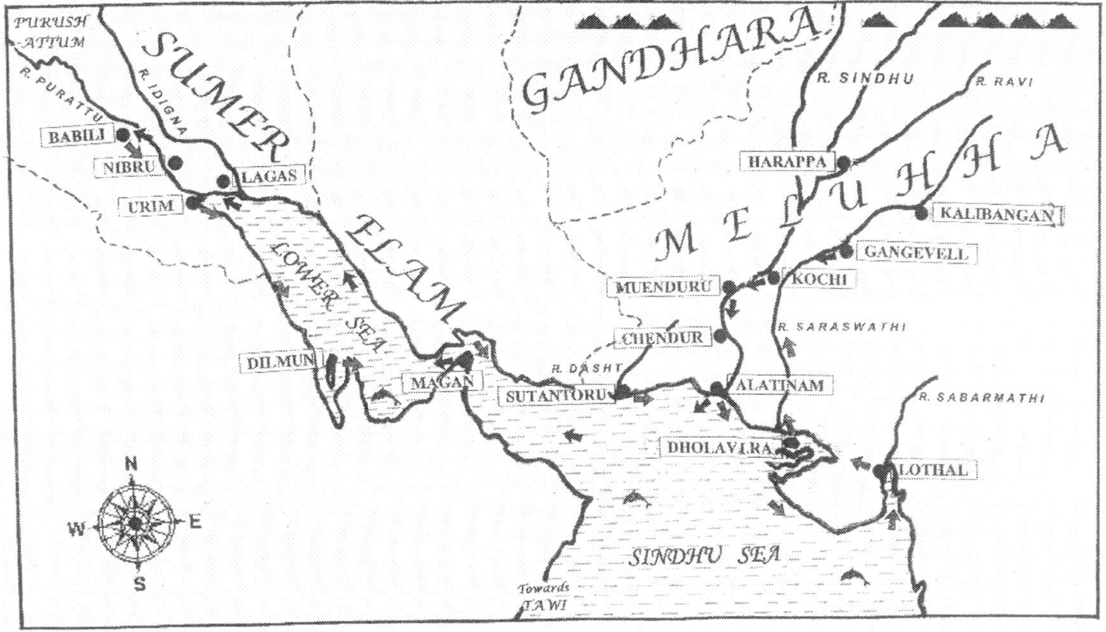

CAST OF CHARACTERS

ANLIL alias Ann – Sumérian woman in Meluhha

ELLA – Single woman in Babili

JITTAN – Meluhhan villain

KAYL – Meluhhan visiting Babili

MURUKU – Siwa's son aged seven

NERGAL (the Fox) – Rich and powerful Babilian, and Ella's ex-husband

PARAVAR – Owner of Meluhhan ship

QWOCO – Sailor on Captain Paravar's ship

RIBBA – Ella's son aged nine

SAMASIN alias Sam – Babilian youth

SIWA SAQRA – Merchant of Meluhha. This character evolved from the figurine of a bearded man named 'Priest King', discovered on the Indus Valley site of Mohenjo-daro.

VELLI – Siwa's daughter. Female protagonist whose character evolved from a bronze artefact named 'Dancing Girl', discovered at Mohenjo-daro. With her head held high and an arm akimbo, the exhibit represented to me the liberated women of the Bronze Age.

YALI – Skipper of small crafts

ZIBIGI alias Biggie – Sumérian villain

1 KING SHULGI'S REWARD

Stable boy Samasin hurried out of his master's mansion in Babili. As he ran up the gentle slope, a dark lean foreigner in blue headgear crossed the road as if to accost him. He reminded Samasin of an elephant trainer from Meluhha working in the palace ground. A black purse swaying from the man's shoulder wobbled his brisk walk, but his cheeks blew in and out. 'Probably whistling one of those horrible Meluhhan tunes,' thought Samasin. The man's wrinkled face broke into a smile and his lips parted.

It occurred to Samasin that he was already late for the King's work. He quickened his pace and passed by the Meluhhan as if the man did not exist. Behind him he heard a gasp of utter surprise.

Soon the two neat queues of date palms gave way to a denser growth of olive trees. The air became cooler, and sweet calls of Meluhhan birds called peacocks told him he had reached the palace ground. From afar he saw the Priest-physician of Babili awaiting him, doubtless carrying that frown which always unnerved him.

Drawing near, he saw the Priest-physician smiling, and let out a deep breath.

"You won't be treating any animal today, Sam," said the old man fishing out a slim package from a cotton bag by his side. "King Shulgi appreciates your year-long service at the Palace, and has asked me to reward you."

Sam beamed, and held out both his palms. "It's the first time, *Belum*, that a person other than my foster parents has appreciated my hard work."

"Your master?"

"Not even Master Nergal." Sam laughed, but there was a hint of choking in his throat. He dug his teeth into the jute string binding the gift package.

The Priest-physician smiled. "Have patience, young man. Open it at home."

Sam knelt, took his mentor's right hand in both of his own, and kissed it. While he was returning, he reasoned that immediate celebration of King Shulgi's reward seemed in order. Just as he was nearing Master Nergal's mansion, his feet took to a narrow path running down from the main road.

It led him to a tavern which sat hidden from the prying eyes of passers-by. "You know how drunkards behave," its heavy-eyed owner had once told him. "I can't risk exposing their vice to the ladies going to the Palace." Sam had always suspected whether that was the real reason.

Even as he entered the tavern, he could hear the chirping of sparrows. It sounded pleasantly different from the evenings when men crowded there after work. Then it used to get so noisy that once he had missed King Shulgi's annual procession to the Temple of Marduk, despite all its drum beats and fanfare.

Sam pushed forth a piece of copper, and the keeper heaved a yawn before moving to one of the large jars behind him. An image of a gaping hippopotamus in the palace pool flashed in Sam's mind, and he chuckled.

Stepping over several tree trunks to reach his favourite spot, his attention was drawn by a man sitting in the shadows, slouching like a wounded leopard. Sam recognized his blue turban. It was the jolly old Meluhhan he had avoided on the way to the palace ground. The man sat motionless as if frozen in snow.

The Meluhhan threw a fleeting glance at Sam and resumed staring at his hand which seemed to be holding a tiny object. Although Sam could not see the man's face clearly, he could well imagine it carrying several furrows on the brow. What had ruined the Meluhhan's mood that even his apparently precious black purse had dropped to the ground?

Sam shrugged his shoulders and sat down. Letting the cool drink fizz around his tongue, he studied the package that the Priest-physician had presented to him. Was it necessary to open it only in the small hut that he shared with his master's cart man? Half way through the second flask, Sam assured himself that it would not do any harm if he slit the package slightly and had had a peek inside.

As he tore a loose joint in it, his finger ran over several smooth grooves. Before Sam realized it, he had unravelled the King's gift. His eyes lit up when he beheld a carved ivory handle in which was ensconced a chiselled flint blade about two palms long. He had always considered his agile physique incomplete without a weapon. He had wanted one for a long time and now he possessed it.

So engrossed was Sam in studying the dagger that he almost jumped up from the log seat when he heard a snort overhead. "That isn't a safe toy you got there, boy," said a voice, and the dagger was yanked out of his hands.

Sam jerked up in anger and saw a small head atop a bulky torso, glowering down at him. On it, stuck a nose which seemed moulded in clay by a child. It occurred to him that probably it had been distorted during a skirmish in the past. He jumped to his feet and his muscles tensed as he considered smashing the queer nose into pulp.

His own dagger pointed at his neck. Behind the villain's back, he spotted the tavern owner springing to life and disappearing behind the large jars of beer. Sam lowered his eyes and sank down in his seat.

The villain with the crooked nose sniggered, and sauntered away towards the Meluhhan. "Hey, you black raisin," he said. "Where's the owner of this place?"

The Meluhhan's brow eased, and his pursed lips relaxed as he rose from his seat and surveyed the villain from head to foot. The villain poked two thick fingers under the old man's chin. "Did I crack a joke?"

The Meluhhan's scrawny face turned serious again, and appeared fumbling for words. The villain jabbed at his turban. The Meluhhan's hand shot up to keep it from falling off. The villain seemed to interpret that mild reflex as an affront. "You want to fight, do you?" he asked, raising Sam's dagger.

To his horror, Sam saw the flint dagger flashing into the Meluhhan's frail chest. A terrifying shriek pierced through the tavern and echoed outside into the date-palm grove. The villain with the crooked nose bent to lift the Meluhhan's black leather purse, and ran out of the tavern.

Sam saw the Meluhhan pressing his chest with both the hands, and tottering. Instinct whispered to him to leave the scene quickly. The goblet of beer slipped from his hand and he leapt over several log seats to reach the entrance. His long hair flowed down his face, tripping him a couple of times. A hammering sound, closely followed by a gasp, made him look behind.

The old Meluhhan's head had hit a log seat and his turban was rolling on the ground. His eyeballs had bulged and his body was shaking as if possessed by an evil spirit. Blood gushing out from his wound had started forming a red puddle on the floor.

It reminded Sam of a horrid scene which was etched in his memory since childhood. He had often wished that somebody had come to his family's aid on that fateful morning in Magan.

The thought made him turn back. Crying for help, he bounded to the distressed foreigner. He looked around frantically but could not see the tavern owner anywhere. Unsure of what to do, he sat down on the floor, and gently drew the stranger's head in his lap.

His left hand pressed the old man's chest around the dagger, and his right clutched the ivory handle to pull it out lightly. Hearing a scream of intense pain, his hand recoiled. He was in two minds. Could he allow the man's chance of survival to reduce by letting the dagger remain in his body? Or was the wound so deep that the old man could not be saved, and it would be inhuman to add to his agony?

Sam took the old Meluhhan's trembling hands into his own. They were cold. The bleeding man pleaded with his eyes. Sam felt a sharp prick his palm, and heard a whisper, "Give Hiwa Haqra."

Sam's eyes filled with tears. A question arose in his mind, "Where?" Instead of asking it, he just nodded. The old man's chest heaved like a pair of bellows as he laboured to continue: "Tell *'Amma nacciyar aru perum ha…hara…'*"

A gargling sound emanated from his throat and he vomited blood. Then he convulsed and slumped lifeless in Sam's lap.

Sam stared at the weapon buried in the dead man's chest. It was his dagger. He wished he had followed the wise Priest-physician's advice. From deep within his heart arose a queer pressure and it burst out into a loud wail. Unable to move away his eyes from the corpse, he kept shaking his head and moaning.

A sparkle from an object that looked like a bird's nest caught his eye in the shady light. Wiping away the tears, he looked intently. It was the Meluhhan's blue turban lying upturned. Tucked inside was an exquisite gold necklace carrying precious stone beads of red, blue and green hues.

Just then, Sam became aware of a long and broad shadow sliding towards him. His sobs turned to sniffles, and he raised his face. A huge man, possessing eyes which could as well have been a pair of cowries, stood gawking at him. Sam thanked Marduk, the patron deity of Babili, that at last He had sent some help. No longer was he alone dealing with a difficult situation. A trace of a smile appeared on his countenance.

The newcomer shifted his gaze to where Sam had been looking. He smirked, exposing uneven teeth, and in one swoop picked up the necklace.

"Put it back," Sam said in a tone not much different from that of a parent speaking to a child. "It could help the guards find who this person was."

"That's very thoughtful, isn't it?" said the thief in a gruff voice, tilting to reach deep inside his robe. In his hand, Sam made out a brownish object shaped like a bird. The thief raised it to his lips and a shrill whistle cut through the afternoon air.

"Put back the necklace," Sam snapped.

"What necklace?"

Sam was aghast. A deep mark across the thief's left cheek made him think that perhaps the man's pursuit wasn't any different from that of the murderer. So here was someone, who he had hoped would be helpful, further complicating the matter. Sam decided he would not allow that.

He gently laid the dead man's head on the ground. Springing to his feet, he took a deep breath and swung a left punch at the thief's nose. It landed slightly below with a thud. Sam howled and his hand started flipping like a fish out of water.

For a moment, the thief stood dazed. Then dropping a string of curses, he charged. A flurry of blows churned the musty air and Sam managed to land a right punch on the villain's mouth.

He heard a clamour and was glad that a crowd had arrived. Some men ran to hold him and he expected some others to pull away the thief too. Instead, they targeted Sam in unison. Had it not been for the innumerable animal bites and kicks that he had suffered during apprenticeship, he would have dropped unconscious by the time a couple of guards ran into the tavern.

"The killer escaped that way," Sam spoke, gasping for breath, to the one who he assumed to be senior of the two, "he had a jagged nose."

The man carried a bushy moustache and an unruly beard, and despite the prominent amulet around his neck which announced him as Head Guard of the Prison, he looked more like the two villains whom Sam had met that afternoon. Sam pointed at the thief. "The big bear over there has stolen the dead man's necklace."

"*Mulla Xul*! Dhat – dhat boy is lying," cried the thief spitting red, two of his front teeth now knocked out and hanging on by a thread of nerve. He seemed to be alarmed by the sudden distortion in his speech as he tried to elaborate. "Dhat – dhat I lifted a necklace isn't true."

Sam could not hold back a chuckle. The guards frisked the thief, and Sam could hardly believe what they found. There were only a few pieces of copper and silver. The thief thrust out his chest and pounded it. Pointing to Sam, he said, "I saw him murdering dhat poor old foreigner. Now he wants to hush me somehow."

The Head Guard narrowed his eyes.

"I was – I was only trying to help the victim," Sam said raising a hand to his heart. "The real murderer has vanished with the Meluhhan's black leather purse."

"Another story," the thief commented, sitting down on a nearby log seat.

The guards looked at each other and the senior jerked his head towards Sam. The other promptly unravelled a piece of rope from his waist and proceeded to tie Sam's wrists together. Sam continued pleading, and received a couple of whacks behind his head. Then he was shoved out of the tavern on the way to jail.

In spite of the alarming turn of events against him, Sam was reassured by the thought that the two most powerful men in Babili – after the King and the Council of Elders – would get to know the facts from him, and then vouch for his innocence. They were Master Nergal and the Priest-physician.

2 SAM'S TRIAL

Sam tossed and turned all night, not because the stone floor was uneven and cold, but because he was eager to prove his innocence in the morning. He jumped up the moment the Head Guard, unchaining his leg, said, "Get ready, boy, to answer the seven wise men of Babili."

He ran to a small, moss covered tank carved in stone. As he stooped to wash his face, he saw his reflection in the water. His left eye was swollen beyond recognition, and there was a dark circle around it. Although it pained, he had not considered the injury to be so severe. Quickly he splashed water on his face. With wet hands, he rubbed his limbs, carefully avoiding several bruises.

Below the waist, Sam's clothes were soiled and stiffened by the poor Meluhhan's blood that had turned black. He went to the Head Guard, trying to wave away flies which persistently swarmed around him. "Could you please give me a pair of fresh clothes?"

Without even looking at him, the man spoke just one word. "Why?"

Blood rushed to Sam's head, and his fists clenched tight. With a great effort, he controlled himself.

The Head Guard bound his hands behind his back and led him after two guards wielding staffs. Glancing behind, Sam saw two more following them. They emerged on the main road which sliced Babili in two halves, with the King's Palace on one end and the Temple of Marduk on the other.

Sam was taken aback at the sight of crowds teeming on both

sides of the road. Servants and labourers, farmers carrying hoes, shepherds with their goats, woodcutters brandishing axes, milkmaids with small vessels balanced precariously on head; it seemed that everybody had forgotten their pursuit just to get his glimpse. Devoid of either expression or voice, they watched him in awe as if he were one of those outlandish animals that he treated regularly on the palace ground.

Among the bystanders, Sam spotted several friends – men and women serving either Master Nergal or the Master's divorced wife Lady Ella – and he smiled at them. Had he been permitted to speak, he would have assured his friends that he would be a free man as soon as the Council of Elders realized that he had been framed by a petty thief. However, it peeved him that none of them, except the young cart man, responded. Only his gangly friend seemed not to be embarrassed at being associated with a person accused of murder.

Had they not known him for several years? Did they believe that he was a murderer? Sam hated them, everybody except the cart man. In that melancholy mood, his foot hit a stone and he stumbled. A strong hand gripped his arm. He turned to thank the Head Guard, but seeing the man's chastising expression, he held back.

At the cross-roads, they turned right and Sam was relieved to see a huge building with its four sides tapering upwards to meet at its apex. He had gathered in his early days as a camel boy, that there was a similar, but much bigger and more ancient structure named the Ziggurat of Giza in a country called Tawi. Its sides were plain, and not stepped as the Ziggurat of Babili. The one they had reached was the place from where all King Shulgi's learned men functioned.

They started climbing the steps of the Ziggurat and he heard murmurs from the crowd getting louder. Looking behind, he was astounded to see just about everybody on the street following them.

They entered the spacious Council hall on the first floor, and walked through an aisle, on both sides of which were long narrow wooden seats. The noise intensified as people streamed in, and it echoed around the hall. Sam wondered whether all those seats could accommodate the crowd that had followed them. The guards led him right to the other end of the hall where he saw a platform.

On it, he counted seven seats arranged neatly in half a circle. The Head Guard signalled to him to enter a waist high bamboo enclosure that faced the platform.

For a moment, Sam's attention was drawn to the crowd which elbowed, pushed and quarrelled to occupy the front seats. Despite many more guards in the Council hall, utter chaos prevailed till the Head Guard climbed the platform and pointed out several noisy men. As the guards got hold of the culprits and pushed them towards the exit, calm gradually crept into the atmosphere. Then suddenly it turned into silence like that of the Temple of Marduk just before the prayers.

Seven elderly men, bent and bald, climbed up the steps of the platform with great effort. The one leading them possessed a round, clean shaven face on which neither cheek bones nor a chin was visible, projecting a strikingly boyish face. Sam recognized Chief Bel, father-in-law of Master Nergal till his divorce from Lady Ella.

Had the Master too arrived in the Council hall? As Sam scanned the public, his face paled. Master Nergal, who he had hoped would vouch for his good conduct, was not seen anywhere. However, the imposing presence of Lady Ella, was evident although she had been the only silent person among a group of chattering women. Sam's eyes met hers. Flicker of a smile appeared on his face, but she looked away.

The Head Guard gave a detailed account of what he had seen in the tavern. He walked to Bel and handed him Sam's dagger, its blade stained dark with clotted blood. "Chief, this is the weapon of murder."

A collective sigh went up in the air.

The Head Guard proceeded to give two knotted handkerchiefs, one looking fleshier than the other. "We found only these two articles on the victim's body."

"Chief," said Sam, waving frantically. The guard standing nearby pulled at his wrist. The Head Guard glared at him.

Bel looked up from the contents of the two handkerchiefs that he was examining. His face did not convey any irritation for Sam's lapse. "You will get enough time to put your case, boy," he said.

One handkerchief contained some pieces of silver, and Bel put it aside. Upon unravelling the other, he turned to a bony man on his right who habitually carried a scowl. "These three identical objects look like –"

He was cut short by Sam's voice. "Excuse me, Chief."

Annoyance clouded Bel's face. "Yes?"

"I'm aware that it's insulting to appear before your Council in as shabby a state as mine. But even before you have heard me, one of the King's men," Sam said, pointing at the Head Guard who turned ashen, "has started treating me like a murderer."

Just as Bel opened his mouth, the Head Guard butted in, "I'll immediately get him clean clothes, Chief." He waved feverishly to four of the nearest guards who virtually lifted Sam off his feet and out of the Council hall. A little while later, they returned, seemingly without the accused. One of them proceeded to occupy the bamboo enclosure and bowed graciously to the Council.

A keen observer in the front row might have detected a glint in the fourteen eyes, but seven serene faces were all that the others saw. Polite laughter rolled through the hall as people realized that one of the guards had been stripped to dress up the accused.

The Chief's irate-looking colleague took up from where they had left. "The three objects look like fish-hooks alright, Bel, but they're too delicate to catch fish."

"I find it odd that each is made of a different metal," said Bel, "including gold."

As the other members squinted over the fish-hooks, a hum grew in the hall. "What's his name?" Bel looked at the Head Guard. "Yes, Samasin," he said. "Tell us what happened yesterday afternoon."

Sam stood before the Council of Elders with his hands firmly locked with each other. Their glum faces had shaken his confidence, and it was some time before he could hear his own voice. "Honourable Council, it all started when I left my master Nergal's mansion to reach the palace ground."

As Sam narrated the happenings, the Council members interrupted at some places and grilled him. The sight of such a big gathering had triggered a creeping sensation inside Sam's stomach. While talking about how the Meluhhan died, and then about the gold necklace inside his headgear, Sam entirely forgot to mention the dead man's last words. Nevertheless, by the time he finished, he was pretty sure that he had convinced the Council about his innocence.

The Priest-physician of Babili rooted his cane on the stone floor and holding it with both hands, slowly rose from his seat. Sam froze as the old man threw a sharp look at him before facing the Council. "Yes, I do recognise that dagger. It's the one I had presented to Samasin earlier on the day of the crime."

Then tapping his way to the bamboo enclosure, the elderly man handed his cane to Sam. Seizing both of Sam's arms with skinny hands, the Priest-physician looked up into his eyes. For the first time, Sam marked narrow whitish rings encroaching into his mentor's black cornea. Releasing his feeble hold, the Priest-physician turned to face the Council. "I am extremely shocked by the alleged behaviour of this boy." He paused, and looked at each of the seven elders. "He has worked with me during the past year. From my experience, I would say that he cannot execute such a heinous crime."

Sam jumped inside the bamboo enclosure. No one could blemish his character now.

The witness who was summoned next was the man with a mark on his cheek, the thief who had stolen the necklace. "I am Zibigi," he said. Invoking all Sumérian gods and bowing to the Council time and again, he vividly described what he had 'seen'. It brought forth from the audience a few snide remarks for Sam. Zibigi summed up: "Dhat is how I saw the accused quarrelling with the Meluhhan trader and then stabbing him."

Sam gulped and managed to say, "I – I fail to understand why a person, whom I don't even know, lies in order to prove me a murderer. The tavern owner knows that a man with a crooked nose, not I, committed the murder."

The tavern owner plodded to the fore as if walking in sleep. In a droning voice, he said, "After serving beer to the accused, I went out for some work. While returning, I heard a commotion – you know Honourable Council, how drunkards behave – and hurried to my tavern. There I saw the accused fighting with Biggie."

"Biggie?"

"I meant Zibigi, the earlier witness," the tavern owner added quickly. "And before I forget – I didn't see any purse or necklace with the dead man as claimed by the accused."

Sam was astounded. Why had the tavern owner lied too? He waved a hand to draw the attention of the Council members, but it seemed that they chose to ignore him.

Just then a woman's voice was heard. "I request your leave to speak, Father."

There was surprise on Bel's countenance as he looked in its direction. Sam thanked Marduk that Lady Ella had decided to speak.

"Girl," said Bel's voice booming through the air, "I'm not your father, nor are you my daughter when we are in King Shulgi's sacred Ziggurat."

For a moment, total silence prevailed in the Council hall. Ella seemed to be taken aback. "I beg your pardon, Chief," she said. "May I request permission to speak please?"

Bel consulted the other six elders, and got up. The two men sitting next to him held each of his hands and appeared to be reasoning with him. Bel said, "The Council permits you to speak after I leave, lady." And he walked out.

Ella came to the fore. "Thank you," she said with a brisk nod. "I know the accused Samasin since he was working as a camel boy in my ex-husband Nergal's village. We employed him to tend to our two horses, and after our divorce –"

"Come to the point," the Assistant Chief cut in. The man's irate countenance reminded Sam of an old farmer who used to chase him in his childhood for sneaking into an orchard.

Ella smiled and raised a hand as if pacifying an indignant child. "We saw a little while ago that the clothes Samasin wore bore the blood marks only below his waist." She paused. "Had it been Samasin who stabbed the victim in the chest the blood would have splashed on the upper portion of Samasin's clothes, wouldn't it?"

"Hear, hear –" said a husky voice, "the flimsy reasoning of a woman's mind."

Most men in the gathering sniggered. Ella gazed so sharply at Biggie that the smirk disappeared from his face. As he cowered, the sniggers subsided.

"Sh..sh…No one is supposed to comment except the Council," said the Assistant Chief. Then he growled at Ella. "Learning doesn't give you the right to meddle in matters of the state."

Ella's eyes blazed dissent, but she seemed battling with herself not to respond. Sam watched her laboriously returning to her seat. With each unsteady step of hers, his resentment rose against the Assistant Chief and his Council.

For a long time, the six Elders discussed among themselves. Sam tried hard to read their lips, but could not make out anything.

At last, the Assistant Chief stood up, and the buzzing crowd turned silent.

"Listen, O Babilians," he started speaking in a squeaky voice. "Listen to King Shulgi's justice, imparted by the learned Council of Elders." He looked exhausted by that time, and a guard ran to hand him a flask of water. After taking a couple of long swigs, he continued, "We have carefully examined all the evidence. The Council declares Samasin, the stable boy of Nergal, guilty of murdering the unidentified Meluhhan."

A robust cheer went up from the place where Biggie sat. Sam had expected to hear a 'not guilty' verdict. He saw the high walls of the Council hall revolving around him, and threw up his arms. The shrill voice came again. "Samasin is sentenced to the Ordeal of the wild bull. It will take place tomorrow, the New Moon in the second lunar period of Spring in the twenty-third year … "

Sam could not hear further. He dropped to his knees. "By Marduk, I don't have blood on my hands. You would be executing an innocent man."

"Honourable Elders of the Council," Ella's voice cut through the hubbub. "May I point out that the tavern owner's statement cannot be accepted?"

Sam held his sobs and looked up. The Assistant Chief looked at his colleagues as if conveying, 'That woman is a pain in the neck.'

"Please listen to me, honourable Chief," Ella continued. "Babilian law states, 'If conspirators meet in a tavern, and if they are not captured and delivered to the Council, the tavern owner shall be put to death.' So in a situation such as this, the tavern owner is bound to give a false testimony to save his own skin."

Sam stood up as hope rose in his heart. The frown on the Assistant Chief's face deepened, and he said, "Would a woman teach law to the Council?"

A loud laugh emanated from Biggie's throat. Most men and a few women joined in, and the Council hall sounded like Sam's ill-fated tavern in the evening rather than a place of justice.

Sam's knees knocked together as he watched the Elders gravely walking towards the exit. A shriek escaped him. "I beg you to behead me. Please grant me a swifter death."

They walked on. Sam gnashed and cursed not only the Elders but all their ancestors too. The Head Guard rammed a rough palm on his mouth.

Sam's legs refused to walk. As the guards supported him to descend the Ziggurat steps, his feet dragged. His tearful eyes spotted two men pushing hand in hand through the noisy crowd. They were the tall villain Biggie and the fat tavern owner.

A question popped up in Sam's mind. What had the dying man pressed in his palm?

He sprang to his feet and the chain that fettered him by the anklc clanged. He screamed. His eyes darted to the red flesh where the skin had been rubbed raw, but pain was overwhelmed by curiosity, and his hand reached into the pocket. It recoiled as if stung by a scorpion. One of his fingers was dripping with blood, and from it hung a tiny bronze fish-hook.

The more Sam stared at it, the wider opened his mouth. But for the metal, his fish-hook was an exact replica of the three which had been found on the old Meluhhan's body. Was it with some purpose that the dying Meluhhan had given him only the bronze one? Was the bronze fish-hook meant to convey a specific message to Hiwa Haqra?

Sam slowly sat down on the rough floor. Had the Meluhhan discovered anything which the villain Biggie did not want Hiwa to know?

As his eyes roved to find an answer, they caught a mouse nibbling at the millet bread from the meal that he had left untouched. It broke an unseen thread which connected his thoughts, and his mind jumped back to what was happening before him. As he wondered how many innocent men condemned to death that the little creature had seen there earlier, it leapt in air and scurried away.

There were footsteps on the stone floor, and he hastened to drop the fish-hook back into his pocket. Stretching his neck, Sam discerned the Head Guard who also doubled up as the jailor, approaching with a torch in one hand. It seemed queer of the brute that he smelt of rose scent even from afar. When he was just a few steps away, Sam discerned under his flickering shadow a gliding feminine movement. From his position on the ground, even the short stature of the Head Guard had hidden a tall lady from his sight.

Sam rubbed his eyes. He had never expected Lady Ella to visit him in jail.

The Head Guard pulled a stool which screeched on the ground, and mumbled 'Half a *mu-eš*, lady,' before withdrawing.

Noticing a gleam in Lady Ella's eyes, Sam could not hold back his tears. She took both his hands in hers and they sat without a word for a while. At last she spoke. "If you wish to be left alone, Sam, I'll leave. I understand."

"No, lady," he said, wiping his eyes with the back of a hand. "I'm grateful to you for all you did to save me. I believe it's my fate that I die."

Ella did not appear to have heard him. "Sam, you stated that the Meluhhan possessed a necklace and Biggie stole it," she said. "How did it look?"

"It had a big pendant and was made of gold beads and gold-capped stone beads, mostly red and blue."

"I thought so. It ought to be one of the three necklaces which my father asked a merchant of Meluhha to supply."

"I saw only one."

"Perhaps all three might not be ready, although it's about a year and a half since Father paid him in gold." Throwing a glance down the corridor, she added, "I suspect that the Meluhhan's murder is related to the missing necklace."

There was a long pause before she spoke again. "By the way, Sam, your master doesn't stay home on several nights every fortnight. I'm aware that he doesn't visit the destitute women's home of which he is a trustee. Do you know where he goes?"

Sam could not bear Lady Ella talking about her ex-husband Nergal instead of sympathizing with his plight. "To his storehouse," he said with indifference. Sam had never been able to figure out how she fell in love with a man who although matching her good looks, fell short of other qualities which she excelled – brains, values, compassion.

"What does he store there?" Ella asked.

It seemed to Sam that she would not give up easily. "Sealed packages so big," he indicated with his hands. "And sachets made from cloth."

"What do they contain?"

Sam protruded his lower lip, expressing ignorance. "I've seen some inn-keepers buying them in bulk." Fishing out a soiled yellow packet from his robe, he said, "This is one of them. I had picked it up to hold silver."

Ella examined it and said, "May I keep it?"

"Of course," he said, reflecting that whatever he possessed would be useless before the sun set again.

She drew nearer. "Now I have a feeling, Sam, that there's more to the murder than meets the eye." Her voice turned into a whisper. "It's shady, and that's why they want you out of their way."

Before Sam could take in her words, he caught a glimpse of someone approaching, and assumed it was the Head Guard. "Lady," he said quickly, "the Meluhhan dropped a name just before he died – 'Hiwa Haqra'."

"Siwa Saqra?" Ella's lips parted to speak again, when another voice which was very familiar to Sam, intervened.

"Ella? Here? At this time?" said Nergal's voice, carrying an unmistakable tone of sarcasm.

Sam looked at Nergal, whose dense brow made him imagine for the first time that it probably symbolized wickedness. His eyes demanded to know, 'Where were you, Master, when I needed you most?'

Over the years, Sam had quarrelled with several Babilians who had talked of his Master as 'Nergal the Fox'. Now he could see the reason behind that perception about the suave, smartly dressed man who had cultivated a smile which camouflaged, and a voice that obscured.

Ella recovered first and looked straight at Nergal. "Couldn't you come to the Ziggurat to help a person who served you faithfully for so many years?"

The Fox guffawed. "Chief Bel's daughter, I'm told you performed quite a drama there."

"The least you could have done, Nergal, was to appoint a person knowledgeable with the laws of Babili to reason for this unfortunate boy."

"Keep your rotten wisdom to yourself," he snapped, raising his square chin.

Although it was the first time that Sam heard Nergal speaking to Lady Ella in such an insulting tone, it did not surprise him. He had lost respect for his Master since the day little Ribba had timidly asked him, "Sam, did your father too whip your *Ama-ugu* like we whip the horse?"

Heavy footsteps getting louder broke his thoughts. He saw the Head Guard hurrying towards them.

"Time's up," the Head Guard said. Both his stiffness as well as tone mellowed as he faced the gatecrasher. "I beg your pardon, *Belum*."

Sam turned away. Did the Fox come to the jail just to quarrel with his divorced wife?

3 'CELESTIAL IRE' ON BABILI

Pressed on by the guards, Sam entered the arena with his shoulders drooping and feet dragging. Had he seen himself in the copper mirror before which the Head Guard often used to twirl moustache, Sam would have noticed that his black hair had attained a distinctly greyish tinge within one night.

The arena was a natural formation of land that looked like a roughly truncated funnel. For easy access inside, the Babilians had dug away a huge chunk of its periphery that faced the country road to Zimbir.

Sam thought that the entire population of Babili had occupied the sloping arena. He was miffed to see a festive atmosphere around.

A cry of anticipation arose as a wild white bull was led in, his huge hump shifting from one side to another as he walked. He threw up his head as if to display his thick curved horns.

Sam recognized the beast. When he first came to Babili as a teenager, he had seen a convict stronger and nimbler than himself being flung and trampled by the same bull. Although several men had been sentenced since then, he had found a pretext every time for not joining his friends to watch the Ordeal.

The mangled body of the poor man killed many years ago flashed before Sam's eyes, and he stepped back feeling sick. He considered whether it might be less painful if he stood motionless and let the bull impart one deathly impact.

The wild bull ogled at Sam, and gave vent to a long drawn out grunt as if expressing his annoyance. It sounded particularly menacing in the utter silence that had permeated the arena. Although sweating profusely, Sam drew apart his legs and stooped as if in readiness to jump out of the bull's path. In his mind, he knew that his response was more a reflex action than defiance.

Just when the guards prepared to set the wild bull free, it seemed that all of a sudden the evening had set in. Sam thought that it was ironic that a sandstorm should blow when his life was caught up in a severe storm.

Someone shouted, "Where is *Šamaš*?" The entire gathering looked up to the sky.

A shaky voice followed, "The heavens are on fire."

"Look," said another, "the sun has sunk into that big black hole."

The noise of scared voices, all speaking together, grew louder. Many among the spectators knelt, touched their heads to the ground and wailed, seeking forgiveness from the heavens for their sins.

The Priest-physician waved like a madman at the Head Guard. It seemed that he had instructed not to release the wild bull because Sam saw the guards desperately trying to restrain the beast.

"How dare you stop the Ordeal?" a husky voice rose above the din. Sam turned and saw Biggie standing up in the front row, looking as if he wanted to release the wild bull on the Priest-physician.

The Priest-physician shook his cane at Biggie, motioning him to take his seat. "The Council of Elders would decide about it."

For the first time since the judgement, Sam saw a ray of hope. If the Priest-physician had sufficient reason to stop the Ordeal, there was a good chance to be let off.

It was quite some time before the Priest-physician walked back to the centre of the arena after consulting the Council members. He put a palm-leaf cone to his mouth and spoke, "The Council of Elders rule that *Šamaš*, the Sun God, forbids this Ordeal to be carried out –"

Even before he had completed, Sam jumped up. "I'm saved!"

"This Ordeal won't be executed in the Sun God's presence again, so now it can happen only at night."

Sam was unable to speak. He dropped to the ground and

pounded his fists on it. He heard Biggie hollering only one demand again and again: "Let's get it over tonight."

"It's the New Moon tonight," said a belligerent voice. "We won't enjoy the Ordeal in the dark." The crowd shouted in agreement.

"Then let it be on the night of the Full Moon," said the Priest-physician, still waving up and down with his cane at the spectators.

"No, no, no. Dhat's too long. *Mulla Xul*! We all want the Ordeal tonight." However, Biggie's voice got drowned by strident cries of 'Full Moon, Full Moon'.

"So it's final," said the Priest-physician over his palm-leaf cone. "The convict Samasin will be subjected to the Ordeal of the wild bull a fortnight from today, on the Full Moon night."

Sam's face looked up tearfully. "A fortnight?" he said aloud. The thought of awaiting death for two weeks was more distressing than the pain of an immediate end.

He staggered to his feet, wondering if that would be time enough to plan an escape.

No sooner did he hear the footsteps, Sam hastened to rub off the words he had just scratched with a piece of charcoal that he had picked up on his way back from the arena. The Head Guard had magnanimously permitted him to keep it, and now the man had dropped in unexpectedly.

"Boy, can you write?" he said, glaring at partly erased words 'bribe', 'silver' and 'cart man' on the stone floor. Sam did not raise his eyes, for he knew his game was up. He was not ready for the next question. "Can you read too?"

He got up, looking doubtfully in the Head Guard's eyes. "I was taught reading and writing by none other than Lady Ella." As he spoke, his foot mopped the floor. He hoped that the telltale words were gone at last.

The Head Guard walked away. Sam heard him instructing the solitary guard on duty to go to the Ziggurat for some work. Mentally, he worked out that he would be under the watchful eye of the Head Guard for twenty *mu-eš*. The man was strolling back towards him, and Sam groped for an explanation for writing those words. Ever since Sam knew him, the Head Guard's face had looked strained as if due to acute constipation. Seeing him smiling,

Sam was deeply perplexed.

"I want you to read something for me, boy," the Head Guard said, delving in the pocket of his knee high gown and producing a roll of tree bark.

Sam's eyes brightened. He unrolled it and read aloud. "*A rich man in Babili, named Nergal, seeks sister's hand. Enquire.*"

Doubting that he heard himself correctly, Sam read the letter again very slowly. There he was face to face with death, and the Master was looking for a new wife.

"He is your master, isn't he?"

"He was," Sam said, spitting. "I'd rather starve than work for him again."

"I've delayed replying to my brother long enough," said the Head Guard, rolling the bark and stuffing it back in his pocket. "I shouldn't postpone further as the message would take a week to reach him."

"Does he live in Magan?"

"Lagaš," said the Head Guard as he left. Shortly he returned clutching a fresh piece of bark, a feather and a small vial. "Write a message for me, boy."

Sam dipped the pointed end of the feather in the dye, and carefully stroked Cuneiform script on the bark, blowing on each letter before he scribed another. As he looked up for further dictation, he perceived sheer wonder and respect in the Head Guard's eyes.

"That's all I have to convey. Now read it to me."

Sam read: "*Nergal does all that Father advised us to shun. People know him as 'the Fox'.*"

As the Head Guard left, Sam wondered why Master Nergal lived in Lady Ella's small house when he possessed a mansion. He had failed to understand how the Fox could afford a luxurious life style when all he did was to visit a storehouse outside the town. Whenever he had asked the other servants, they had avoided replying. When Lady Ella visited the jail, she too sounded suspicious of the Fox's activity.

That evening his friend, the cart man, came to visit him. No sooner was the guard out of earshot, Sam whispered, "Can you obtain some opium?"

The cart man drew a long face, making its bony features look so comical that had it been a less serious occasion, Sam would have laughed. "Yes," he said, "I'll get you a dose from the tavern near the Palace."

"Does that sluggish traitor deal in opium too?"

"Can't you make out that he consumes probably as much of it as he sells?"

Sam had little time to discuss tavern owners. "I don't want it for myself, though I think it might take my mind off my fear," he said. "I want the wild bull to consume it."

The cart man had a twinkle in his eye. "But, Sam, how would you make the beast eat it?"

"Once the Priest-Physician administered it to a horse that fell sick, and it remained drowsy for the rest of that day. The old man sent me away, saying I was too young to deal with the poison. I assume that he dissolved it in water."

"You would need much more opium to sedate a bull, and that would cost an arm and a leg."

"Go to Lady Ella. She trusts you. Tell her that I need some silver." As Sam spoke, he saw the Head Guard approaching. "Then buy all that's available in Babili."

"Time to leave," said the Head Guard to the cart man, who immediately got up from the floor, thrashing his gown with both hands to dislodge dust.

"Wait," Sam said holding the Head Guard's leg and eying him. "I believe you know that my friend too works with Nergal the Fox?"

"It doesn't matter a bit to me. Come on, boy, get going."

"It does," Sam said, giving a jerk to the Head Guard's leg. "Should I tell him about your letter? Would you like the Fox to know? Or would you grant my request?"

There was a pause. Sam saw the strong sentinel cringing. "Fool. You know I can't let you escape even if I wanted, because then I would be facing the wild bull instead of you."

"It's much safer than that. You won't raise any suspicion. My friend will meet you with a stack of damp hay before the Ordeal," Sam said, winking at the cart man. "All you have to do is to let the white brute devour it."

The Head Guard scratched his thinning hair. Helplessness was evident on his face. "The white brute?"

"Yes," Sam beamed. "The one your men had a hard time holding back from killing me."

The Head Guard nudged the cart man towards the exit. "Deliver the hay fifteen *mu-eš* before time. My promise won't hold if you're late."

Never before had the Babilians seen a convict, who had been sentenced to execution, walking faster than the guards.

Reaching the wide open space where he was going to face death once again, Sam surveyed the arena. Torches moved all around its periphery as people poured in. It seemed that many more spectators had come to watch the Ordeal than on the earlier occasion. He surveyed the expectant masses, and smiled to himself. They hoped to be entertained by his scamper for survival, but they would be going home very disappointed.

The Priest-physician took up his palm-leaf cone. "Put out all the torches. They distract the wild bull."

After several appeals, the last of the flames died down. It looked eerie under the moonlight. The noise subsided as the guards led the beast into the arena.

Sam rubbed his eyes, and stared in disbelief. Even under the scarce light, there was no mistaking that his adversary had changed to a huge black bull. Standing beside him, the white one which Sam had faced earlier would have looked just a healthy calf.

He was aware of a sudden need to empty his bladder, and looked around uneasily. Then he gestured to the Head Guard and spoke in his ear. The man led him out of the arena towards a long line of roofless cabins that stank more and more as they drew near. When they were returning, Sam could not keep silent any longer. Looking accusingly at the Head Guard, he spat. "You went back on your promise."

"No, I didn't," the Head Guard said. "I let the white bull eat the hay that your friend brought." There was a definite stress on the word 'white'.

Sam blinked. He could not but appreciate the man's ethics. While keeping his promise, he had stayed true to the King by getting another wild bull from a neighbouring town. Sam rued that his attempt at fighting injustice with craftiness had failed.

As he waddled to take his position, he looked up at the heavens for a last prayer, and saw the Full Moon. He gazed at it more intently. It did not appear normal. Had his mind started playing tricks already?

The guards prepared to set the black bull free. Despite pressing both his palms on his eyes, Sam could clearly 'see' the wild bull lowering his head to the ground and throwing up his tail. Sam 'heard' one of the animal's ram-like front legs scratching the earth. He prayed that the beast charged without further delay, and that he lost consciousness instantly.

However, what Sam heard were voices all around goading the bull. He also heard a distant bellow. His experience said its tone was far from enraged. Was he still hoping against hope?

Scared to open his eyes, he wondered about what was happening. Then amidst the general mayhem, someone spoke clearly, "Behold, Babilians –" It was the Priest-physician's voice. The first thought that passed through Sam's mind was that he was turning crazy just before his impending end. Then he heard the voice again. "Behold the wild bull."

Very cautiously, Sam peeped through his fingers. The Priest-physician was leaning upon his cane, holding the palm-leaf cone close to his lips. The guards had taken charge of the black bull, which stood like a slave waiting to be relieved after a hard day's work. Sam's hands dropped down, and he peered with eyes wide open.

The din died down and the Priest-physician spoke again, "Babilians, have you ever seen a wild bull behaving like a tame dog?" He turned to where the Council of Elders sat, and added, "It seems to be a divine signal indicating that the convict isn't guilty."

After being shocked to the core by the entry of the black bull instead of the white one, Sam could respond with nothing more than a blank stare. In the meantime, the Head Guard had come up to him and tied his wrists.

"*Mulla Xul*!" Biggie's voice cut through the murmurs. "How can Babili let a murderer go unpunished?"

The spectators answered in chorus, "We can't. We shouldn't."

"We, the people of Babili, demand dhat justice be meted out," shouted Biggie. He turned to face the crowd and throwing both hands in air, flapped his fingers and sang at the top of his voice, "Get our own white bull."

A roar went up as the spectators picked up the chant. The arena echoed with their demand. Sam's eyes met the Head Guard's and he perceived fear in them.

"Listen –" The Priest-physician waved furiously with his cane. "Listen to me. It isn't a question of this bull or that. The animal's behaviour is driven by heavenly forces." He pointed the cane to the mooing bull. "It's apparently responding to the fierce sentiments of *Sîn*, the Moon God. Just look up in the sky. See how His face has turned scarlet."

"A red moon isn't as rare as you're making out." Biggie seemed to be enjoying the argument as he turned to the spectators. "We see dhat every year or so, don't we?"

"What we see occasionally is a blush on *Sîn*'s face. Tonight it's His entire countenance," said the Priest-physician as he tapped his way to Sam. "And that's just a fortnight after the Sun God *Šamaš* turned away from Babili. Have you ever seen such a celestial ire?"*

"We Babilians are concerned dhat a dangerous killer is getting away," said Biggie, not willing to lower his voice. The crowd booed in his support.

The Priest-physician beckoned to Biggie, who walked to the centre like a rooster looking for a fight. "You accused this boy of the murder, didn't you?" the Priest-physician asked, extending a hand to Sam's shoulder.

Biggie glowered at the old man. "What has dhat to do with dhis?"

"A lot," said the Priest-physician. "The law says, 'If an accused who is sentenced to be thrown into a river doesn't drown, then the accuser should be put to death and his house be given to the accused'."

"Dhat's irrelevant here." Biggie clenched the fists and rested them on his waist. "You're helping a criminal to get away."

"On the contrary, I'm trying to help you," the Priest-physician said. "The Council could as well reason that 'If an accused who is sentenced to the Ordeal of the wild bull does not get gored, then his accuser should be put to death'."

Biggie's face wilted, and so did his enormous physique as he returned to his place without a word.

The Priest-physician walked slowly to the Council members, resting on his cane after every few steps. A short consultation later, Chief Bel stood up holding the palm-leaf cone to his mouth: "The Council of Elders orders that the convict be released. He has faced the wild bull for the required time. Therefore, he has fully served his sentence according to the laws of Babili. For similar circumstances, the law says that 'If the condemned is thrown into the river as a punishment, and he escapes unhurt, the river proves he is not guilty'."

Sam stood there as if under a spell. Gradually an image of a face bearing a wild growth of beard became clear. The Head Guard was removing his bonds. Sam stared at his free hands and laughed like a maniac. "I'm free," he shouted, raising his hands to show to the spectators. "I'm alive!"

Before Sam's mind recognised what he was doing, he had seized the Head Guard by both his ears and smacked a smouldering kiss on the man's pate. There was a furious swearing, and a powerful force threw Sam backwards. He tottered to his feet only to fall back on his knees, sobbing.

The guards propped him up and gently led him on the way out of the arena. He overheard several groups of people as they overtook the guards. None of them was convinced that he was innocent despite the judgement passed by the Council of Elders. He knew that he must identify the assassin to clear his name from the stigma. Hiwa Haqra, the man mentioned by the dying Meluhhan, could probably help.

Sam looked around but did not see either Biggie or any of his cronies. Ella had said on that evening that his enemies wanted to get him out of their way. A shiver passed through his body. He would not live to prove himself innocent if Biggie and his gang had decided to get rid of him. A voice that sounded very close to Ella's told him to get away. He looked around and only saw the milling crowd.

Sam determined to follow his inner voice. He shoved the guards and ran for his life. The next moment, he had mingled in the crowds streaming out of the arena.

Hurrying past a wayside tavern, Sam heard a loud ribald song floating out from there. He recognized the voice as well as the 'dhis' and 'dhat' in its wordings. He halted and his teeth grit together. Picking up a rock, he aimed it at the tavern.

He thought he saw Ella's face on the wall of the tavern. It seemed to be admonishing him.

The rock dropped from his hand and he turned and ran till he reached home exhausted. If he wanted to get far from Biggie and his gang, he needed a horse. Heading straight towards the stable, he saw a lamp floating in there. He came to an abrupt halt and slipped behind the trunk of an ancient cedar. The cart man was setting the saddle on the horse.

Where would be the Fox riding so late at night?

Sam thanked Marduk that he had reached the stable before the horse was gone. No sooner had the cart man left on his way to the only lighted window in the mansion, Sam came out from his hiding. His hands shook as he stroked the horse, for he was about to repay his friend's invaluable help by putting him in trouble with his master. The horse gave him a lick, which brought back the sense of urgency to his mind. Un-tethering it, he led it out of the gate. Once there, he scampered upon the horse and spurred it towards the port of Babili.

As the clip-clop of the hooves broke the silence of the night, Sam heard the cart man's desperate cries behind him, and pitied the man for the explosion he was about to face from the Fox.

* *Author's note: A double eclipse – total solar on May 9th and total lunar on May 24th – took place in Babylon in 2138 BC, i.e. King Shulgi's 23rd year of reign.*

4 ON THE RUN

A gush of air, accompanied by a flapping sound and a screech, passed over Sam. He sat up with a start, and yawned. As he wondered how long he had slept after reaching the port of Babili, he heard voices floating in from the wharfs. In the sparse light of dawn, he saw several slaves on one barge labouring to raise its stone anchor.

He ran towards it shouting. Had the owner hired stone deaf men on his barge? By the time he reached the wharf, it had slipped into the river currents. Without a second thought, he dived into the waters. Although he could not stop his teeth from chattering, he splashed vigorously in pursuit of the barge.

Then he saw a slave pointing towards him. Others on board peered in his direction. Sam noticed some quick movement on the deck. He was delighted to see them throwing a long rope at him. Clenching his teeth, he stroked through the waters and just when his limbs had started refusing to take further strain, he managed to get hold of the rope. A loud cheer went up on the barge, and he was fast drawn towards it.

As Sam pulled himself up on the deck, smiling with a sense of achievement, he stared into the face of Nergal the Fox.

A smirk twitched the corners of the Fox's mouth. "Ha, ha, crafty rascal," he bawled, "you gave them the slip, did you?"

Hearing him, a brawny young man drew nearer. Sam frowned at the Fox. Couldn't he hold his tongue about what nobody on the barge knew? The young man stroked his arms menacingly and asked, "Boy, are you dodging the law?"

Sam narrated how he had been set free, hoping that the man would not hand him over to guards at the next river port.

"Yes, we saw the moon turning copper red, and they say it's a bad omen," the skipper said in a shaky voice. "I too would've rested today like others, had it not been for the silver plates I've to deliver at Urim to a vessel going out to sea."

"Please drop me there," Sam said. "I don't wish to stay in this cursed place any longer."

The skipper's eyes roved all around and settled on Nergal.

"I know the boy, Skipper," said the Fox extending a hand to his employee's shoulder. "He's the last person to run from the law. I'll pay his fare." Sam's hand rose to lift it and drop it away, but held back. An impulsive action could ruin his chance of remaining on board. The Fox dragged him away from the crowd. "The boy is freezing. He needs dry clothes." Pulling out a gown from a sack, he flung it at Sam. "Don't worry about work. I'll recommend you to a friend in Urim."

Sam smiled as he peeled off his wet clothes. Perhaps the Fox wasn't as bad as he had started believing lately. He was the least prepared to face an abrupt hostility in the Fox's voice. "Ungrateful wretch, you continued calling on my enemy even while serving me."

Sam took his time to pull the gown above his head.

"Tell me, mite," the Fox spoke again. "What did the sow want to know?"

Sam's lips pressed together. Why was the Fox so concerned about Lady Ella's conversation?

The Fox gritted his teeth. "Why don't you speak, stable boy? Have you stuffed chick peas in those horse-like cheeks?"

Sam laughed in an obvious imitation of the Fox. "Horse-like cheeks," he echoed with delight. He inflated his cheeks, but barely able to control mirth, let the air out through tightly shut lips. "Phoo-phoo-"

Several sweating slaves, who had finished the work on hand, drew closer to the two men, presumably hoping to share their little joy. The Fox glared at them, threw a reprimanding glance at Sam, and walked away.

Deep in sleep, Sam sensed something touching his head. His hand rose to push it away as he turned to rest on the other side. Then a greater force whacked him. It was a foot. Sam's hands shot up to grip it. He pulled himself nearer and planted his teeth into the sinewy part just above the ankle.

"Aw.."

On recognizing the voice, Sam dug the teeth deeper. A cry emanating above drew nearer as the man who had kicked him crashed on the deck. "Leave me, stable boy –"

Letting go, Sam got up and stood with legs apart over the Fox. Yawning and stretching out his arms he asked, "Where have we reached?"

"Urim," said the Fox sheepishly as he too rose to his feet. It did not take him long to regain the master's mantle. "You slept through the entire daytime, lazy boy."

By then, Sam had seen the slaves pulling the barge along the dockside, and he started walking towards them to do his bit.

"We'll leave as soon as the sun's rays light the sky," he heard the Fox behind him, "so don't waste my time again."

Sam made a face in the dark.

The work did not last long and everybody on board went back to sleep. Sam tossed and turned. What perplexed him was the Fox's suspicion about Lady Ella's visit to the jail. He thought he faced two unrelated problems – one created by the Fox, another by Biggie. One man was after the peace of his mind, the other after his life.

Sam got up and looked around. The frame of the barge reminded him of the lower-half skeleton of a blue whale he had seen as a child. Noiselessly, he moved towards the bow.

As he stood on the forecastle breathing in the salty air, he experienced a novel freshness invigorating his entire body. A voice within told him that Urim, where the Purattu merged into the Lower Sea, was too near Babili for safety. He looked out in the dark, rubbing his chin. Perhaps Magan was a safer place than Urim, in fact the only option, because Sam was not aware of any other port on the Lower Sea. But should he go where long ago he had lost his parents and baby sister Anlil?

As he continued scouring the sea with wide eyes, he made out a dark form that looked like a vessel several times larger than his barge. It stood like a rock in the open sea. Could it take him to

Magan? Could he pay the fare?

His hands went to the pocket of his gown. The little silver which he possessed had been given to his friend, the cart man. Only the bronze fish-hook scratched his fingers. The murdered Meluhhan had not told him where to find Hiwa Haqra. Anyway, he had more pressing problems at hand than searching for an unknown man. He pulled out the fish-hook to fling it into the sea.

It struck Sam that Babili would remember him as a murderer who had escaped execution through a stroke of luck. If he wanted to clear his name from the stigma, he had to identify the queer nosed assassin. It seemed that the dying Meluhhan wanted to tell Sam the reason behind the fatal attack on him. Unable to survive long enough to narrate it, the man had mentioned Hiwa Haqra. Sam thought that Hiwa ought to help him reach the assassin.

His hand jerked back. Tearing a long ribbon from the gown he tied the fish-hook in it. He put it back into the pocket, undressed and tied the gown around his waist. Then he climbed over the port side, lowered himself till his knees felt the cold water, and let go.

The flow of the river seemed to be helping him swim towards the ship. By the time he reached halfway, he was breathing so heavily that his mouth opened wide. To his surprise he found the water smelling different and tasting salty. The feeling of swimming in the sea for the first time was quite exhilarating, but acute pain gnawed at his muscles.

Only after reaching the starboard side near the stern of the ship, could Sam consider catching his breath. It seemed that a double rudder was installed on the vessel.

As he bobbed with his hands pressed against the broadside, he heard a rumbling sound overhead. Looking up, he saw a huge box jutting out from the deck. It looked big enough to accommodate a man. "I wonder what it is."

The next moment he knew it. A warm and sticky substance splashed on his face. A curse dropped from his lips and he dived. Emerging a little farther, he looked back angrily at the over-hanging box, and then swam to the bow. A thick and taut rope extended from the deck into the sea. He reasoned that there ought to be a pretty heavy anchor at its other end.

Sam scaled the rope to reach the quarterdeck. Vigorously shaking his head like a dog, he put a hand behind an ear to pick up any telltale sound. He could hear only the flapping of a loose portion of a wrapped sail. Heaving himself up, he slinked into the shadows.

From that vantage point, he studied the ship. With her planks secured together by thick ropes and wooden fastenings, she was divided in two parts by a wooden cabin in its centre.

Untying the gown from his waist, he squeezed it and put it on. Then he crouched towards the nearest hatch, and descended a rope ladder leading to the hold.

His head reeled as he groped in the stuffy darkness. His fingertips pressed on soft bales which he thought were probably packed with woollen textiles, and touched cool jars which he was sure were filled with fresh water. The hull appeared to be made of bound reeds that smelt so badly of bitumen that his hands flew to his nose, but they could not stop a sneeze.

There was a noise behind the bales on his right. A green glow, the size of a small pot, emerged in front of him like a spectre. Before he could duck, an eerie face stared at him in the light of hundreds of fireflies bound in a piece of gauzy cloth.

"A Sumérian?" said a surprised voice. Then it turned into a bark. "Stowaway?"

Sam saw an angry pockmarked face with thick lips and a prominent chin. The man spoke Sumérian with pronunciation which sounded similar to how King Shulgi's elephant trainer spoke. Scarce light reflected from a big red bead swaying from his neck. It momentarily drew Sam's attention from the spotty face and he reasoned that the wearer of a carnelian bead could not be just a sailor.

"Captain," said Sam. There was a tremble in his voice. "I seek your mercy."

"I'm the head sailor, and I suppose you're a rapist or a murderer escaping from the guards of Urim?"

Sam fell on his knees. "I swear by Marduk that I'm neither. I'm running from a gang of murderers."

Looking up, he imagined the head sailor's eyes softening in the green glow around, and prayed that his hunch was right. The man stood there like a statue as if he had slid into his past. Then he flinched. "I'll report you to my Captain."

"Do it by all means," Sam said, getting up. "But I pray, not now." He raised his palms and brought them together just as the elephant trainer did when seeking a favour. "No sooner does the ship leave the port, I'll come out. Please let me hide as long as we're in Urim. My life's in your hands."

The head sailor took his time studying Sam from head to toes. At last, he spoke. "Come."

Sam's face lighted up. He followed the head sailor as the man fumbled his way to the farthest end from the overhead hatch. There he rearranged some bales to make a little space between them. Sam hurriedly climbed the bales and descended into the niche. He smiled as he huddled inside. Total darkness enveloped him as the head sailor pulled up a bale to cover the narrow opening.

The steps were withdrawing when Sam heard a voice booming one word, "Betrayer." From little of the Meluhhan language that he had picked up from the elephant trainer, he not only understood it but also realized that someone else had seen him.

"Qwoco?"

Sam sensed concern in the head sailor's voice.

"I'll wake up the Captain and tell him everything," said the man who had been addressed as Qwoco.

Sam waited with a baited breath. He fought an urge to lift the covering bail and see what was happening. Then he heard the head sailor's resolute voice. "Go ahead. Do it."

"You know you'll get blacklisted," said Qwoco. "No Meluhhan captain would employ you."

The head sailor's voice lowered. Sam could catch hardly two words, which he thought sounded like 'purse' and 'beads'.

There was absolute silence for a while. Then Sam heard Qwoco roaring with laughter. "I was just pulling your leg," he said, and his voice sounded dramatically different. "Got a nasty scare, didn't you?"

"The trouble with you, Qwoco," the head sailor's sober voice was heard receding up towards the deck, "is that you only understand the tongue of threat."

Sam listened intently, but it seemed that Qwoco too had gone away.

Despite the pervading stench and dampness, he slept soundly, unaware of the hubbub his desertion had created on the flat-bottomed river-barge.

5 STOWAWAY

The sound of short breaths awoke Sam inside his dark hideout, and set worms crawling inside his stomach. A whistle came from the direction of the hatch, and a voice followed. "The mongrel refuses to return. I think it has found him, *Belum*."

Sam sat still. A second voice came from farther off, apparently from the deck above. "You better wind up fast –"

A third voice, again sounding nearer, cut it midway, "Mind your tongue, boatman Paravar." The speaker seemed to be standing in the hold, near the man who had spoken first. "You're in Sumér's waters, not in your blasted Meluhha. I can seize this raft and 'wind you up'."

Sam's heart started emitting drumbeats. The port officials were out there and they seemed to be trying to reach the mongrel which barked overhead, announcing his presence.

The intimidating voice spoke again, but in a lower tone. "Your dog has smelt a rat. This bloody place is so congested that anything larger would have stuck out like a palm tree in the desert."

Sam's sense of ease was short-lived. Dim light flooded on him and a face peered in. It carried a long soft beard which made him think that the man was trying to convey he was older than he actually was. Two hands clasped Sam's hair, and he felt it being uprooted from his scalp. He squeezed out of the hole and tottered after the young official.

In the patch of sunlight streaming through the open hatch, there stood a sturdy red-faced man with his arms akimbo. He caught Sam by the neck and shoved him towards the rope ladder. As they reached the deck, Sam saw several sailors standing under the shadow of a huge square sail eyeing him with apparent rebuke.

The red-faced official kicked him as they approached the captain's cabin. He stumbled, and would have fallen to his knees had he not caught hold of a big cage hanging from the cabin roof. Two rock doves fluttered inside as he regained his balance.

"See boatman, you aren't even aware what's wriggling under your rump," his tormenter said with a grunt.

Paravar, the ship captain, turned pale. He reminded Sam of a bald gorilla in King Shulgi's palace. Despite his woes, Sam hoped the creature would bare his teeth and pound his chest. Instead, the Captain stomped a foot and stared at the head sailor. The poor man whimpered: "The rat was hiding under the sacks, Kavintu."

The bearded young official slapped Sam and demanded, "Who the devil are you?"

"Samasin of Babili, *Belum*." Sam revealed a baked-clay amulet that he wore around his neck. It was a lucky charm from the temple of Marduk, the patron deity of Babili.

"You must have committed a crime in Urim."

"I haven't set foot in your town," said Sam as his hand shot to his heart. "Last night I reached here on a barge and swam across to this vessel."

One of the officials addressed their red-faced leader. "Then why did our superior make such a fuss?"

"A powerful Babilian tipped him off," the leader muttered as he started walking towards the starboard where another rope ladder was tied hanging down to the sea.

Sam's ears pricked up. Powerful Babilian? His hand rose to his lips and he bit the forefinger. Which man other than Nergal the Fox would have guessed that he was on the Meluhhan ship?

"Aren't we arresting the stowaway?" asked the young official trailing behind the rest of the troupe.

"No, the State prison is teeming with our villains," said the red-faced official. "We can't harbour others' too."

"What do I do with him?" Captain Paravar shouted at the man's receding back. The red-faced official looked behind but, instead of replying, made a vulgar gesture. The Captain simmered till the entire team had descended to their boat. Then all his anger at the arrogant official boiled over on Sam. "Now let's cleanse my ship of the last Sumérian bastard."

Two hefty sailors pounced on Sam and tied his wrists and ankles. Sliding a long pole between the bound limbs they carried him towards the parapet like a deer that had been shot dead. From his awkwardly swinging position, Sam tried to focus his eyes on the Captain.

Luck had favoured him beyond his wildest dreams and Sam was aware that it would run out sooner or later. Despite that, he tried clutching at a straw. "Let me live, my *Belum*, and I'll be your slave for lifetime," he shouted, swinging from one side to another between the two carriers. "I'll tend to your horses. I'll deliver the mares."

The Captain waved a hand. "We don't have horses in Meluhha."

The men were nearing the parapet, and he had to think fast. "I'll scrub the *zooly* toilets. I'll – I'll –"

"We're chock-a-block. You're a burden on my ship," called out the Captain.

"Please untie me before dropping," wailed Sam. "I don't want to die."

"My men have better work to do."

Only a few steps remained before the sailors tossed him overboard. Sam screamed and words flew out of his mouth, "I'll wash the dishes for your wife, I'll change the baby's nappies."

"Now you talk sense," said the Captain. "Leave him." The two sailors did just that. Sam fell on the deck with a thud like a sack of dates. They unravelled him. He got up and, with a bowed head and hunched shoulders, scuttled to the master.

"What are you running away from?" the Captain bellowed.

"From some men who're mad at me," Sam said, assuming that only the basic instincts might appeal to the gorilla's savage brain.

"Mad for what?"

"A fema– I mean, a woman," Sam mumbled, looking intently at the Captain's rough toes.

The skipper batted an eyelid. "Aren't you a tad unripe for such matters?" Then he guffawed with a knowing glint in his eye. "You bloody amorists are a happy breed of pest on this earth," he said. The sailors laughed out aloud.

Sam grinned as he took the Captain's right hand in both of his, and bent low to kiss it. "*Belum*, you've a pearl of a heart inside that harsh –"

"Get lost," said the Captain, pulling away his hand. "You've wasted enough of everybody's time." Then he called out to the head sailor, "Give him something to eat. And make him slog for his food and passage. We'll kick him off at Dilmun."

A chunk of warm millet bread remained in Sam's suspended hand when he heard a clip clop sound of hooves. Jerking up, he saw a man riding a white horse passing by the inn where he had spent his first night in Dilmun.

"He could be my next master," thought Sam as he stuffed the piece into his mouth. Wiping a hand over his lips, he hastened towards the entrance of the small hall congested by log seats and customers.

As if his action were reflected from a smooth surface, there was another hasty movement near one of the walls too. Sam was momentarily distracted, but he had no time to look. His eyes were fixed on the horse which was smoothly cutting though an oncoming flow of labourers going towards the port.

Sam ran, squeezing through narrow gaps and bumping several men. He swore that it was tougher than swimming upstream of the Purattu. That was when two men coming right in his path moved swiftly to hold him.

"Stole someone's purse?" said one of the men, his eyes looking over Sam's shoulder.

Sam looked behind and saw that a man following him had abruptly turned back. The disproportionally small head on that massive physique was unmistakeable. It could not be anybody but the villain with the crooked nose, who had murdered the old Meluhhan in Babili.

The two men exclaimed when they saw Sam's pursuer running away. "We're sorry," said the second man, "for obstructing you in hurry."

"I was chasing the horseman," said Sam. " I'm a stable boy. I just landed in Dilmun, and thought he might hire me."

"He already employs one, I know it," said the first man. "But someone else might need your services. He is a Meluhhan, and the only other person in Dilmun to possess a horse – rather a mare, a beautiful black mare."

"Where can I find him?"

"In Eduru Meluhha, a colony of merchants hailing from the east."

Sam thanked them and resumed walking. His thoughts returned to the man with the crooked nose. Probably the assassin had recognized him as soon as he landed at Dilmun the previous evening, and was shadowing him since. There was no doubt that he had been closely watched as he took the breakfast, and was chased when he ran out of the inn. Sweat beads sprang on his brow.

Sam turned into a lane and slipped behind an idle ox cart. It was risky to stay in Dilmun any longer. Where should he go now? The last port on the Lower Sea was Magan. It was one place which he never wanted to visit, but Fate was leading him there. Could he avoid the crooked nosed killer by escaping to Magan?

After a fairly long dilemma, Sam came out of the lane and joined a gang of noisy labourers going towards the port. As he jostled among them, he thought hard about how he would board a ship before the assassin caught up with him again.

He was arguing and reasoning with himself when his thoughts were interrupted by a cart pulling up beside him. A voice struck his ears: "Amorist?" He turned to find a grinning Captain Paravar sitting behind the cart man.

"Captain!" he exclaimed. How relieving it was to see someone he knew in a strange place. Just then, a white roly-poly foal tethered behind the cart attracted his attention. A large black spot on its forehead gave it an impish look. He went to the foal and scratching it on the chest, said, "It's a healthy little beauty you have bought, Captain. She'll grow up into a fine mare."

"What are you going to do now?" asked the Captain, and Sam wondered why he had a mischievous glint in his eye.

"I've decided to go to Magan," Sam said as his fingers combed the baby animal's soft slippery mane.

"Have you given up on Dilmun so soon?"

"Only two merchants own horses here," said Sam, searching for a believable reason, "and they have already hired the stable boys. I hope that many more merchants in Magan own horses. Could you please drop me there?"

The Captain smiled. "How about joining me to Meluhha? I need someone to care for this baby."

Sam pinched himself, perhaps so apparently that the Captain burst into laughter. In the blink of an eye, all the uncertainty clouding his mind had blown away. "My *Belum*, you don't ask Samasin; you order him," he said grabbing the Captain's hand and pressing it warmly. Turning to the foal, he added, "It seems just about five lunar periods old. How many days is it to Meluhha?"

"Five or six days to Alatinam, the first port of call, and three or four from there to Port Lothal, our destination."

Before Sam realized it, his values rode roughshod over self-interest. "I suggest that you return it to the seller, Captain, and get back the silver you paid him."

"Why?"

"This sweet little thing is too young to pull through," Sam blurted out, not realizing that he was jeopardizing a godsend to escape from a professional assassin who had been taking undue interest in him. "Draught and dampness always sicken a horse. It also requires plenty of space to romp. A ship is the last place for that."

"Moreover, we're likely to run into thunderstorms which precede the South-West Monsoons," said the Captain wryly. "Unfortunately, the poor thing wouldn't live a day longer on land because its mother died last week, and my friends planned to slaughter it for a feast. So I decided to take it along for my kids."

"Nothing short of a miracle would save it at sea."

"That won't happen unless we give it a chance, young man," said the Captain motioning him to take a seat beside him.

"*A-la-la*!" Sam's hands shot up in air as he gave out a full throated cry, stopping several passers-by in their steps.

"What would you like to buy for my foal, Samorist?" asked the Captain as the cart started rolling again.

Sam beamed. He found the new moniker more agreeable. "Alfalfa hay, barley and linseed," he said raising a finger for each. "Sesame and salt blocks too, if available."

As they neared the market, the air turned dense with a mixture of smells – fish, meat and vegetable. Vendors loudly announcing their wares, seemed to be doing a brisk business.

Just as they finished their purchase, a sailor slinked up to the Captain and grinned. Sam noticed that his forehead sloped to the nose, from where his face receded to a small chin. The sailor's closely spaced eyes shone. "Is the baby horse replacing the goat for the mid-sea feast, *Kavintu*?" he said, fondly pressing a big mole under his left nostril.

"It isn't for a meal, Qwoco." The Captain replied with a frown. "Hurry up, load all those sacks and baskets on the cart."

Sam's teeth pressed his lower lip. He was face to face with the lout who had threatened to expose him on that night in Urim.

6 VELLI'S DILEMMA

About a lunar period before Sam was recruited to look after the foal, an incident happened in the city of Muenduru in distant Meluhha. It was going to affect both the man and the animal.

As Velli dipped in the cool flowing waters of River Sindhu, she had a hunch that she was being watched. Like all pretty Meluhhan girls, she had learnt two lessons early in life – to take voyeurism on the river bank for granted, and to carry a sling and baked clay pellets along with the toiletries. Compared to other young ladies in Muenduru, Velli had been compelled to use the sling more frequently.

Pretending that she was unaware of somebody's presence, she waded out of the water. Slanting rays of the setting sun caressed her nude body and pulled away its long shadow behind her. A necklace flowing over her ample bosom seemed to intensify its quiver as she strutted towards her clothes like a peahen. Its golden beads and pendant twinkled against her dark skin, and beads of precious stone – red, blue and green – added to the effect of sky at night.

From the corner of her eye, Velli sensed some movement behind a bush far to her left. She raised both arms to tie her hair in a bun, and perceived a head slowly rising behind the bushes. She took her time in the act, and discerned that the intruder's head remained unmoved. "Paralysed, as expected," she murmured with disdain.

Facing away from it, she bent down and casually placed a pellet in the sling. Rapidly regaining her full stature, she revolved it over her head. Before the peeper could retract, she swung around and shot at him. "Go to watch your mother."

The whiz of the sling was followed by a doggish yelp. She saw the egg-shaped pellet ricocheting upwards, spinning wildly. A portly man staggered out in the open, pressing hard his balding temple with both hands.

"You?" A shriek escaped Velli, and she stooped to grab her varati, a long piece of coarse cotton cloth. "When did you arrive?"

"I want to speak with you alone," said the man, labouring to steady his heavy frame. Her father Siwa Saqra's trading associate in Gandhara, he had offered to marry his daughter to Siwa whose wife, Velli's mother, had died some years ago. In exchange, the Gandharan trader had asked for Velli's hand.

"In this condition?" she said, her dark eyes steadily looking into his oblique ones. He lowered them, and she hastily wrapped the varati around herself. "Didn't my father tell you I don't want to marry you?"

"I'm the one you'd marry, you rude girl," he said, slapping his flabby chest upon which hair had started turning grey. Her lips pouted as she picked up another missile. He smirked. "Velli, I know your secret."

She shot upright. Did he really say what she heard?

"I know what you're hiding," he said, eyeing that portion of the varati which covered her abdomen. The sling slipped through her hands. "So now you know what's best for you, silly girl," he said grinning, exposing a set of uneven teeth. The sparks in her eyes fizzled out. His voice stung her again. "I'll meet Hiwa tomorrow to finalize our wedding."

She looked at him aghast as he turned to leave. Sauntering away with a feminine gait that she could not stand, he looked back at her. To Velli, the smile on the retreating Gandharan's face did not appear any different from that of a handsome Sumérian in those very woods just three lunar periods ago.

Her teeth clenched. "Pig," she murmured, "I'd have chased you all the way to your sty but …" Both her hands moved over her belly. Her heart pounded as she slumped on her knees. "How will I face Father when the Gandharan spills the beans?"

Velli sat weeping until a steady noise of parrots arriving to their nests broke her thoughts. It was getting dark. She got up instinctively. It seemed that all her senses had numbed, and a mysterious force was propelling her towards that portion of the river bank where not long ago a young girl had been carried away by a crocodile.

She walked on the narrow path whose slope started dropping rapidly. Her feet picked up speed, and she could now see the river approaching her fast. That was when a voice penetrated her consciousness. It was too familiar to be ignored. She halted. Looking behind, she saw a white haired lady carrying a walking stick, limping in a hurry as if a dog was chasing her.

Velli recognized the wife of an ascetic who lived in the forest and was known as the Horned Hermit. "Why are you going that way?" said the woman, red in face and breathing so heavily that her nostrils emitted low whistling sounds.

Velli did not reply. Unable to bear her dilemma, she had opened her heart to the hermit's wife few weeks ago. A tear rolled down her cheek. A soft wrinkled hand gripped her wrist and feebly pulled downwards. She did not resist. As she sat on the grass, a bony arm moved to her shoulder.

"Do you see those weaver birds?" the hermit's wife said, pointing to a pair of yellow birds fluttering before a flask-like nest hanging on a nearby tree. Velli nodded. "A crow trashed their nest and devoured all their chicks last week. You should have seen those poor little things grieving." Velli looked more carefully at the chirping birds. "Did they ever think, 'Life is not worth living any more'?"

All that Velli could do was draw squiggles on the earth. The hermit's wife said, "Why, dear, why?"

Velli found her voice. "A man I had rejected saw me bathing, *Amma*, and discovered what only you and I know. He threatened to expose me to my father if I turned down his proposal again."

"Let him," said the old lady, pulling her lips between toothless gums.

"*Amma*?" Velli looked at her wearily.

"He will have to explain how he came to know what he claims to know. The way he did it would make any young lady's father wild on the speaker."

"I am very scared to face Father, *Amma*," said Velli, holding the old lady's hand. "You're aware about his frame of mind after my mother's death. If he gets to know my condition, he would break down completely."

"Would Hiwa suffer any less if you were to kill yourself, my child?" said the hermit's wife. "Your father will believe you more than anybody else. And by the way, haven't you already sent a messenger to Sutantoru-on-Sea?" Velli nodded. "So just stand up to the pressure for a few days, Velli. Your aunt will come soon and take the situation in her hands."

Velli could not agree more. Her father Siwa felt cornered whenever her aunt confronted him with pursed lips which looked like (–).

The two women sat talking, till Velli got up with resolve in her eyes, and took the narrow path leading out of the woods.

The following morning, as Velli fed leftovers to their colt, she heard a snort like that of a bull approaching a herd. She perceived a rotund form materializing up the street. Although its top was wrapped in a bandage, and it leaned forth as if carrying some weight on its back, its gait was too familiar to misinterpret.

Flinging the mango skins towards the colt, she ran. She was so anxious to return behind the safety of a curtain that she missed seeing a mango stone flipping to the entrance.

The Gandharan trader did not see it either. Smiling at Velli's retreating derrière and humming a bawdy song, he stepped on the little yellow pit. For a moment, he turned into innumerable limbs beating in the air. His brief performance commenced with a shrill cry and ended with a loud thud. The flap of the sack that he carried gave way under his impact and a large sealed package shot out of it.

Siwa Saqra, still burping after a heavy breakfast of ripe mangoes, scurried to help him. First the trader's shriek, and then the bang echoed just as in high mountains, which made Siwa look back and bark, "Shut up." Velli knew that the words were directed at her parrot, whose cage swung from a low branch of a huge neem tree in the centre of the courtyard. Unconcerned of its master's discomfiture, the bird merrily repeated the sounds, and a giggle escaped Velli despite her woe.

Red in face, the Gandharan trader looked at Siwa like a priest eyes a sinner. "I loathe women laughing aloud, Hiwa. It speaks volumes about how your girl was brought up."

Siwa looked stunned, but mumbled 'I'm sorry' as he helped his guest to get up and walk to a cot. The trader sat on it, giving vent to a long series of 'ouch's in varying tones. In the kitchen, Velli danced merrily to each of those sounds.

The trader lowered his voice. She strained to hear but failed to pick up even a word. Then her father called her, and suddenly she started feeling cold. Somehow she made it to the foyer.

Siwa motioned to her to sit beside himself. Velli reflected how sharply her father's trim beard, a shaven upper lip and immaculate dress contrasted from the Gandharan's looks. Siwa said, "I understand that now you don't have any objection to marrying my friend?"

Velli's heartbeats eased. The blackmailer had not yet disclosed her secret. She could simply nod 'yes' and resolve an issue which had lately dampened her pillow with tears every night. On the other hand, how could any woman spend a lifetime with a boor like the Gandharan trader? As she gazed at a crack on the floor, she could not hold her toes from squirming. "Father," she said in a low voice, "I don't wish to marry so soon."

"Velli, we'll arrange the wedding only after the next monsoons."

"Right now," added the trader, lovingly moving his fingers between the jute-string woven in the cot, "we'll only announce our engagement – that's all."

Velli's brow knitted, but then she hastened to say, "Could we speak alone, Father?"

"Why?" Siwa said in a voice that she perceived as meaning 'Is that necessary?' Her head inclined and her eyes narrowed. "Excuse me," he said getting up and following Velli through a flowing curtain into an adjoining room. He folded his hands under his arms and grunted.

"I – I don't want to marry him, Father."

"Why not?"

"I don't like him," she said, fighting to suppress a sob.

"Velli, you're too young to know what's good for you. Give me one good reason for your dislike."

"Father, he's older than you."

"Men never age," said Siwa, pounding a foot on the floor.

Was her father trying to justify his covert desire to marry the Gandharan's daughter, a girl half his age? The next moment, she admonished herself for such a thought. It was most likely that he was simply parroting the ancient wisdom of the Meluhhan men.

Siwa's tone softened. "You'll be happy in a large prosperous family, dear. I've met the trader's wives – three wives." Without noticing that Velli's mouth and eyes had attained a perfectly round shape, he continued, "Also his daughter. They all are nice ladies."

"But Father," her voice trembled, "he is – he's cun– he's so different from you."

"Velli, I've already committed to him," said Siwa holding both her arms. "I never go back on my word."

Velli sensed a strange internal force thrusting out her chest. A firm voice emanated from her throat, "I won't –"

She had hardly spoken when a resounding slap smacked her cheek. Her hands flew to cover her face. Never had her father treated her in such a manner. Her mother's memory flooded her mind and burst out as a whine. '*Amma…*'

Through tears, she saw anger leaving Siwa's face like a passing cloud. He sank to the floor, as if that one word had drained out all his energy. She sat down beside him, and her convulsing body found solace in his strong arms.

Just then there was sound of a cart pulling up at the gate. A cheerful voice followed it.

"Auntie!" Velli gasped, leaping up and rushing out of the room. A radiant woman aged about sixty was alighting from a donkey-cart as if the ground below were a pit full of mud. Velli flung herself into the woman's arms and clung to her like a creeper on a tree. Her brow sensed a warm kiss.

"Don't worry dear," she heard her aunt saying in her ear, "I received your missive. I've decided to take you to Sutantoru."

Fear left Velli's mind. It was high time to pay back the Gandharan who had scared her in her dreams throughout the night. She let out a loud wail. "Father's forcing me to marry a doddering man, Auntie."

Turning red with anger, the trader staggered to his feet. "Hiwa Haqra," he cried, and his round cheeks quivered. "I want to tell you a thing or two about that daughter of yours."

Velli shut her eyes tightly and embraced her aunt harder. The trader's voice trailed in again. "Before I do it, I would say that I've seen many hen-pecked husbands, but never a chick-pecked parent like you."

There was a moment of silence. Then, over her aunt's shoulder, Velli caught sight of the trader's sealed parcel flying across the street. It landed with a loud crash raising a small cloud of dust. Roughed up a second time that morning, it tore open, ejecting a lot of pieces looking like brown stones.

"Gandharan," Siwa's deep voice came as a blast. "I've had enough. Will you leave or shall I throw you out?"

Velli could not believe what she heard till the caged parrot reassured her with a steady chant of the last three words.

The Gandharan trader, despite his recent mishap, darted to the street and started gathering the strewn pieces with a swiftness which made Velli blink. "I'm sorry for what I blabbered," he implored. "Siwa, please calm down."

"I don't care about anybody's views. I stand by my daughter," said Siwa, thrashing one palm with another. "I don't wish to continue our contract. I'll introduce you to Merchant Jittan, my client's man in Meluhha. You may directly sell your stone dye to him."

The trader behaved as if he had not heard Siwa. He produced only a wailing sound when he said, "I'll repack the material and send it to you tomorrow." Then he turned and left hastily before Siwa could speak again.

Velli wondered why the Gandharan trader chose to bear a stark insult. Was her father's involvement so crucial in sending the stone dye to Sumér?

7 GIRL FROM SUTANTORU

Swells higher than a man's height rocked Captain Paravar's ship. His sailors sniggered as Sam sat at the base of the mast, gripping it like a child hugging its mother. Although he was used to the howling desert winds, he had never heard such ominous rumbling every time the lightning stabbed the darkness. The waves slapped the vessel whose woodwork screeched eerily, making Sam wish he could shut his ears just like his eyes.

Had fate saved him from execution only to drown him at sea?

Shouts accompanied by a fluttering sound told Sam that several sailors were busy taking down the sail. From the Captain's bellows, Sam guessed that he was fighting hard along with his sailors to drain out the deluge of water from the vessel.

Perhaps the situation was not as grim as he feared. Shouldn't he too perform his duty? 'The foal would have been scared to death by now,' was his first thought.

He got up like a baby learning to walk, and tottered to the animal. One look at it threw the storm out of his mind. It lay sprawled on the deck, soaked to the skin and staring at the sky.

Sam's arms slipped around the foal's neck, and he broke down.

He was not aware when the storm showed signs of abetting, and the sailors started gathering around him. A hand gripped his shoulder. He knew it was the Captain, but was unable to look up and meet his eye.

Then he heard the Captain's soothing voice. "We could save it from man, but not from nature. Perhaps it was its destiny to be buried at sea."

As the Captain's footsteps retreated, Sam thought that his palm sensed a throb. He sat up and perceived a weak pulse. Spinning around, he shouted. A couple of sailors ran to bring warm water and dry cloth as he bade. Another hurried to fetch an earthen pot containing smouldering coal to start a fire.

Cajoling the foal, Sam cleaned and rubbed its limbs. Little by little he poured warm broth into its mouth. He saw its hide shudder, and its chest heave. Then it neighed as if under unbearable pain. He patted and cheered it. "Captain," he yelled, "your little one has got over the worst."

Sam heard the Captain hollering 'thanks', and then asking his deputy to set free one of the two rock doves in the cage. They watched the bird taking off towards the stern and fluttering away. "Turn her around," ordered the Captain.

As the crew started the exercise, Sam went to the head sailor and said, "Why did you release the pigeon? Wasn't it meant for the Captain's dinner?"

"No," said the head sailor. "Those birds are our best friends. When we lose our way at sea, we release a dove. It always flies away in the direction of land."

Sam saw the Captain studying the mast which whipped at the top. There was concern on his face. Summoning two sailors, he instructed them. They tied a piece of rope around their waists and scaled the mast. Suspended high above the deck, they commenced a long struggle to fix a supporting strut to the mast.

The foal had slipped into a nap and Sam watched the Captain with interest as he gave periodic instructions with one eye on the sky. At one point he said, "There, the *Vata-miin* is now visible. Get me the *kamal.*"

Following his gaze, Sam recognised the Pole Star Thuban shining in the northern sky. The head sailor came, carrying a wooden card with a hole in its centre through which passed a string. The Captain held the string between his teeth and moved the card to and fro at the Thuban. Then he marked a position on the string with a knot.

He walked towards his cabin, measuring the length from the knot to the card with his fingers. The head sailor ran ahead of him, lighted a couple of lamps and flung open an ebony chest. Selecting a pile of barks bound by jute string from several similar tomes stored inside, the Captain studied it for quite some time. "We're somewhere near Sutantoru-on-Sea," he announced at last, and strode to the rudder to take charge.

Around midnight, an excited cry woke up everybody. The Captain strained to see in the direction pointed by the sailor. "Yes," he agreed, "we were closer to the port than I reckoned."

Sam discerned a weak flicker of light far away. "That's one of your regular ports of call, isn't it?" he asked.

"No, it's one port that prefers foreign ships to our own."

"Any ship, whether local or foreign, pays the port for the facilities, doesn't it?"

"Sutantoru has its reasons," said the Captain. "One, the monsoons don't affect its route to Suméru as they do in Alatinam and Port Lothal. This port is accessible to Sumérian ships all the year round."

Sam waited for him to continue, but there was silence. He turned to see the Captain's face in the dark. "What is another?"

"Sutantoru is notorious for some sort of slavery, which would never be permitted at other ports."

"Slavery? With Sumér?"

With a sigh, the Captain started walking towards his cabin. Sam considered it best to resolve an issue that was on his mind. Catching up, he said: "The foal is too weak to continue the voyage, Captain. Shall we leave it in Sutantoru?"

"I can't abandon it, Samorist."

Sam thought that since he did not know where Hiwa Haqra lived, he might as well start his search from Sutantoru-on-Sea rather than from Port Lothal. "I'll go along with the baby if its buyer provides me shelter and food," he said.

The Captain shook his head. "Who will buy a sick animal?"

"It's not just any animal," said Sam, and he immediately realized that he had given away annoyance in his voice. He quickly added, "As I told you, Captain, it's going to grow up into a lovely mare."

"To the people who have never seen a horse, Samorist, it's no more than an exotic breed of donkey."

Sam considered it practical to postpone his search for Hiwa Haqra till the foal had grown up. A mare could be an invaluable help in Meluhha, the land of long distances.

"Suppose nobody takes it away, Captain," he said quietly. "I'll stay back in Sutantoru to look after it."

As the ox-cart carrying the sick foal rattled along a narrow muddy track, Sam jumped down to look closely at some wooden poles erected by the sides, and then ran to catch up.

"Those poles indicate the place where the dead are buried," the Captain informed.

After a long ride, they passed through a fortification wall built with semi-dressed stones. As they entered the village, Sam heard vendors enticing customers, women haggling, and children crying. Thrilled, he watched farmers, herdsmen, hunters and fishermen socializing with full vocal gusto.

"We're lucky," the Captain said. "It's the weekly barter day when people living along the shore and in the wilds gather in Sutantoru-on-Sea."

They found some space near a banyan tree. Several women, wearing their hair in long plaits, were lighting earthen lamps at the foot of its imposing trunk. From the devoutness on their faces, Sam assumed that they were worshipping the banyan tree.

A whiff of acute fragrance drew Sam's attention to one who had broken away from the crowd and was approaching them. Her oiled hair was adorned with a trumpet-lily held in place with long pins made from bone. She was escorted by a young lady aged about twenty, whose eyes reminded Sam of a doe in King Shulgi's palace. A lose robe of thick cotton made the girl appear like one of those water jars on their ship. He wondered whether she too bore tattoos on her dark skin like her elder companion.

By then the two women had reached them. "Now the mariners have stooped to selling animals," said the elder woman, looking askance. Sam could not miss that she pursed her lips in a peculiar way which looked like (–).

"She isn't interested in our foal," the Captain mumbled, producing an ivory comb from his *vesti* and running it on his bare scalp. "I tell you, boy, that female is 'shopping' for small talk with a handsome man."

As the woman bent and patted the foal, Sam studied her young companion. She gave an impression of being plump, and yet her face was not so. It radiated an unmistakable glow. She too stooped to fondle the baby, and her long jet black hair fell over her shoulder upon the animal. Tickled by its touch, the foal shook its head. She broke into a peal of laughter, making Sam gape wider.

The girl moved her hand over the skin of the foal. Then she opened its mouth and peeped at the teeth. She watched its breathing and prodded nearby droppings with a stick. Sam could not hold himself. "You seem to understand horses well," he said.

She eyed him as if he were one of those burial poles by the wayside. His sight fell on her necklace and got locked on it. It was just like the one he had seen inside the dead Meluhhan's turban before Biggie performed the vanishing trick.

Sam's head trembled as he became aware that the woman was speaking to him. He caught the words "She already owns a colt," and they stiffened his relaxed posture.

"Colt? Here in Sutantoru?" he asked, glancing at the Captain. "I was told there weren't any horses in Meluhha."

"You were told the truth. Recently one has come to Meluhha, although not in Sutantoru." The woman put her hand around the girl's waist. "Her father brought it from Gandhara –"

"Is it for sale?" the girl cut in, smiling at the Captain. Just those four words made Sam imagine that her voice might have vibrated many a young man's heartstrings.

"Yes, lady," the Captain answered, steadily looking at the girl's necklace.

The woman asked, "What does it cost?"

"Nothing, if you promise not to make a meal of it."

The woman smiled. "I've come to buy a horse, not horse-meat (–)"

"Then it's all yours," said the Captain indicating the foal with both his hands.

The girl clapped hers. Sam heard the woman telling her, "The foal would give a pleasant surprise to your father when you return home."

The girl giggled. Sam started untying the foal, when he heard her speaking to Captain Paravar. "Do you also call on ports farther than Dilmun?"

"Yes, I do," said the Captain. "My young companion boarded it at Urim."

Sam turned to face them with a broad smile, only to find that she had not thrown even a fleeting glance in his direction. Turning serious, he led the foal to the woman and handed her the rope.

"Is there a man named Kayl on board?" the girl asked.

"Owlish? Possessing a tortoise head under the shell of a turban?" said the Captain as his hand rose to his chin. "Habitually whistling tunes?"

"That's him," she cried, clasping both her hands together. "Is he here?"

"No, he isn't on board, but he travelled with me from Alatinam to Urim on this voyage."

The woman addressed the girl. "Kayl is your father's right-hand man, I suppose – the one who delivered your message to me?"

"Yes, Auntie."

With a subtle wave of his hand, the Captain beckoned Sam. "This young man Samo– I mean Samasin – possesses a deep understanding of horses," he told the woman. "He would serve you well."

"Sure," she said. Sam flashed a smile at her in general and at the girl in particular. The girl tapped her aunt's elbow, leaned and whispered in her ear. "On second thought," added the woman, "we could do without any help."

"As you wish," the Captain shrugged his shoulders, and turned to the girl. "By the way, young lady, I've rarely seen as beautiful a piece of jewellery as your necklace."

Sam was glad that the Captain had noticed the necklace too. He looked forward to knowing more about it.

"Superb, isn't it?" she cooed. "My father gifted it on my birthday."

"I would like to buy one for my wife," said the Captain. "From where did he get it?"

"From Gandhara, I guess. Lately he travels there often."

The Captain sighed, "The old girl will have to make do with local jewellery then."

Sam wished that the Captain had sought details about her father instead. He walked to the foal and gave it a big hug. As it weakly followed the women, Sam's eyes shone with tears. Then they shifted to the taller of the two departing forms. More the naïve Sumérian observed the girl, faster did his heart pound.

His arm received a soft punch. "Samorist," he heard the Captain's voice. "Let's rush to the docks. I want to leave before dusk."

Sam boarded the cart, pondering how to elicit more information from the Captain without raising interest in his tender feelings. "Which products do you carry from Meluhha to my country, Captain?" he asked.

"Cotton textiles, ivory products and gold jewellery with carnelian beads," the Captain said, stretching out his legs. "But from the next season, I'd be mostly carrying timber."

"Wouldn't timber be difficult to handle in a storm?"

"Storms only hamper you after the monsoons arrive," said the Captain. He picked up a crane-necked flask, drank from it and passed it to Sam. "This time we got caught because we were late leaving Sumér. My client in Lagaš refused to sign his order in the temple of *Šamaš* when the Sun God disappeared from the sky."

"It happened in Lagaš too?" Sam's hand holding the flask remained suspended half-way to his lips. Had the Captain's ship not been delayed by the Sun God, he couldn't have escaped the killers.

"Yes," said the Captain. "I had to wait for a week till the following Day of Šamaš to get my big timber contract."

Sam realized that he was not getting anywhere, so he asked straightaway, "Where is Gandhara, Captain?"

"It's high up in the mountains," said the Captain with a knowing glint in his eye, "where lapis lazuli is mined."

"The Sumérian connection."

"Yes, your country is a big market for lapis beads. The man about whom the girl enquired –"

"Your passenger named Kayl?" Sam asked, brightening up.

"Yes, he was carrying lapis to Babili."

"Babili?" Sam's head reeled as his hand slipped inside his gown to the piece of cloth holding the fish-hook. What he had not realized earlier was that the Captain's description of Kayl perfectly matched the murdered Meluhhan's appearance. The stunning similarity between the necklace found in the dead man's turban and that worn by the girl also supported the assumption that he was none else than Kayl.

Was Hiwa Haqra – the man Kayl had mentioned – the father of the damsel who had stolen his heart?

8 DRUNKEN SAM DROPS HINT

Landing at the village of Alatinam, Sam felt like a king when Qwoco held his hand and guided him through its lanes, responding to his queries with "Yes, *Belum*" or "No, *Belum*".

Despite Alatinam handling trade between Sumér and all towns on River Sindhu, it lacked the sparkle of Dilmun. With fish laid out to dry everywhere, it not only looked like a big fishing village but also smelt like one.

Sam spit out once again as if he were enjoying the act. Nothing could irritate him any more, not even the repellent odour.

How beautiful was Hiwa Haqra's daughter! Now who cared even if the Babilians thought he was a murderer? His future was not in Sumér, but in Meluhha where he would marry and raise a large Suméro-Meluhhan family. He marvelled at the power of Woman, and how she could turn a man's priorities on their head.

Sam inhaled a whiff of mustard oil. Looking behind, he saw a cock-eyed sailor whose primary task on their ship was cooking. He had heard through the ship grapevine that old women in Lothal used to allude to him while cautioning young mothers not to tie oversized scarves on their babies' head. The 'cock-eye' was following Qwoco like a disciple, lugging a big packet bound in date-palm matting. Sam wondered about what kind of a person Cock-eye was that he worshipped, of all men, Qwoco.

Shifting his attention to the package in Cock-eye's hands, he asked, "What does that contain?"

Cock-eye hesitated, and Qwoco replied instead. "Date

sweetmeat for my friend's kids."

Doubt flickered on Sam's face for a moment. A parcel of dates wouldn't be as heavy as it seemed to burden Cock-eye.

"Come, *Belum*," Qwoco hastened to add, and pulled him towards a thatched hut on the river bank. An unfamiliar but pleasant aroma drifted in the air. He pushed the door that was a little ajar, and a volley of merry voices hit them. In the dim light, Sam made out that several men were seated on the ground, drinking and chatting. All three of them were promptly served the drink.

Sam raised his goblet to his lips. "It's sweet, so different from beer."

"*Tanni* is derived from Palmyra trees," informed Qwoco. "Let's enjoy it to the fullest, for we have plenty of time in our hands."

After drinking a few goblets of the novel drink, Sam blinked his eyes and smiled benignly at everybody. He heard Qwoco saying, "We are friends, you and I."

Sam was delighted that what was at the back of his mind since that morning had been expressed by Qwoco.

"Yesh, clozh friends," he said, extending a hand to the sailor's shoulder. His tongue seemed to be faltering, but that was a little inconvenience everybody put up with when they enjoyed a good drink.

"So close that we share our secrets," Qwoco said in a low voice.

"Of coursh, we do."

"Tell me yours – because I'm your friend." Sam sensed Qwoco's warm arm creeping on his shoulders.

All of a sudden, he felt that the trauma which he had undergone in Babili had weighed upon him for too long. He had to vent it out to a friend. Taking a deep gulp, he pulled Qwoco closer. "I shaw shome people killing a Meluhhan."

"A Meluhhan?"

There was utter disbelief in his friend's tone. He had to be convinced.

"A pedigree Meluhhan – like you." Sam tapped Qwoco's chest. "Hizh name was Kayl. He told me a shikret. And I'll tell it to you. Becauzh we are friends."

"What is that, Hamasin?"

Sam sensed thrill in his friend's voice.

"Sh..." He raised a finger over his nose and looked around

stealthily. Cock-eye, with his eyes half closed, was blissfully sipping his *tanni.* Sam continued, "Kayl ashked me to meet Hi – Hiwaqra. Now that is my shikret."

"Meet where?"

"He didn't tell."

Sam failed to understand why Qwoco laughed heartily. "Secret within a secret, Hamasin?" he asked.

"It isn't that. Poor Kayl couldn't tell me." Sam choked as he spoke. "He died." He sprawled on the ground, held his eyes wide open and put out his tongue.

"Boo-hoo..." Qwoco sounded overcome by the tragic turn of events.

"Boo-hoo-hoo..." Sam got up and wailed on his friend's shoulder. "Kayl gave me shomething. And died."

He felt gentle patting on his back as Qwoco whispered, "Gave you what, Hamasin?"

"A teeny-weeny fish-hook." Sam attempted to reach inside his robe, but his trembling hand refused to do his bidding.

"To catch fish?"

"No, stupid. To show it to Hiwa – Hiwaqra."

Qwoco ordered one more drink, and Sam did not know what happened after that.

When his eyes opened, he was only aware of a sharp pain shooting through his head. He found himself lying under the open sky. For quite some time, he kept staring at everything he saw around. As he rose with a great effort, a small boy playing nearby ran into the hut and returned with the man whom Sam vaguely recognized as one who had served the drinks. He paid the man, who nudged him in a certain direction. As he staggered ahead, he wondered if he had aged suddenly.

Sam was endeavouring to turn a corner when a moist, muscular and breathless body collided against him. He fell, and the stranger tumbled over, his weight pressing Sam to the ground. Much of the *tanni* that he had consumed flushed out from his stomach, drenching the dazed man.

"Shorry, my brother," Sam apologized as he clasped the stranger in a firm embrace.

The man struggled to get free. "Leave me you *tanni*-tadpole," he cried. Sam suffered a pang on his shoulder. The stranger had bitten him. Anger swept over him, and he planted his teeth on the stranger's ear. The resulting yawl made him smile. By then a crowd arrived shouting, and started beating up the stranger.

The collision, the bite and the commotion combined to sober up Sam. Several shining objects lying on the ground caught his eye, and he picked them up. They were a heavy silver waist band and two silver necklaces. He got to his feet, wiping away the dust from the ornaments, when he heard a series of annoyed quacks drawing nearer.

A tall man joined them, clasping a rebellious duck close to his chest. He had his curly hair cut short. Sam imagined that were he to wear it long, the abundance of curly locks would be the envy of women.

Someone in the crowd asked Sam to give the jewellery to the tall man, and pushed the thief forward.

"Everything's in order," said the man loudly. "Let him go."

As the crowd dispersed, the man turned to Sam. "Thank you Sumérian," he said with an approving nod. "I presume you arrived on Paravar's ship?"

"Yes," said Sam, wondering why the man spoke as if everybody around was deaf. "I'm Samasin from Babili."

"I'm Yali – better known as Tall Yali – skipper of a sea-going vessel," said the man. "Paravar's a good friend of mine."

'Maybe,' thought Sam, 'but you haven't learnt from the Captain to lower your voice when you aren't instructing your sailors.'

In the meanwhile, a plump woman in her fifties, her nose pointing in the air, had wobbled up to them. Red in face and panting, she waved a lotus leaf that she held, apparently without getting any relief from the heat.

"She's my elder sister," said Tall Yali. "Sister, he is Samasin. He caught the thief and saved your jewellery."

Sam detested snobbishness, and Tall Yali's sister impressed him as conceit incarnate. He bowed because he was supposed to look courteous.

The woman beamed, and Sam tried to spot her eyes which got more or less covered by her rosy cheeks. Her smile erased all the arrogance from her face. "Come home for dinner, Hamasin," she said.

"I'd be delighted, Sister." He bowed again, but with sincerity. "However, I need to reach the docks immediately as my ship's leaving at sunset."

"I'd give this duck to you if your ship hasn't left already," said Tall Yali. "Had it been any captain other than Paravar, there was a sliver of a chance." Sam gaped at him. Tall Yali handed the fowl to the lady. "Meet me at the docks, Sister. I'll get him there nevertheless."

"I'll join you as soon as I've bought everything on your list," she said flapping the round leaf which, Sam noticed, was etched with nail marks all over it.

Tall Yali hailed a donkey-cart and they jumped on it. Amidst the noise of the rapidly rolling cart, he asked, "By the way, Samasin, do you know Nergal of Nibru?"

"I know only one man named Nergal, and he lives in Babili."

"How silly of me to ask you," Tall Yali said with a shrug. "Sumér is a vast country, and there would be several Nergals in each of its towns."

"Yali, my friend," Sam said scratching his head as if to locate a deeply buried thought. "Do you know any merchant named Hiwa Haqra?"

Tall Yali winced. Sam was not sure whether what he saw on Yali's weathered face was disbelief or reflection. He repeated his query a little louder.

"You mean Siwa Saqra?" asked Tall Yali as if he had been shaken out of a dream.

"No, Hiwa Haqra."

"That's the same," said Tall Yali. "In Meluhha, most sailors, farmers, women – those who are illiterate – pronounce the words starting with 'sa' and 'sha' with 'ha'."

"Well, then do you know Siwa –"

"No, I don't." Tall Yali sounded like a boy carrying a catapult, asked if he had broken a pot. "I guess Siwa Saqra is someone with whom you'd like to hobnob?"

"No," said Sam, and paused. "I met a countryman of yours in Babili. While on his deathbed, he asked me to meet Hiwa – I mean, Siwa Saqra. But before he could say where, he passed away."

Tall Yali's jaw dropped. "Did you make so big a hullabaloo on such a flimsy matter?" he exclaimed.

Sam wished to avoid narrating his initial objective of clearing his name from the murder in Babili by exposing Kayl's assassin. Nor did he want to confess that he liked a girl he had met in Sutantoru-on-Sea, and had discovered later that she was Siwa Saqra's daughter. "Not at all," he said in a shaky voice. "Captain Paravar had a foal on board and asked if I would take care of it."

"Foal? What's it?"

"In our country, we have an animal called a horse. It looks like _"

"I know. Paravar told me that horses are very strong like the khurs, the wild asses of our desert, but they can be tamed."

"A foal is a baby horse," said Sam, relieved.

Reaching the port, they saw that Captain Paravar's ship had advanced so far that the sail appeared to have merged with its body. Sam pressed his temple as he stood staring at the blob on the horizon. "When could I get the next ship to Port Lothal?"

"You're on your beam-ends, Sumérian. One won't call at this port for four lunar periods."

"Four?"

"Yes, because no longer are the winds suitable for sailing," said Tall Yali.

However, Sam was not listening. He was thinking about the two ladies of Sutantoru. From their conversation, it was clear that the girl was just visiting her aunt at Sutantoru-on-Sea, and that she lived elsewhere. He had to locate her father to seek her hand. "Reaching Lothal is not important for me, finding Siwa Saqra is," he said. "Which are the major trade centres upstream of the river that we saw, Yali?"

"There are Chendur Village and Muenduru City. Further up on the course of the Sindhu, a river named Ravi meets it. Somewhere along that, sticking up like a sore thumb is a fort named Harappa."

"Sarappa," rejoined Sam.

"You learn fast," Tall Yali said with a smile. "But it is indeed 'Harappa'. That's one word which everybody pronounces right." Sam noticed that as Yali spoke, his eyes were fixed on the dockyard gate. Following his gaze, Sam saw that a heavily loaded cart had just entered it, and a woman held the reins of the oxen. Tall Yali clapped and waved, and Sam recognized his sister.

When the lady came to know about Sam's misfortune, she gave vent to a sound like 'tch-tch-tch'.

"He's searching for a man named Saqra," Tall Yali told her.

"Haqra!" she exclaimed. "One of my childhood friends in Fort Harappa belongs to the Haqra family. Do you remember a famished woman we met in the market last year?" she asked Yali.

"Her husband works on Lothal port."

"Samasin," said Tall Yali, slapping Sam's back. "I can take you to Laketown Dholavira from where you could reach Port Lothal." He pointed to a small ship anchored at the docks. "That's mine and we'd be leaving soon."

"Yali, my good friend, call me Sam," he said, letting out an audible breath. "I'd surely go with you to Laketown Dho – Dho?"

"Dho-la-vi-ra," said Tall Yali laughing. "Sumérian, you've started discovering that we Melluhans have created the most outrageous names on earth."

A little later, Sam stood on the deck of Tall Yali's vessel waving farewell to the helpful lady.

With new hope, he turned away; and his hand casually slipped inside his pocket. A low scream escaped him. The piece of cloth carrying the bronze fish-hook was missing. Perhaps he had dropped it in the skirmish with the robber. Although he no longer cared about proving his innocence in Sumér, the fish-hook would have provided a handy excuse to meet the father of the girl he loved.

Sam woke up, cursing the sailors whose raucous chattering had disturbed his sleep. They sounded as excited as teenagers participating in a camel race. He got up stretching, to find out the reason. Long way ahead of them lumbered a larger ship, and it seemed that theirs was fast catching up with it.

He looked again. The other vessel, seen in the dim light of dawn, looked no different from what he had seen on the full moon night in Urim. "That's Captain Paravar's," he said, leaping and running to the skipper. "Yali, could you get me on it?"

Tall Yali ordered a sailor who went to the forecastle, lighted a torch and waved it. A little later, Sam saw a flame moving from side to side on the bigger ship. No sooner did they reach within a hearing distance, Tall Yali took up a funnel speaker and informed about Sam. They watched a tiny boat being lowered from its deck. When it neared, Sam recognized Cock-eye. Sam embraced Tall Yali and descended down a rope.

The smell of mustard oil reached him long before he set foot in the boat. Taking up the two extra oars, Sam asked: "How's our friend Qwoco?"

"We left him in Alatinam," said the sailor. "Weren't you two together?"

"You were with us too, clutching Qwoco's tail, weren't you?"

"I left after drinking just one goblet."

"Then I guess Qwoco was too drunk to recall I was with him," said Sam, scratching behind his ear. "I wonder why I didn't see him again. Alatinam is such a small place."

Cock-eye went on rowing, looking the least interested in Sam's monologue. After a considerable time of silence, they reached the ship. They climbed up to the deck and pulled the boat after them.

As soon as he saw the Captain relaxed, Sam said, "Tall Yali told me he knew someone back home – not in Babili, but in Nibru."

"Nergal?"

"You too know him, do you?"

"As well as the reed of my ship," said the Captain gravely, "although we haven't met." He started walking towards his cabin.

"A person who should be given a wide berth?" asked Sam, falling in step.

"Didn't Yali tell you how Nergal was instrumental in striking our friendship?" The Captain entered the cabin, holding the door open for him.

Sam looked around the Captain's lair. A few times earlier, he had got a glimpse of the cot and the ebony chest, but for the first time he saw a terracotta basin containing several long necked jars wrapped in pieces of damp jute cloth. "No," he said, "how did you come to know Tall Yali?"

"It's a long story." The Captain motioned to him to sit on the chest. "Crooks like Nergal disgrace their mother land."

"Nergal of Nibru," Sam assured himself aloud as he took the seat. Despite not having any love for his former Master, he would never think of Nergal the Fox as a crook.

"It happened about four lunar periods ago in Alatinam," said the Captain, as he picked up two jars from the basin and offered one to Sam. "No? Are you sure?"

Sam declined politely. After all that he had gone through in Alatinam, he had determined to shun liquor.

"Nergal of Nibru met Yali and both became close friends. After visiting several places upstream of the Sindhu, he returned and gifted a necklace to Yali's sister, who was alone as Yali had left for Dholavira."

The Captain took a long draught from the jar. Sam feared the worst for the jolly lady, and wished that he was wrong.

The Captain continued. "Nergal told her that he could replicate any jewellery when the planets attained a certain position, and asked for the necklace which he had gifted. He wrapped it in a piece of black cloth and retired into a room. Emerging from there a little later, he handed the package to her, saying, 'Unwrap this on the third day, Sister. However, if any doubt arises in your mind, your ornament would turn into a stone.'"

Sam rose to his feet. "Did it?"

"Not the first time. She found two identical necklaces on the third day when she untied the knots. So expecting to make hay while the sun shone, the greedy woman handed all her jewellery to Nergal. That was the last time she saw it, because the cheat had boarded a ship that had called on Alatinam port earlier that day, and was gone."

The Captain got up to get another flask of beer, and as he neared the basin, his nostrils quivered. He reached the door like a pouncing tiger. As he flung it open, a sailor stumbled and fell. "You, son of a warthog," roared the Captain. "Eavesdropping, weren't you?"

"I – I –" Cock-eye stuttered. "I came to ask, *Kavintu*; what will you have for dinner?"

"Your balls!" blasted the Captain, "Scrambled and peppered."

The sailor scurried away as the Captain fumed, and Sam considered it apt to leave him alone.

Both Qwoco and Cock-eye's strange behaviour perplexed Sam, but someone more important was now occupying his mind, and he considered it trivial to bother about a couple of crazy sailors.

9 QUEST IN LOTHAL

Sam hurried to the stern, curious to see what happened after their ship entered Port Lothal from an inlet channel which was connected to River Sabarmathi. He saw lock gates being closed after them. As the ship approached the dock, a group of labourers there pulled at ropes tied all along its broadside. Their dark bodies shone under the sun, and a strident chorus of '*haisho*' reverberated in the air.

No sooner had the ship touched the wharf, Sam was roughly jostled by a mad rush of hefty men, each carrying a long staff. He shivered at the thought that they were going to beat someone on the ship to death. As each man tied a load to either end of the staff, and carried it across their shoulders, he laughed at his unfounded fear. The porters jogged down to the wharf and struggled upwards on a ramp that led to a brick building which stood on a high platform.

Upon landing at Port Lothal, Sam shuffled to the tallest Palmyra tree he had seen from the ship. The searing hot weather had forced him to abandon the Sumérian gown for the Meluhhan *vesti*, which not only hindered his movements but also made him think that his walk now resembled a woman's. He folded the loose portion high above his knees and tied it around the waist before climbing the tree.

A bird's eye-view of Port Lothal threw out all his complaints against the *vesti* from his mind. The town looked like a giant mesh. From the main road which cut right across it, several streets emerged, running parallel to each other. They were flanked by low buildings. Black smoke arose from many of them. Crossing the streets at right angles were narrower lanes lined with higher buildings.

"Those ought to be residential houses," Sam thought, "and I need to visit them to find the lady whom Yali's sister mentioned."

Sliding down little by little, Sam reached the ground. An intense search led him up a flight of steps to a row of houses whose dung plastered walls were painted with motifs of flowers and birds. Among those identical houses, he found the one which he sought.

Inside, a bent old woman was sweetly singing a lullaby to a baby. Hearing his footsteps stopping at the door, she turned. Suddenly faced with two yellow eyes, Sam stepped back before realizing that she suffered from cataract.

"Daughter-in-law," she called out in a sharp voice. "See who's at the door."

A woman wearing a short silver necklace came out wiping hands on her varati. It struck Sam that although she looked tired, she was not as sickly as her very healthy friend in Alatinam had described. He joined his hands in typical Meluhhan greetings and said, "I am a friend of Tall Yali. His sister said that you belong to the Saqra family of Fort Harappa."

"Yes, yes," she said, her face radiating warmth. Her shell bangles clanked as she pulled out a mat from a niche in the wall and spread it out on the floor. "Please sit down. I'll be back soon."

She returned carrying a black terracotta bowl in both her hands. She placed it before Sam and squatted down resting against the wall.

"I'm searching for Siwa Saqra," said Sam as he sipped the salted buttermilk and experienced a gentle coolness spreading under his scalp like canal water in a dry field.

"Hiwa," her voice hit a high pitch. "He's a distant cousin of mine."

Sam saw the blind old woman twisting her lips in a sign of apparent contempt. "I believe, lady, that your parents and brothers live in Fort Harappa?" he said.

"They did, a long time ago. Now they're in Gangevell – Rocky Gangevell."

"I presume Siwa is still in Fort Harappa?"

"I'm not sure." Her lower lip extended sideways. "A lot has

changed since I left Harappa a decade ago."

Sam finished the rest of the buttermilk in quick gulps and got up. As they walked to the door, she said, "When my brother came from Gangevell, he told me that Siwa had been passing through a rough patch. First, his trading venture failed. Then, he lost his wife."

"That might have happened many years ago," said Sam, recollecting the costly necklace that Siwa's daughter wore in Sutantoru-on-Sea. He was on the verge of asking a question, when he decided against it. His overt purpose for Siwa's quest should not be perceived any other than carrying a message from Sumér.

In order to meet Siwa, he had to reach Fort Harappa which was roughly a hundred *da-na* away. The long voyage called for earning and saving considerable amount of silver. Sam bit his tongue. "They have neither horses nor camels in Meluhha. Here, all my experience is as useless as pits of ber fruit."

Visiting the northern part of Lothal in search of work, Sam met men either melting copper ingots in a huge furnace, or casting and rolling the metal. Sweeping away sweat from the brow, they told him they had enough workers, and did not need any more.

Sam stared at distant trees. The little silver that the Captain had given him had disappeared in rent and food. Without any work, the fate of living by the road and going hungry stared him in the face.

As he trudged aimlessly, a heavy hand fell on his shoulder. "Come with me, foreigner," said a commanding voice. Sam looked into the eyes of a burly man, who possessed a moustache that was twisted and waxed to point upwards. He wore a broad leather belt, and carried a long bamboo staff. He ought to be a guard, thought Sam. "Wandering like a bull on the street," said the guard, thrusting a square jaw at him.

"I'm looking for work," Sam said.

"You won't get it anywhere in Port Lothal, because sailors have filled all the vacancies till the time their ships go out to the sea again."

"And that won't happen till the monsoons are over," Sam gasped, pressing his head with both hands.

"We need lots of additional hands to do the annual maintenance of our drainage system," said the guard. "You'll be doing that as a slave, and –"

"Slave?" Sam's desperate cry arose above the clangs of a

hammer on an anvil. The only person who could save him was the Captain, who had left for Tamilakam that morning.

Sam sprinted, forgetting that he was dressed in an ankle long *vesti*. His foot got entangled in the flowing cloth, his fingers groped in the air, and he crashed to the ground.

The guard walked up to him and offered his hand. Holding it, Sam got up sheepishly.

"Slavery in Meluhha isn't as bad as you fear, Sumérian," said the guard in a kindly tone that Sam thought was not natural to a man in his profession. "You'd be a temporary slave until you find work. Lothal will provide you a roof over your head and two square meals a day for your labour."

The deep furrows on Sam's face were replaced by a smile. It remained there over the following few weeks despite his repulsion to food after a long day of descending into manholes and removing solid waste.

In his search for freedom, once he visited a workshop manufacturing stone beads. The owner, his hair greying at the edges, greeted him in Sumérian. Sam pressed the man's hands in his own and shook them vigorously. "Where did you learn my mother tongue?" he asked in a choked voice.

"My uncle has settled in Dilmun. I worked with him for a few years," said the workshop owner.

"In Eduru Meluhha?"

The man smiled. "Buying and selling keep me away for long periods. I need someone to overlook this unit. Can you write?"

"Not in your language," said Sam, "but I know the Sumérian Cuneiform."

"That's good enough," said the owner, as he started walking. "Come, I'll show you my workshop."

When the authorities learnt that Sam had found work, they immediately released him from slavery. That night, Sam got up time and again and knelt in prayer. "God Marduk, bless Lady Ella for teaching me reading and writing."

In his first week at the bead factory, he chipped away impurities of raw stones with a stag horn. In the second, he grinded the beads in shape while a husky colleague rotated an abrasive wheel. The third week saw him boring the beads, and polishing by rolling them in a leather drum filled with sand slurry.

Trained to assuage animals' pain, Sam had now learnt to make ornamental beads which pleased humans. As a result, he could put aside more silver in every lunar period than he had ever done before.

Counting his savings one night, Sam thought, 'It won't be long before I travel to Fort Harappa to meet Siwa –' Then he heard himself speaking aloud, "Saqra's daughter."

10 VISITOR FOR SIWA

After deserting the Meluhhan master's ship in Alatinam, Qwoco reached Muenduru City to execute his Sumérian master's order.

Early that morning, he squatted before a barber and watched his long trusses falling to the ground. He had grown up travelling with a group of street performers, and that early experience came in handy when working behind the scenes and creating obstacles in an adversary's path. However, Qwoco was at sea in personal interactions like the one he was about to carry out.

The Sumérian master's deputy, Biggie, had met him in a tavern on the docks of Urim a few days before Captain Paravar's ship set sail for Meluhha. "The Master wants you to deliver this to Siwa Saqra in Muenduru City," Biggie had said, handing him a package of date-palm matting. "It contains a purse."

Biggie had instructed him what to tell Siwa Saqra, adding with a guffaw, "If you mix it up, *Mulla Xul*, I'll roast you alive."

Qwoco was aware of how Biggie had eliminated the Master's earlier agent in Meluhha, and therefore did not take his words lightly. No sooner than he had paid the barber, he sprinted on his third visit to a public toilet that morning. Later, after having calmed down his nerves with a flask of *tanni*, he knocked on Siwa Saqra's door with Biggie's heavy package pressed under his arm.

He heard a child's voice saying 'I'll be back soon', and looked behind. A boy aged about seven was prancing towards him. He did not see anyone else nearby except a brown colt. The boy stood before him, looking with bewildered eyes.

"Go away," said Qwoco, raising a hand.

The boy pushed the door and ran inside. "Father, there's a tonsured man standing out there." Through the partially open door, Qwoco spied the boy narrowing his eyes and pouting his lips. "He looks like this, and has stuck goat manure under his nose."

Qwoco's hand went up to his dear mole, and quickly fell back. His fingers curled with an intense urge to clip the little fiend's ears. A suave bearded man came to the door. Instantly, Qwoco brought forth a smile upon his face. "Hiwa Haqra?"

Siwa sniffed, and his nose twitched. "Yes?"

"I'm Qwoco the timber trader," he said, wishing he had chewed a few grains of pepper to suppress the smell of *tanni*. "I recently visited Huméru."

"What brings you here, Trader Qwoco?"

"I bring a message from Babili." He held out a little bronze fish-hook in his palm. Siwa picked it up, turned it over and over again, and looked at him questioningly. Qwoco cursed Sam for passing out before he could extract more information. "To – to provide identification?" he said in a low voice.

The merchant pondered for a while, and gave a quick jerk of his hand signalling him to follow. The sailor's lips stretched in relief. He had successfully convinced Siwa.

The two men passed under a huge *neem* tree right in the centre of the courtyard, and reached the foyer. No sooner did they sit down on the floor, Qwoco opened the package, pulled out a black leather purse and handed it to Siwa. "Kayl requested me to deliver it to you, and convey that he had finished all tasks allotted by you."

Siwa looked concerned. "Where's he?"

Qwoco's voice broke. "Fell very sick and died."

"Is Kayl dead?" Siwa exclaimed. The sailor found it difficult to bear the long silence which followed. At last, Siwa spoke again, "How did you know him?"

"We sailed on the same ship. I met him again in Babili."

"How long were you with him before he died?"

"Only two days."

Siwa looked at him without batting an eye. "Was Kayl in his senses till the last breath?"

"Yes, he was," Qwoco said. He congratulated himself for his alertness. How else could Kayl have asked him to meet his master?

"Was there anything else that he wanted you to tell me?" said

Siwa, closely examining the outer skin of the black leather purse.

"That – that he had finished all his tasks," said Qwoco, fearing that any more lies might expose him. He became aware of Siwa looking at his hands which had started trembling.

Siwa slowly turned the purse, and as he inspected it, his eyes narrowed. He raised a finger to his tongue. Qwoco watched with curiosity as Siwa rubbed saliva on the purse, and then checked the finger. It carried a very light reddish tinge.

Siwa looked into his eyes again, and he felt a strange force fluttering one of them beyond his control. "Trader Qwoco, what's the wholesale rate of sandalwood?"

Qwoco realized that his tongue had stuck in his throat. Siwa got up, and he too stood up hastily.

"Muruku," Siwa called out. The boy came running. "Muruku, did you see any guard passing by on the street?"

"Yes, father. Just a while ago," said Muruku, beaming at Qwoco and starting to jump. "Shall I call him?"

Qwoco weighed the pros and cons of passing the blame on Biggie. No, that would be stupid. He ran the risk of exposing the Master too. His watchful eyes had convinced him that unlike Biggie and the Master, Siwa was a man whose heart would bleed for the tears of the helpless.

His hand rose to his tonsured head and scratched it, and it promptly responded by suggesting a story. Hurriedly, he dropped to the floor and stretched face down before Siwa. "I lied to you, *Kavintu*," he said, thumping his forehead on Siwa's feet. "I'm just a labourer at the port of Sutantoru-on-Sea."

"And my man Kayl didn't die, he was murdered," Siwa said, stepping back.

"Forgive my wretched soul, *Kavintu*. I didn't go to Huméru and I never met Kayl," Qwoco wailed, raising a tearful face. "A Humérian offered to pay me a bar of silver for delivering that purse to you. My wife's long illness made me do what I shouldn't have."

"Before I change my mind," Siwa shouted, pointing at the door. "Go away."

"Go away," repeated a caged parrot in the house. "Go away."

Qwoco did not need to be told so many times. He got up quickly, and holding a loose *vesti* in place with both his hands, hurried out of the house. He did not intend to stop till he had put it far behind. He knew that the little pest Muruku was closely following him. He heard the boy saying 'shoo..shoo' in an instigating tone, which set off a series of barks. Qwoco sprinted all the way to the end of the narrow lane, where Muruku's street dogs came to a halt, but kept on growling at him.

Out of breath and cursing 'Hiwa's boy', he walked past the corner on the main road. It seemed someone was calling him. He turned and saw Jittan, the Master's new local agent, standing at the entrance of a tavern and waving to him with a beaker in hand.

Over a year ago, Qwoco had overheard the Master talking to Biggie about the type of man he wanted in Meluhha. His brief had been terse: "I want someone just clever enough to carry out my bidding." Subsequently, Biggie had introduced him to Agent Jittan in Urim, and Qwoco had put two and two together despite his blissful ignorance of arithmetic.

Qwoco was in no doubt that Agent Jittan too had reached Muenduru City to meet 'Hiwa Haqra'. He winced with a passing thought that should Siwa happen to share with the agent his frustration about a recent visitor – one 'Trader Qwoco', it was just a matter of time before his misdemeanour reached Biggie's ears. He felt a strange sense of vacuum inside his belly, and he sighed. "Nothing is going right today."

"Agent Jittan," Qwoco grinned, revealing teeth and hiding thoughts.

"Sailor Qwoco, what on earth are you doing so far from the sea?"

Instead of replying, Qwoco asked enthusiastically, "Landed from Chendur Village?"

"Yes, this morning," said Jittan.

Although Qwoco wished to know why Jittan wanted to meet Siwa, he decided not to broach the matter. Why push the man into asking him too about his purpose for being there? From the amused look on Jittan's face, Qwoco suspected that the agent had already inferred that he had met Siwa.

With an unspoken understanding, both men talked about the rains, the sowing and the fishing – carefully avoiding any mention of their work. As they talked, the sailor's eyes roved to a pottery workshop across the street. Inside, a hunched man sweated at a potter's wheel producing small jars.

His attention was broken when Jittan lowered his voice and asked, "Do you know of a good physician in Muenduru City?"

Qwoco straightened up. The agent's tone pointed to an issue that might provide some leverage against him in future. "There was an excellent physician here. Last year I ran into him in Coppertown Khetri, where he has now settled down," he said, gazing at Jittan as if he could read about his malady. "Feeling sick?"

"Hm," Jittan grunted. "I go through hell while passing water."

"I know a man who makes conch bangles in Gola Dhoro. He too suffered from that problem."

"Is he cured?"

Qwoco perceived doubt in Jittan's voice. "Completely," he said, ordering a drink. "A few weeks ago we met in Laketown Dholavira. He was very happy."

"So it can be treated," said Jittan, easing in his seat.

"Certainly," said Qwoco, rueing that the agent had not shared anything that could be used against him.

Jittan leaned nearer. "Qwoco, you travel far and wide, and know a lot of people." The sailor nodded, absent-mindedly watching the tavern owner serving his drink made from raw mango and honey. The agent added, "I need your help."

All of Qwoco's faculties were attentive again as he pushed his beaker aside. "Yes, Agent Jittan, what can I do for you?"

Jittan took his time pulling out a few nasal hair before he whispered, "Could you keep a lookout for a fair-skinned woman named Anlil?"

"Humérian?" Qwoco asked. The big black mole under his nostril quivered.

"Yes, part of my very first 'consignment' from Huméru. Got away."

"Big loss to the Mas–" Qwoco checked himself. "I mean big loss to Biggie," he said, putting on a sad demeanour.

Jittan sighed. "I paid for her."

"Such losses, Agent Jittan, are part of your trade. Biggie would understand. Why don't you tell him?"

"And get butchered like my predecessor?"

"That's possible," said Qwoco, "and we need to save each other from such a fate." He smiled, looking at Jittan from under his brow. He knew that his message had reached home when he saw the agent cringe.

11 DACOITS OF NAL FOREST

Sam's caravan was trudging over a moist spongy track winding through tall trees when dogs started barking, and it slowly came to a halt. About twenty scraggy men riding donkeys and carrying bronze spears, bows, and bone arrows, closed in on them.

A one-eyed man among the weird group bared his teeth at the noisiest dog and shot it. As it howled its last, the remaining dogs scampered into the bushes. Sam wondered if the shooter had lost an eye as a boy while learning archery, or as an adult in a shooting duel for the leadership of the gang.

Cutting through the crowd, came forth a huge man riding a water buffalo. He sported a garland of small bones. With a start, Sam realised that they were human finger bones. Swellings all over the man's hairless chest, apparently the handiwork of a witchdoctor, gave it the appearance of a crocodile hide. His eyes looked so devoid of any feelings that children ran into their mothers' arms.

"Drop your weapons," he commanded in a cold voice. "Fall out in two groups – men on one side, women on another." They obeyed. "You – sons of a harlot," he growled at the group of men. "Hold out all your gold and silver in your hands."

Then the ringleader turned to the women and his expression changed to what could be deemed a smile. Several small children let out a wail. "Consider me your brother. No harm will come either to you or your cubs." Sam blinked. Was he listening to a robber? "Your ornaments will go to feed our little ones. So all my sisters will retain only their matrimonial necklace and part with everything else."

From his experience in the bead industry, Sam knew that every Meluhhan woman wore a special necklace as a talisman for the long life of her husband. "What a noble gesture from a criminal," Sam marvelled in his mind.

"However," the ringleader added, "if I find anyone cheating, I and my men possess effective tools to reform her." His followers eyed the women longingly and guffawed.

Sam sank his head into both hands. "His instincts aren't any different from the marauders of Magan."

Just then, there was a call from afar, loaded with urgency. Sam saw everybody in the caravan looking behind on the forest path which they had travelled. A lanky man was jogging up to them with a raised hand. Sam thought that his slim nose and slanting eyes made his face look like an antelope's. The man went straight to the ringleader.

"Why have you left your duty?" the ringleader demanded even as the messenger was trying to speak.

The man pointed at the group of travellers with a jerk of his head. "Are they from Port Lo – Lothal?"

The leader turned to the caravan owner, a muscular man sporting a roughly square shaped black beard. He joined his hands and bowed.

"Foreigner – gems," said the messenger gasping. "There's a Humérian among them. He's loaded with gems."

The leader's eyes popped out. "Gems?"

"Yes, Chief. Humérian gems."

The ringleader grunted. "How do you know?"

"I overheard someone who had had a flask of *tanni* too many," said the messenger. "So I travelled all the way from Lothal to alert you."

"The drunkard might be babbling."

"I asked him. He said he had seen the gems with the foreigner."

Sam realized that everybody was looking at him. The ringleader pointed at him and said, "You, who are prettier than my prettiest wife. From where do you hail?"

An uneasy peal of laughter rang through the group of travellers.

"Babili," answered Sam, peeved with the comparison.

"Where the hell is Babili?"

"It's in Sumér."

"That's it," said the ringleader, patting the messenger's back. "Take him along. Let's go."

The one-eyed dacoit batted an eye. "What about the jewellery, Chief?"

"Humérian gems would fetch us far more than all that scrap put together," said the ringleader, jerking the reins to turn his buffalo around.

One dacoit snatched Sam's bronze knife. Another tied up his hands while a third blindfolded him. In the meanwhile, irritated by Sam's desperate pleas, the one-eyed dacoit shoved a gag of dry grass into his open mouth.

They led in the donkey carrying his luggage, and lifted him to sit astride on it. Then one of them whipped the overburdened animal. It broke into an awkward trot and Sam lost his balance. Two strong hands held him just in time.

They rode in utter silence. For a long time, he heard only the sound of animals' hooves over the chirping of birds.

At last, some children's shouts broke the peace. Sam's blindfold was pulled off. Rubbing his eyes, he saw that they had reached a clearing. Two teams of boys were hurling pellets of dry dung at each other. The one-eyed dacoit yelled at them and the mock battle broke off. Several caves lined the periphery of the place. Women and children came running out to watch him.

The one-eyed dacoit pulled out the gag and led him to the ringleader, who demanded, "Give me the gems."

"I don't have any," Sam said, coughing. "That's what I was trying to tell you."

"Where are they – the gems of Huméru?"

"I don't –" Before Sam could repeat, the one-eyed dacoit slapped him. He staggered and fell down. His ear started hearing a screeching sound. One dacoit pulled off his *vesti* and started examining it. A cheer went up amidst the children, and Sam hurriedly covered himself with both his hands.

Two others opened his sacks and checked the contents. An identical announcement came from each of them. "Nothing."

The sound of the ringleader's whip sounded in the air. "Carve out his stomach," he bawled. Two men standing nearest to Sam pulled out big knives from their waistbands.

Sam felt dizzy. He recollected his foster father's advice just before he had accompanied Lady Ella to Babili to serve the Nergal household: "If you are right, and your Master doesn't believe you, appeal to the Mistress."

Sam looked at the women and pointed with his chin at Marduk's amulet that he wore around his neck. "My sisters, I swear by my patron deity, that I am not hiding anything from your men. I don't want to die –"

His voice gave way to a sob. While the men sniggered, the women looked helplessly at each other. The two armed men raised their knives. The shine on the chert blades was enough to collapse him on his knees.

A screeching voice arose from the crowd. "Don't."

Sam saw an elderly woman step forth with the aid of a staff taller than herself. She held a hand over her brow.

"*Amma*?" The ringleader's surprised voice kindled some hope in Sam's mind.

"I'm sick of your wanton butchery, son." Sam detected angst in the old woman's feeble voice.

"*Amma*, the bastard has swallowed my gems," said the ringleader, sounding like one sibling complaining about another.

"You thick-headed boy, can't you think of a simpler way to get them out?" snapped the old woman, pointing a crooked finger at him.

The ringleader threw a blank look at his followers. They all seemed at their wits' end. Perhaps sensing their confusion, another feminine voice came from one of the caves, "May I speak, Husband?"

It was a woman carrying a child on her hip. Although she might not be more than thirty, her drooped breasts made her look much older.

The ringleader spat and looked as if he were considering a very weighty matter. His silence seemed like an age to Sam. At last, he spoke. "What do you have to say, woman?"

"Give him laxative," said the young woman, hastily retreating to the shadows.

The ringleader roared with laughter. His one-eyed assistant squinted in a merry response. Sam tried to decipher their reaction. Was the mirth generated by what they considered was a woman's stupidity? Or was it a smoke screen to obfuscate their own?

"Fetch some castor oil," commanded the ringleader, and a man ran towards one of the caves.

Carefully holding his hands in place, Sam bowed reverently to the ringleader's mother. Before he could regain his posture, the one-eyed dacoit forced a heavy dose of castor oil down his throat. He coughed severely and pressed his stomach as it rumbled in rebellion. The dacoits' children clapped in sheer delight.

Over a long time, Sam suffered severe attacks of loose motions. Every time a man analysed the output and waved crossing his arms, it raised the ringleader's temper by another notch.

Sam was not aware when he fainted. When he regained consciousness, he realized that he had been abandoned at the same place in the forest where the dacoits had intercepted the caravan. They had thrown his *vesti* nearby. He appreciated the dacoits' thoughtful action. He could return to civilization without undergoing further embarrassment.

He got up, but slumped back, too weak to stand. Anxious to get out of the forest before it was dark, he cut a dry branch and started hobbling with its support.

The croaking of frogs resonated all around. Sam thought that probably it was their last chorus for the season. The rains appeared to be lingering over the Nal forest before departing from Meluhha.

Emerging out of the woods, his face lighted up seeing several plumes of smoke twirling upwards in the rays of the setting sun. As he drew nearer, some children recognized him and ran to greet him. He lifted up the youngest and they reached the camp amidst a lot of talking and laughing.

Late into the night, the travellers rejoiced Sam's safe return. He cautiously sipped a goblet of *tanni*, his first since the outing with Qwoco in Alatinam. He saw the caravan owner's thick lips moving. "Sam, I'm sorry that they robbed you of all your precious gems."

Sam laughed. "I didn't possess any."

The man smiled doubtfully. "You wouldn't be sitting here if that were true."

Sam narrated the entire sequence of events as it had happened. In the light of the camp fire, he watched the caravan owner's face turning serious.

"Sam," he said, rubbing his thick square beard between a thumb and two fingers. "In Port Lothal you have an enemy who's deadlier than the dacoits of Nal Forest."

12 SIGNS OF TROUBLE

As the ferry carrying the passengers and the goods of Sam's caravan approached land, he stood first in the queue to disembark at Laketown Dholavira. Anxious to meet Tall Yali at the shipyard, he smilingly suffered a co-passenger who wanted to impress upon him that the lake town was thirteen times larger than Port Lothal. He was told that all goods traded between Sumér and the towns on River Saraswathi passed through the port of Dholavira.

Sam thought that the sheer number of carts there was indicative of the trade. Just as in Port Lothal, the total absence of camel carts made him pity the hundreds of oxen and donkeys which were loaded inhumanly to transport the steady flow of goods.

Upon landing, Sam hurried through a thick wooden gate set in a high brick wall, which was so wide that two ox-carts could have passed each other if it were possible to move on its top.

A storm channel ran along the road, and women balancing water pots on their head met him in twos and threes. The air became cooler as he reached a gigantic water tank lined with banyan and *pipal* trees. As unfamiliar birds of various colours chirped above, several men leisurely fished under the shade, turning Sam green with envy.

The atmosphere changed into that of din and toil the moment Sam crossed the gate of the shipyard. Tall Yali was overseeing the repairs on his vessel, the one on which Sam had caught up with Captain Paravar's ship. No sooner did Tall Yali spot Sam enquiring on the wharf, he shouted and ran down the ramp to embrace him.

As Yali showed him around in his booming voice, it seemed that Sam's eyes had stopped blinking. Had he been told earlier that some Sumérian shippers had inducted in their fleet the vessels built in Meluhha, he would have laughed. Now he had a reason to believe it. He had never seen so many huge boats under construction at a single location.

"The most crucial work on my ship is over," said Yali. "I've taken a river craft on lease to sail between Dholavira and Gangevell till the winds enable sea voyage again."

Sam whooped. He had not expected to get Tall Yali's company for part of the long tedious journey to Fort Harappa. "When are you leaving?"

"The day after tomorrow. You're welcome on board, provided –" Tall Yali stopped, looking as if he was in two minds.

"Go ahead, my friend, what do you want me to do?"

"I suggest that you visit the northern gateway of the city to see a huge signboard. We'll discuss the details later."

Sam reached the north gate in such a hurry that he failed to spot a person who was closely following his movements.

Looking up at the wooden board, he figured that it measured as much as one and a half times the length of both his arms stretched wide apart. On it were engraved ten glyphs, formed by careful placement of well-chiselled pieces of gypsum. Each symbol seemed to be as high as the distance from the elbow to the fingertips.

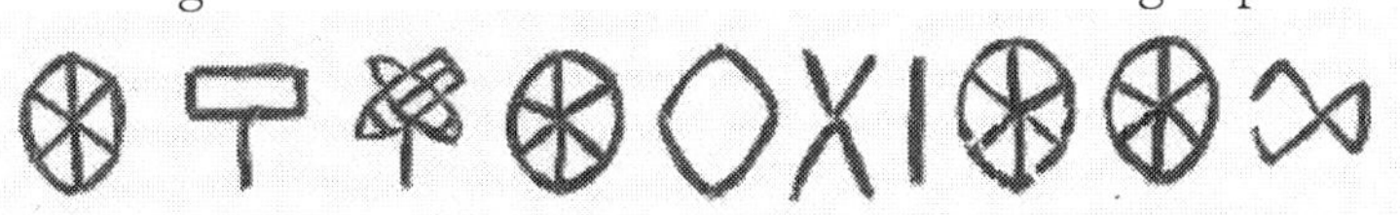

A wrinkled old woman selling ber fruit watched Sam in utter delight. A load of silver rings which hung from her nostrils and ear lobes tinkled as she shook her head approvingly.

A little away was a stall selling areca nut where several idlers stood gossiping. It struck Sam that they were chewing the nut flakes quite like a camel leisurely masticating cud. He walked up to them, and raised a hand in greeting. "I can't read your language," he said pointing to the board. "Would you please tell me what it says?"

The loafers seemed to take the white man's query as a smart attempt to humiliate their illiteracy. They surrounded him. The old woman, familiar with their ways, shouted hoarse for help. A small crowd gathered and the idlers considered it wise to rest the matter. Sam thanked the people and added, "I just asked them what that board read."

"Absolutely nothing," said one man whose eyes were lined with black oily soot. "They just don't add up to make a sensible word."

"Some say they denote a secret code to a treasure," said another.

Sam looked up at the board again. "That sounds intriguing."

"It is," said the first man. "Do you have the time for a story?" Saying 'yes', Sam squatted down besides him. The man called out to the old woman. "*Amma*, tell him about our great grandfather."

The woman took rather long to get up, but then nearly ran into them. Seeing the eagerness on her face, it occurred to Sam that she might have narrated the family history to anybody who cared to listen.

"My husband's grandfather hung it up when he settled in Laketown Dholavira," she said, as the man with the soot-lined eyes helped her to sit down.

"From where did he come?"

"Rocky Gangevell," the woman said. "He was a crackpot."

Sam smiled, egging her on.

She narrated that the old man had been a black sheep in his family. He never took any interest in either farming or trading as his brothers did. He loved roaming in the forests and the ravines. One day, fed up of his waywardness, his father scolded him, and he ran away down south leaving behind his wife and a baby. He slogged in the mines of Tamilakam for fourteen years, by which time his wife had died and the son had grown up.

People said the truant had discovered a big diamond, earned a lot of gold, and had returned home to enjoy the fruits of his labour. Then a notorious man in the area started calling on him. Again he left home, this time with his boy. They came to Laketown Dholavira, changed their names and settled down.

"My great grandfather was quite poetic," said the man with the soot-lined eyes. "In Dholavira he went by the name of Kuraivil Otticai – 'Kutti' for short."

"Why poetic?"

"It means 'Rainbow Melody'." He chuckled. "Is a rainbow meant to be heard?"

The woman gave vent to a long sigh and said, "Mad Kutti had never grown out of childhood fantasies – the light and the sound, the rocks and the rivers – any subject other than a means to earn a decent living."

"An unusual character," Sam said, getting up.

"If you consider him queer, more so were my father-in-law and my husband," the woman groaned. "Together they spent their entire lives trying to discover Mad Kutti's wealth, and left us all paupers."

Sam clicked his tongue several times in the Meluhhan way of expressing sympathy, and left to meet his friend again.

Tall Yali finished instructing his head sailor about some repairs, and said, "Let's go to meet Ann, the woman I intend to marry. She's a widow. There's no expert with a razor in the entire Laketown Dholavira as Ann. She might cut your hair free of cost if you co-operate with us."

"First the signboard, and now co-operation? I don't understand this riddle, Yali."

Yali showed him his palm on which were sketched all the signs of the board.

"Once I drew this on a piece of cloth and tied it around my wrist so that I could think over it in spare time," Yali said. "And I saw the signs in a new arrangement. I ran all the way to share it with Ann."

"What was it?"

Yali showed him another palm. Sam saw that the first two glyphs from the right had been shifted to the extreme left.

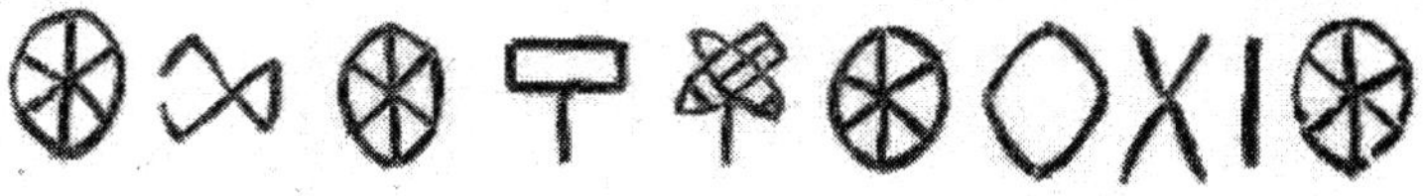

"You know, we read the Meluhhan language from the right to the left."

"That's how we read Sumérian too," Sam said, pleased that he could get in a word, "but I was told that this arrangement of letters doesn't mean anything."

"Despite that, they tell us a lot. Both Ann and I are convinced that we've pretty much deciphered the secret code to a treasure trove." Sam looked askance. Did his friend really take the rumour about Mad Kutti's treasure seriously?

"We discovered that in the new arrangement, the number of symbols between successive wheel signs decreased from three to two to one, thus throwing up a definite logic."

Sam held Yali's right palm and saw that they did, going from the right to the left.

Yali pointed to the three symbols between the two wheels on the right. "If we draw this stick, this cross and this circle over each other, we get this wheel over here, and all other wheels are now irrelevant."

He wetted a finger on his tongue and rubbed out the three extra wheels, and Sam saw the code that the couple believed would change their fortune.

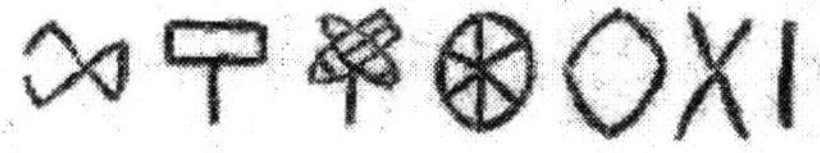

By then they had reached a brick house. From the other side of its wooden door, a sweet lullaby floated to Sam's ears. Yali knocked on it. The words got louder and clearer, and the door opened slowly with a chirping sound.

A tall young woman as fair as a Sumérian stood before them. Sam was tongue tied as he stared at her. She raised a finger to her nose, which he thought was quite sharp. That was a rare feature among Meluhhan women. She smiled as if she had been expecting them, and led the way inside.

Sam was perplexed as to how the woman's smile rekindled childhood memories. Somehow it had reminded him of his mother.

Inside, a bamboo cradle was rocking. A tiny blanket covering a slightly dark faced baby gently rose and fell with its breathing.

"Ann, this is my friend Samasin," Tall Yali said, "who, I told you might be helpful to us."

Ann looked at Sam. "How much has Yali told you so far?"

"Till you boiled down to seven glyphs," said Sam absentmindedly. He had expected a heavily accented speech like his own. Hearing perfect intonation of Meluhhan words, he started doubting his guess that Ann too hailed from Sumér. He watched her quickly drawing the seven signs on the brick-paved floor with a piece of charcoal. It seemed she had had a lot of practice doing it.

"Seven is a wonderful number," said Ann. "There are seven days in a week, seven colours in the rainbow, seven major rivers in Meluhha, seven openings –"

Sam, who had been feeling a strong urge to yawn loud and long, jerked visibly upon hearing the word 'rainbow'. He genuinely lent an ear to what Ann was telling. "Suppose the first three signs from the right represent the primary colours, we can co-relate all the seven symbols with the colours of the rainbow – with several guesses along the way, of course."

"The long and short of all this is that I want you to go with Ann to explore Rocky Gangevell." Tall Yali put a hand on Sam's shoulder. "Unless we see its surroundings, we won't know how the code would help us to reach Mad Kutti's treasure."

"Why don't you go?"

"You know, Sam, I'm 'married' to my ships –" Tall Yali caught Ann's eye, and faltered. "I mean, until the two of us get rich and get married. Presently, sailing leaves me little time to do anything else."

"If what we've found indeed leads us to a treasure, we'll share it with you," said Ann. Sam detected a glint of hope in her eyes.

It was rather embarrassing to refuse to such a nice couple. However, Sam feared that a futile treasure hunt would drift him away from his main objective of meeting Siwa's lovely daughter. He wanted to get out of the situation without sounding rude. "Ann, Yali, excuse me," he said in a voice that sounded slightly louder than a whisper. His eyes remained firmly fixed on the symbols sketched on the floor. "Hadn't it been for utmost urgency to reach Fort Harappa, I'd have grabbed this fantastic opportunity."

Yali as well as Ann looked stunned. An uncomfortable silence engulfed the room. Sam wished that Tall Yali put in a word, but all his friend did was to stop rocking the baby's cradle.

Ann jumped to her feet. "Why did you make me divulge everything to the Sumérian when you weren't sure that he would co-operate?" she cried, rubbing her soles over the symbols. The otherwise sweet ring of her silver anklets sounded like a warning gong to Sam. "Yali, you will sail without your friend," she said. "Do you get it?"

Sam looked up with a start. He too got up as quickly as Yali had done. Murmuring a vague apology, he walked towards the door. Tall Yali promptly followed at his heels, and the heavy door banged after them.

13 MAD KUTTI'S CODE

Feeling as if all his energy was sapped, Sam dropped at Tall Yali's feet. He had scoured through the port and the shipyard since the morning, contacting several skippers and ship owners. None of them was going as far as Rocky Gangevell during the following few weeks.

"Tell your bad tempered woman," he said, looking up at Yali's face like a dog which had missed a meal for biting the master's child, "that she has succeeded in enslaving me for her hare-brained venture."

Reaching the port the following day, Sam saw Yali talking with a tall dark woman. Tied to her back was a bundle from which a baby looked around inquisitively. Yali waved, calling him to join them. Sam could not see Ann anywhere, and wished that she had dropped the idea of going after Mad Kutti's treasure.

Getting nearer, he found that the woman was none other than Ann. "You look shocked, Sam," Tall Yali said laughing. "She has dyed her skin to prevent undue attention."

Sam could well understand the embarrassment of a fair skinned woman in public. The way the Meluhhans ogled at him had been a constant source of uneasiness in Lothal. It had taken him quite some time to get used to the impolite stares.

About a fortnight later, Yali's little craft entered the port of Rocky Gangevell with Sam and the dark skinned Ann on board. Three-quarters the size of Laketown Dholavira, it was the last port on River Saraswathi that was connected to the sea. It impressed

Sam as one swarming place of utter chaos.

As he packed his belongings, Sam watched the two lovers from the corner of his eye. He was curious to see them preparing for, what Yali had told him, 'a few weeks' parting' till Yali returned from Dholavira in the following trip.

Surprisingly, Tall Yali's usually loud voice was inaudible. He appeared livid as they talked. Ann raised her palms at him and gave them a quick jerk. Perhaps she did not want to discuss some matter which Yali insisted. He reacted by raising a forefinger and moving it in a circle on the side of his temple.

Then he held her by her shoulders, as if making a last ditch effort to persuade her. She seemed to be asking him a question as she moved a finger across her throat. Her hand tapped her chest while another formed a fist that rose to the level of his shoulder.

Yali pointed down at her toddler which was chortling at her feet, screening its face on and off with part of her flowing *varati*. The repeated movement of her head from one side to another was telling about her disagreement.

Yali threw up both his arms. They talked a little longer before his voice burst out. Only one word was heard – 'crazy' – before it lowered again.

Sam could not avoid looking directly at them. Tall Yali was stooping, akin to a camel in the process of sitting down. Ann smiled as he lifted up the baby and showered it with kisses amidst squeals of dissent.

From what he had seen, Sam inferred that the couple was parting for a long period, not just a few weeks, and that Yali was deeply concerned about Ann and her baby's safety.

Upon disembarking, Sam and Ann joined several other passengers who walked up a rough slope to an inn. It was made of two long and narrow thatched huts. Each was a hall in which people rested on the mud floor along its walls. One was allocated to men, and the other to women and children.

"You wanted to meet someone in Gangevell, didn't you?" said Ann as she softly patted the baby to sleep.

"Yes, some people carrying the clan name of Saqra."

"I'll come with you," said Ann, "for I want to learn about all places in this town which are connected with colours in one way or another."

They searched out the family of the lady whom Sam had met in

Port Lothal. Its head, the lady's father, was a man aged over seventy. His jet black hair was reddish-brown near the roots. It was woven in a plait which curved like a dog's tail, seeing which Ann whispered, "It's the latest craze among the youngsters." Sam thought the elderly person, who was smiling warmly at them, was yet to reconcile with the passing of his youth.

"Siwa chose to leave Fort Harappa and settle in Muenduru City," the man spoke, raising a hand to screen his mouth which Sam doubted had probably lost half the teeth. "Failure of his trading venture due to a corrupt partner was very embarrassing. So he sold his wife's entire jewellery, paid his creditors, and left Harappa for ever."

Sam nodded with the wisdom gained from his own experience with the Babilians, but before he could utter a word, Ann interrupted. "By the way, while we're in Rocky Gangevell," she said, and Sam frowned at her. "We want to visit the special places here, for instance, caves with ancient paintings, or perhaps trees with differently coloured foliage."

Siwa's relative said, "No, lady, there isn't anything of that nature around."

Ann's smile faded away. Sam pitied her for what he had always believed was an unrealistic analysis of Mad Kutti's code. In the collapse of Ann's dreams, he saw a ray of hope to meet Siwa's beautiful daughter sooner than he had expected. Now that he knew the girl's exact location, it was a matter of weeks before he would see her again.

After a pause, Siwa's relative spoke again. "Perhaps the Ringing Rocks might interest you, lady. Any boatman at the river bank would take you there."

"What are they?"

"Boulders which emit a sound when they're struck."

Ann looked unimpressed. As they walked back to the inn, Sam tried to lift her spirits. "Why don't we visit the place? Who knows, some of those rocks might be coloured."

Ann turned to him, her eyes shining. "You might be right, Sam," she said tugging at his arm, "let's rush there."

At the river, they hired a long shallow boat that had been carved out of a tree trunk. Its young boatman seemed so happy with the foreigner's assignment that, despite his broad chest heaving as he rowed against the current, he puffed from time to time to share whatever he knew about the surroundings. As they travelled north, the low hills on the left bank started rising gradually till Sam noticed that they looked like the high wall of a fort.

"There's a narrow path near the top of the range," said the boatman. Sam squinted and discerned a long line of cattle moving against a background of mostly black rocks.

Little further on, the hills started getting lower till the boatman moored the boat at a rather dark place shaded by dense foliage. He led them on a narrow path lined with bushes bearing flowers of all hues. Ann tried hard to find a pattern among them, but soon gave up.

Reaching the top, the boatman pointed out several brownish boulders, roughly egg shaped and higher than a man's height. Standing in sharp contrast to the black rocks all around, the brown boulders stood like children forming a circle.

The boatman picked up a granite stone and struck it on two nearby boulders which stood closer to each other as compared to the rest which seemed equally spaced. Both emitted a sound. Passing on her baby to Sam, Ann ran round the circle, examining each boulder visually instead of striking it. Seeing her reaction, the boatman tossed the granite stone over his shoulder, and walked away to sit on a smaller black boulder.

"This formation reminds me of Stonehenge," said Sam, as he gently moved a hand on the baby's back.

"Stonehenge?" said Ann, as she finished going around the circle. Her shoulders had drooped and her face had turned morose.

"It's a circular arrangement of huge chiselled rocks. It's on an island in the sea that's located very far, west of Sumér."

"Have you travelled there too?" she asked, tapping with a granite stone the two close-by boulders.

"No. A man with auburn hair and blue eyes, hailing from the land of Stonehenge, told me." Sam said, remembering a tough foreigner who he had accompanied across the desert, in his first independent journey with his foster father's camels. "He believed that it was the handiwork of flying visitors from another world."

"Bird-like men from the sky?" she asked as she struck yet another of the ringing rocks.

"Or perhaps men like us, riding giant birds," said Sam. "Could they have flown to Rocky Gangevell after visiting Stonehenge?"

Ann had reached the seventh boulder by then, and was smiling.

"I've made an interesting discovery."

"What?"

"Starting from here," she said, striking the second of the two close-by boulders, "they emit the ascending notes of our music. Listen."

Ann walked along the circle, striking each of the boulders, and identifying the note. "*Sa, Ri, Ga, Ma, Pa, Dha, Ni,* and *Sa.*"

Sam murmured the notes and counted them on his fingers. "These rocks together emit all eight notes of Meluhhan music, do they?"

"Not eight," she said, striking the two nearest boulders alternately. "These two emit the low and high notes of *Sa.* There are seven unique notes." Her eyes widened as she repeated, "Seven."

Sam glanced at the boatman who was busy sucking nectar from a heap of blue flowers that he had plucked. He gasped, "Kutti for Kuraivil Otticai, means 'Rainbow Melody', Ann."

"That's what occurred to me too," she said, snatching the child from him and giving it a long kiss.

They took far lesser time to come downhill, and the boatman rowed silently on its return voyage downstream. They passed that portion of the hills that appeared like a wall, and had a road on which cattle had been spotted from afar. As they watched, Ann looked at Sam. "Have you seen those brown boulders appearing intermittently among the black ones?"

Their shape and colour was strikingly similar to the eight ringing rocks which they had just visited.

"How could I miss them?" he said with a knowing smile. "They stand out like an albino tiger in a jungle."

After sailing some distance downstream, the brown boulders ceased appearing just as suddenly as they had started. "They're about a hundred of them up there," said Sam. "I doubt if they all ring like the eight we saw."

"I'd be happy to take you there tomorrow," said the boatman.

Ann pressed her lips and stared far away. Sam started clucking at the baby which responded by gargling heartily.

Walking back to the inn, Ann related the colours of the rainbow starting from its outermost arc to the order of the musical notes *Sa Ri Ga Ma Pa Dha Ni*, so that Red represented *Sa*, Orange represented *Ri* and so on. "There you are," she cried. "Through his queer signs, Mad Kutti wanted to convey the musical notes in the sequence *Sa Ga Pa Dha Ri Ni Ma.*"

"Your logic would serve some purpose only if that entire lot of brownish boulders along the mountain road gives out sound," Sam said.

In response, Ann looked up at the sky.

14 '*HARSAG ZALAZALAG*'

No sooner had they pulled their hired boat up the river bank, and tracked to the mountain road, Sam picked up a granite stone and ran to the nearest brownish boulder. As a series of sharp ringing sounds echoed over the hills, Ann raised her babbling toddler over her head. "We're nearing Mad Kutti's trove, Sam."

The path running on the mountain side was not wide enough for an ox-cart to travel on it. On one side were the rocks, including the ones they wished to study. On the other was a steep slope, dropping all the way to the river bank. After gobbling some boiled grams which Ann had brought along, Sam pulled out from his sack a large piece of cloth and a wax-sealed miniature flask. Picking up a peacock feather from several fluttering on the ground, he said, "I'm ready, Ann."

"Let's go southwards and check if we have missed out any ringing rock," she suggested. They found three more brownish ovular boulders, after which none appeared for a long distance.

They returned to what they believed was the first ringing rock on the mountain path. Ann struck each brownish ovular rock that came on their way and announced its musical note, while Sam jotted down. They found that several rocks were surrounded by reddish brown anthills. It was difficult to reach such rocks and carry out the sound test. Sam hurled small granite stones at them and after listening carefully several times, Ann decided which note each rock emitted.

Twice they travelled up and down the hilly road to ensure that their record was complete. Descending the hill, Sam spotted another boat which had been dragged up on the bank.

"It wasn't there when we came," he told Ann. "We didn't meet any visitors up there either."

However, Ann was so occupied pacifying her adamant toddler that she glanced at the other boat but did not reply. The matter was soon forgotten.

At night, Sam studied the piece of cloth under the light of a small lamp, making several patrons at the inn curious. "I have to perform at a rich man's party," he told the nosey ones who asked. "So I'm practising for it."

"Practising without singing the song?" asked one who had caught a glimpse of the musical notes.

"You find that curious, don't you," Sam said laughing, as he silently cursed the man for his prying nature. "With lots of practice, my ears can hear the music as my eyes read the notes."

Late into the night, amidst the cacophony of masculine snores, Sam found that a portion going from the South to the North matched Mad Kutti's sequence: *Sa Ga Pa Dha Ri Ni Ma.*

As the sun arose, Sam and Ann bought a bronze hoe, a shovel, bamboo baskets, and a long piece of jute rope and reached the boulders which followed Mad Kutti's sequence. There, the path narrowed even further. Surveying the seven special boulders before they started work, they found that one was teeming with red ants.

"We'll take it up last," said Sam. "Six out of seven chances are that we'll find Mad Kutti's treasure without having to deal with the ants."

They started from the South and did not find anything under the first two boulders which emitted the notes of *Sa* and *Ga.*

"Seeing so much moist earth around, any fool would guess what we're up to," Ann said, shovelling the loose earth back into the holes. Then she quickly covered both with dry leaves.

When Sam was digging under the third boulder, Ann ran to him and touched his arm, raising a finger to her nose. They heard a sound of sporadic coughing down the road. Sam clambered up a nearby mango tree and stretched his neck. "It's an old man, sporting a thick moustache as white as cotton wool."

The man approached them slowly, pushing a donkey. He was hunched and looked oblivious of their presence.

Sam shouted, "Grandpa, is your donkey troubling you?" The

man walked on without responding. Sam repeated the question more loudly.

"Grandpa is stone deaf," Ann observed.

"He's dumb too," said Sam. "At his age he ought to know the peril of walking so close behind a donkey."

The man grabbed the rope around the animal's neck and started pulling it.

"He has heard you," she said, and they laughed.

The old man passed them, not even throwing a cursory glance at them.

"He appears partially blind too," Sam sighed with relief. As soon as the man and his animal were gone, they resumed digging.

They laboured till the sun came overhead, but failed to find anything under four more boulders which gave out the notes *Pa, Ri, Ni* and *Ma.* Only the one sounding *Dha* remained, and it meant challenging the red ants that had made it their home.

"Let's take a break while I spend some time with the tot," Ann suggested, "and we'll think out a way."

"You go ahead," he said, surveying the anthill. "I just can't wait to find out."

Sam raked away the porous earth, and before he knew it, innumerable little legs crawled up all over him like rising flood water. The shooting pain of ant stings forced him to throw down the hoe and run to a patch of grass. As he rolled on it like a merry donkey rolling in the dust, Ann laughed at the vanquished warrior.

Just then they heard leaves rustling on the mango tree, and saw an animal descending slowly, holding on to the bark with long sharp claws.

"It's a pangolin," Sam tried to whisper, but his words came out so loudly that he almost scared away the animal. "This is what I'd call 'Help from the heavens'." He recalled the first time that he had seen a pangolin in Meluhha, and someone had told him that it ate ants and termites and was a welcome guest around granaries and wooden structures.

They watched in silence. Every time the pangolin inserted a sticky tongue inside the anthill and withdrew it, Sam shook both his fists. A little later, when the pangolin started moving away, he could still see countless ants scurrying around on the ground.

"I hate unfinished work," he said, preparing a lasso. As he went after the animal, it broke into an awkward jog. He threw the lasso which landed near the pangolin's neck. It scampered to the edge of the hill. When Sam chased it, it stopped in its tracks. "You're trapped," he cried with glee, rotating the lasso over his head. Just as he released it, the pangolin cuddled itself into a ball. The loop landed on it and slid down.

Then they heard a clanging noise and saw the scaly sphere receding downhill, bouncing on rocks and colliding with tree trunks. In the blink of an eye, it seemed to have reduced to the size of a small pot as it reached the level ground. Sam watched with open mouth as the pangolin uncoiled itself and sauntered into thick bushes by the river.

The rope slipped from his hand as he stood there gaping. Then he heard a peal of laughter. "With a meagre payment," Ann said, putting down the baby, "we could get a hunter to snare a pangolin."

As they searched in the woods, they came to a natural recess in rocks which had been later widened by man. Built in that space, was a circular mud hut with a thatched conical roof. The door, decorated with purple crown flowers which abounded on the mountain, was ajar. Sam knocked on it.

There was a sound of quick steps, and a neatly dressed woman came out. She smiled at Ann and lightly pinched the baby's cheek. She nodded and withdrew without a word. Sam heard her talking with a marked stammer to someone inside. Heavy footsteps came nearer and a brawny man with long hair and beard stood before them, looking at them enquiringly.

"Can you trap a pangolin?" Sam said.

"Yes," he said clearing his throat, "better than any other hunter in Rocky Gangevell."

Sam briefly told him what they wanted. He went inside and returned with a bundle of twine. "Let's go."

After a long wait, they spotted another pangolin coming along. Noticing the handiwork of the earlier visitor, it started leaving when it stepped into the hunter's snare. While trying to get free, it squealed so much that the baby startled and woke up. The entire hillside was filled by a chorus of human and beastly noises as the hunter laboured to tether the pangolin near the anthill.

"There you are," he said at last, forming a bowl shape with his palms. "It should clear out all the remaining ants after it resigns to its fate."

"How soon would that be?" Sam asked, dropping a small piece of silver in them.

The hunter watched the pangolin as it bit into the twine that restricted it. "From the way it behaves, I guess it would be nightfall."

"What?" cried Sam. "It can't escape if a predator comes this way at night."

"Don't worry," said the hunter. "No animal can break its scales open once it coils itself in a ball."

Ann interjected, "Except one."

"Yes, lady," the hunter said, looking at her with respect, "except a python."

"Let's release it," Ann said. "We'll again seek this man's help tomorrow."

Sam considered her suggestion. The risk to the pangolin arose only if a python came along, which he thought was a rare chance. But could they afford to take it? If there happened to be just a couple of pangolins in that territory, it was unlikely that the one which had visited the ant hill earlier in the day would return on the following day.

"No, we'll have to stay here to protect it," he said.

"Sam, think of the child. I can't expose it to the cold under the night sky."

"You need not. I'll leave you at Gangevell, and row back to spend the night here."

"The lady could stay with us," said the hunter, making a monkey face at the enthralled toddler. "We are childless, and baby guests provide us a good change in our dull lives."

Ann agreed immediately, and Sam joined them to borrow a spear. It was a bamboo pole with a long sharp flint stone fastened at its end.

Returning to the spot, Sam climbed the mango tree. He chose a cleft between two thickest branches, where he prepared to pass an uncomfortable night.

At midnight, shrill shrieks jerked Sam out of sleep. He turned away from the disturbance only to feel rough wood underneath which brought to his consciousness that he was not in bed. He awoke to find the pangolin squealing. A thick long shape flowed towards it like a stream reflecting the dim moonlight.

"It's a python," exclaimed Sam, "the pangolin's worst enemy."

His hand tried to locate the hunter's spear. It had dropped to the ground. Without a second thought, he jumped down from the tree. He saw the reptile winding itself around the huge scaly ball. Rushing to where the spear lay, he picked it up and with both hands planted it into the python's body.

It fixed two cold eyes on him. Pulling out the spear and shouting at the top of his voice, he lunged forward and aimed at one of them. The lethargic reptile avoided it with surprising agility. A soft but heavy object hit Sam's legs with a great force and knocked him off his feet.

Seeing the python's tail slithering to curl around him, Sam trembled. Rolling away over the stony terrain, he leapt to his feet and ran towards the brute, aiming the spear at its head. A quick slight pressure against it told him that it had brushed the body. The python swayed its head around but he leapt away.

Sam decided to attack the tail, and continued planting his spear in the brute's body as he danced in a circle, avoiding its jaws.

At last, Sam saw it writhing and gradually releasing its prey. Once its reactions turned slower, it did not take long for him to kill it.

The sun had reached half-way overhead, when loud voices coming from the ground awakened Sam on his perch. Several shepherds, milkmaids and woodcutters were gathered around the dead python. Among them he spotted Ann as well as the hunter whose spear he had borrowed. He descended from the tree and was surprised that they were not talking about the injuries which he had wreaked on it. Instead, they were pointing at one side of its mouth where there was a long yellow cut, on which more flies were swarming than on any other cut. It looked like an old injury which had turned septic

Two men lifted Sam off his feet, and the crowd cheered as they carried him on their shoulders and danced. An elderly shepherd, his weathered face framed by silver hair and beard, smiled at him and said, "Foreigner, you have killed the notorious 'Demon of Gangevell'."

"With my spear," the hunter said proudly.

Sam looked vacantly at them.

"We feared that lately a demon was carrying away our children," said the shepherd. "Its last victim was a small boy whose sickle was found in the woods."

"It had blood marks on it, and we believed that the brave child had injured the Demon," the hunter added.

"That seems to have been inflicted by the boy's sickle," said the old shepherd, pointing his staff at the septic cut. "Hence this creature ought to be what we thought was the 'Demon of Gangevell'."

The men got busy collecting firewood to cremate the python as per the Meluhhan convention for a dead snake. "We could bury it faster," suggested Sam, anxious to disperse the crowd.

"No, we can't," said the shepherd. "Don't you know that a snake gets alive again to take revenge on its killer?"

Sam was about to argue when there was a tug at his elbow. "Don't," Ann whispered. "Cobras are in abundance in Meluhha. People cremate dead cobras. I think that's to protect anyone getting accidentally cut by its fang, which could still be carrying venom."

"But, Ann, that's not a cobra. It isn't poisonous either."

"That's what you and I know," she said. "These people consider anything that creeps as fatal."

So Sam joined the men in placing firewood all over the python's heavy body and setting it on fire. As it burnt emitting an oily substance, the air filled with black smoke and a horrible stench of reptile flesh.

Just as two men were pushing some unburned pieces of its body in the centre of the fire, a mendicant pushed forth through the crowd. He wore a long beard and a headgear that covered almost his entire forehead. So much ash was rubbed on his body that Sam wondered whether the man had crawled out of a furnace.

The mendicant caught Sam grinning and seemed to get angrier. "Atheists," he said, staring at the gathering through his closely-placed eyes. All the villagers looked at him in awe, and a couple of men quietly slipped away. "You've killed God's creation," he shouted. "Who hit it first?"

Sam, to whom the mendicant's voice sounded a tad unnatural, received a powerful push from behind.

Whatever little was visible of the mendicant's forehead, crumpled with creases. "I should have known," he exclaimed, moving a hand over his flowing beard, "that it couldn't be anybody from the sacred land of Meluhha." Pointing a finger at Sam, he continued, "O you colourless outsider. You have brought misfortune upon the God-loving people standing here."

A buxom woman, who carried a big pot under her arm and two even bigger ones upon her head, said in a wailing voice, "Is there any way to save ourselves, O Learned One?"

"Only one," the mendicant announced, turning to Sam. "How did you kill it?" he asked with disdain. The hunter stepped forth and reverently placed his spear at the holy man's feet. The mendicant stared at Sam, who recoiled as if he had been singed. "This gathering of believers," the mendicant said with finality, "will deal with you, a sinner, in the same way as you have harmed God's creation."

The villagers looked at each other. Sam watched the men with an eye on the spear. Ann passed her child to a milkmaid standing next to her, and faced the mendicant with her arms akimbo. "Are you really what you look?" she asked calmly. "Would a holy man call as God's creation, a demon that swallowed three of our children?" She turned to the women. "How could anyone, who has saved our offspring from the 'demon', ever be a sinner?"

A murmur arose among the onlookers. Then the women cried out their support, led by the buxom woman who briskly passed all her pots to others. Sam thought that she had made up her mind to flatten the mendicant's neck in her arm pit. In the meanwhile, Ann had stooped to pick up a rock.

The mendicant started running clumsily down the narrow road. His queer movements made everybody except Ann and Sam laugh. The mendicant fell time and again, and his false beard slipped off, making even Ann join the mirth.

"I'll get him," said Sam, bending to pick up his coil of jute rope. He did not expect the sham mendicant to cuddle himself in a ball like the pangolin. He was distracted by soft fingers closing over his arm.

"Is he worth your efforts and time?" Ann asked, emphasizing the last word.

Sam looked at her appreciatively, and dropped the rope.

After the crowd dispersed, they watched the pangolin trying all tricks to get out of the snare. At last it gave up and slurped up the ants. Sam scratched the ant-hill with a long dead branch. "It's safe at last," he called out. "I'm releasing our little helper."

He commenced digging under the rock of *Dha*, and Ann waited with her baskets to carry away the loose earth. In their anxiousness to make up for the lost time, neither of them noticed the quiet arrival of a donkey carrying the hunched old man they had seen the previous day. The animal loitered a little distance away as its master dozed, his bony toes nearly grazing the ground.

As Ann straightened her back, she spotted him. "The deaf grandpa has returned," she grinned. "I have a feeling that I've seen him before."

"All men in your country look alike," Sam said without even raising his head from work. He had dug deep enough, and had started wondering whether their labour would bear any fruit.

Suddenly he heard a ringing sound and the hoe fell out of his hands. "There's a solid object down there," he told Ann. Picking up the hoe, he carefully excavated deeper. "It's a stone that seems to be chiselled flat on top," he said, gesturing at Ann to have a look at it. Then he scraped around it. "Ann, it's widening at the base."

Sam pulled the stone with both hands but it did not give way. "Wait," she said, "I'll fetch some water."

Once the earth got moist, it softened and released the stony object. It was a mortar that had been buried upside down. It had a recess in its mouth where a stone disc was sealed. Sam scratched away the wax and lifted the lid with his knife.

"Leather packets," he cried. Ann put a finger on her lips, shifting her eyes in the direction of the donkey and the old man. "You know he's totally deaf, Ann," he said, without lowering his voice. "Even if he weren't, he is too stupid to figure out what we're talking about."

He found it difficult to cut open a packet with his trembling hands. They gasped as a fistful of shining yellow pellets, each like a slice of jujube, stared them in the face. "We are rich!" he exclaimed.

Ann echoed him as loudly, not bothered any more by the presence of the old man on the donkey. Sam picked up the smaller packet and pressed it. "Feels like a stone," he looked up at Ann. "Probably it's a lump of raw gold or silver."

"Let it be gold," said Ann, clasping both hands over her bosom. Sam tore open the smaller packet, and out fell a diamond about the size of a goat's eyeball. "*A-la-la! Harsag Zalazalag*!" Ann cried in awe. "See how radiant it is."

The diamond slipped out of Sam's hand. He looked up at her with a dropped jaw. "Are you Sumérian, Ann?" he asked in astonishment.

"No-I-am-not," she uttered. Her lips, which were parted in a smile, pursed firmly. And she lowered her eyelashes.

Sam was distracted by a sudden movement. The donkey threw back its head and trotted a few steps before it settled down to grazing again. He looked at her askance. "Then how do you know what '*Harsag Zalazalag*' means?"

"I don't," she giggled. "Do you become a Meluhhan because you speak our language?"

"But that isn't a common expression," Sam said, looking into her eyes. "It means 'The Peak which emits Brilliance', which I agree is very appropriate for this diamond."

"I picked up those words from Yali who used them to describe a small diamond that a Sumérian guest had gifted to his sister."

"Are you talking about his elder sister in Alatinam?" Sam asked, remembering the incident about Nergal of Nibru that Captain Paravar had narrated to him. Ann nodded her head rapidly. Sam wondered that when Tall Yali could use such appropriate Sumérian words, why his friend had never spoken to him in that language.

The gold and the diamond glittering before his eyes ultimately threw out all other thoughts from Sam's mind. He could not control his laughter as he stared at Mad Kutti's treasure filling both his hands.

Ann picked up the baby and gyrated round and round. It slept, unmindful of their exhilaration. So too snoozed the hunched old man upon his perch on the donkey.

They hurried downhill to reach the bank of the Saraswathi. Ann started singing and Sam clapped the time. Suddenly she broke off and cried, "I recollect it now –" Sam raised a brow. "The deaf grandpa on the donkey –" she said, "he's the same person as the mendicant we met this morning."

"We got to get him, Ann," Sam yelled, smacking a hand on his thigh. "There's some mystery around the man."

They ran out of breath as they hastily climbed the mountain path. Both the man as well as the animal had disappeared.

15 DEMON OF GANGEVELL

Hearing constant barking all around, Ann imagined that she had been trapped by a pack of wild dogs. Her dry throat struggled to shout for help when her eyelids fluttered open with sporadic light falling upon them. She sat up in her bedding. A scream escaped her when she saw their tent on fire, and Sam still sound asleep.

Yelling out to caution him, she ran and picked up her baby. Smoke hurt her eyes and choked her. The toddler clawed at her breasts as it coughed. She groped to get out of the tent and stumbled. Two strong arms pulled her out of the burning tent just before it collapsed.

"Is the baby alright?" asked Sam's voice. "Are you hurt?"

The flames spread to two other tents despite the caravan having camped under some crumbling walls which shielded it against strong winds. Ann watched with concern the ruins which looked eerie in the light of red flames. Earlier in the day, Sam had gathered in the nearby town of Old Kochi that the ruins were seven centuries old. Flaunting his knowledge, he had told her that the walls ought to be three hundred years older than even the Step-less Ziggurat of Giza.

Ann did not understand what Sam was talking about, but then it was his habit to display all that he had gathered from his experience as a camel boy and from reading Cuneiform scriptures. At that moment, her only thought was, 'I hope that the decaying structure doesn't catch fire and come crashing down upon us.'

The men razed all other tents and quickly cleared the area.

Middle-aged women tried to calm down the bewildered oxen and donkeys and led them away to safety. Ann joined the crowd of younger women who stood confused as their children bawled. She wept and kissed her wailing infant over and over again.

Their caravan had started from Rocky Gangevell and had reached Kochi that morning on its way to Muenduru City. Its owner, a skinny young man whose stooped shoulders seemed to be carrying an invisible burden, summoned the two night guards. They approached him as if ready take to their heels at his slightest displeasure.

"I saw a person near the Sumérian's tent, *Kavintu*, and challenged him," said the elder guard whose knees knocked as he spoke. "He ran, and I chased him."

"I heard him shouting," said the younger one who looked a tad confident. "When I reached here, I saw the fire and raised the alarm."

The caravan owner growled. "Couldn't you catch the arsonist?"

"It wouldn't have helped, *Kavintu*," said the first guard. "The strange way he ran was enough to show that he was the insane man whom we had shooed away several times last evening."

Ann's eyes met Sam's. Both withdrew from the crowd unobtrusively, and met a little distance away. She murmured, "The guard said the mad man ran oddly. That's how the sham mendicant moved too." Sam gave out a low cry as she continued, "And the mendicant was none other than the dozing grandpa of the Ringing Rocks."

"Oh my Marduk," Sam spoke under breath. "Ann, for the two of us, that mysterious man has turned out to be 'the real Demon of Gangevell'."

"He's after our gold and diamond," said Ann.

Fearing to sell the *Harsag Zalazalag* in a strange place, Ann had suggested to take Siwa Saqra's help and Sam had readily agreed. Therefore, she was accompanying him to Muenduru City instead of awaiting Tall Yali's return to Rocky Gangevell.

"No, Ann, he is after me," Sam said. "This was his third attempt to kill me."

"Which was the first?" Ann asked, recollecting how the man whom Sam had nicknamed 'Demon of Gangevell' had under the guise of a mendicant, tried to instigate the crowd against him.

Sam told her about the message sent to the dacoits of Nal

forest. "Perhaps the 'Demon of Gangevell' works with a Sumérian gang that wants to prevent me from meeting Siwa Saqra."

Ann shuddered. The name 'Siwa Saqra' had been the sole reason of her undertaking that long risky journey. Upon returning from Alatinam six lunar periods ago, Tall Yali had informed that he had met a young Sumérian who was searching for Siwa Saqra. He was aware that she too was on the lookout of the same man. So when Yali unexpectedly called on her one afternoon saying that Sam had reached Dholavira on his way to meet Siwa, she decided to join him without raising suspicion. She and Tall Yali had planned to conduct the hunt for Mad Kutti's treasure after she had settled her score with Siwa. However, the treasure hunt provided the most convincing reason for her to want to go with Sam.

"Sumérian gang?" she said, looking confused. "How's that connected with Siwa Saqra?"

"Ann, I'll confide in you a part of my past which I haven't told even to my bosom friend Yali," Sam said. "I was witness to a murderous attack on a Meluhhan in Babili. Just before dying, he requested me to meet a person named Siwa Saqra. Obstacles were created in my way in Babili and Urim. I even saw the Meluhhan's murderer following me in Dilmun."

Thinking that Sam had paused to see her reaction, Ann kept a morose face, expressing neither belief nor doubt. Sam continued. "Till I worked in Port Lothal, nothing untoward happened. As soon as I started on this journey to meet Siwa, the Demon started creating trouble."

Ann wondered how much of Sam's story was true. She could not believe that he had nothing to do with the villain she knew by the name of Siwa Saqra.

Ann and Sam had relished a few pieces of mutton that she had cooked for dinner, when a woman's wail arose from a nearby tent. "Oh, no," said Sam putting down his bowl and getting up, "the carver got drunk again." He sprinted in the direction of the noise.

The miserable woman had confided in Ann that her husband, once a well-paid ivory-carver, had lost work when his hands started trembling. The abrupt loss of earnings had forced the family to leave for their village, and prompted the ivory-carver to start drinking heavily. Under the influence of liquor, he often targeted the wrath borne of frustration upon his wife.

Ann glanced at her sleeping infant. Tying the tent flaps, she turned to join the swelling crowd when she heard a commanding voice, "Don't move, woman."

She stood transfixed. It was a voice which had mimicked the sham mendicant. Anger engulfed her like the fire of Old Kochi. She spun around and was face to face with the 'Demon of Gangevell'.

The stranger did not sport a flowing beard like the mendicant. Nor did he have a 'cotton wool' moustache like the grandpa on a donkey. In the dim light, a mole looked as big as a dry date that had stuck under his nose instead of going into his mouth. He carried himself straight and was much younger than both his earlier appearances. Something reflected in his hand as he spoke, "Take it easy, Anlil."

The fire in her eyes doused. Only a few Meluhhans in a village named Chendur knew her real name. "You are mistaken," she said, finding her voice. "I am not Anlil."

"You can't fool me, Anlil." He grinned, exposing yellowish teeth. "I spied you colouring your beautiful white skin."

"Who are you?" Ann said, failing to conceal a quiver in her voice.

"Never mind who I am," he said, switching over to fluent Sumérian. "Ask me 'What do you want?'"

She could not speak. If his address had worried her, his speaking her mother tongue terrified her. It boded ill for safety.

"What – what do you want?" she echoed.

"All of Kutti's gold and his diamond."

She feigned ignorance. "What are you talking about?"

"About how I could help you from getting your real identity exposed before Samasin of Babili." He looked at her from under his brow and smiled.

Ann could not see any way out but to part with Mad Kutti's treasure. After that, how could she face Sam? "My brother," she begged, "why would you ruin me and my baby? What harm –"

"I hate drama, woman."

"I can fetch only the diamond," she said, thanking *Sîn* for a flash of quick thought. "The gold – Samasin always carries it with him."

"Bloody stable boy," said the 'Demon of Gangevell', and Ann

perceived a hint of admiration in his voice. "Get the diamond, woman."

"I will, but you've got to help me get away."

"Meet me at the well," said the 'Demon of Gangevell', and withdrew into the shadows.

Ann heard the drunkard arguing. She had to act fast. Her hands trembled as she untied the flaps of the tent.

Rushing to the corner where the sacks lay, she moved some of them and located the end of a hairpin planted deep into the ground. As she scrapped a hole at that spot, she thought she heard a noise at the entrance, and swung around. No one was there. She drew out a ball of cloth from the cavity, and her fingers sensed that it had turned damp. With shaking hands, she tied it securely inside her *varati*.

Pushing back the sacks in place, she fumbled inside one of them. She found a flask-shaped vial about the size of a finger and scratched open its seal of wax. Pulling off one of her bone hairpins, she dipped it in the flask. She waved it to dry, and inserted it back in her hair. Then she crushed the vial under her foot and dashed out of the tent.

With her mind occupied with the thought of a quick escape, Ann missed seeing a shadow slipping into the tent as she left. In the distance, she heard a spurt of slaps, and the drunkard's wife begging Sam to forgive her husband.

Just when she had left the camp behind, it struck her that her back was lighter than usual. Her hands rose to check her shoulders and she cried, "My baby?"

She ran back. Hearing the commotion coming from the direction of the drunkard's tent, she knew that Sam would not have returned as yet. Then her foot hit a soft object. With a low scream she tumbled to the ground. It was a camp dog frothing at the mouth. Nearby, she spotted a big piece from the mutton she had cooked.

She froze, thinking about what might have transpired during her short absence. The wicked 'Demon of Gangevell' must have poisoned the mutton and tried it on the dog to make sure it worked. "I can't leave Sam to his fate," she mumbled, grabbing the pot of mutton and hurling it out of the tent. Cursing the 'Demon', she kicked both the bowls into the dust.

Then she snatched the toddler from its cradle, and fled.

Slipping out of the camp, Ann scurried towards the hamlet. It reminded her of a night in Chendur Village when she was fleeing from an evil villain. How ironic it was that she was now rushing to meet another villain who was just as wicked.

She spotted a flame from afar. It lighted up a brick wall whitewashed with lime. Drawing near, she could distinguish the silhouette of a buffalo cart against the wall. Then the flame seemed to have moved because the silhouette disappeared. Ann saw the Demon's features being caricatured in the flickering light of a torch that he held. She imagined that the shadow looked like the head of a mongoose.

She considered how she would deal with the 'Demon of Gangevell' once she was seated in his cart. The Demon deserved one scratch of her specially prepared hairpin before she used it on Siwa Saqra.

No sooner did the thug see Ann, he jumped down from the cart. She reached inside her *varati*, untied the knot, and placed the *Harsag Zalazalag* in his hand. He raised it to his eye, and rotated it against the torch.

Ann thought, 'It won't be long before I wipe that stupid grin off your face.'

The 'Demon of Gangevell' tied the *Harsag Zalazalag* to a loose end of his *vesti* and tucked the knot under his belt. Leaping to his seat, he said, "Get on." As she clambered up, he extended his hands. "Give me the tot."

"That's all right; I'll be able to hold it."

"Woman," he said grinning. "I am not your dim-witted Jittan."

Ann stared at him. The 'Demon of Gangevell' knew her every secret.

Even before she became aware about what she was doing, she had handed the infant to him. He slid a hand upon the sleeping toddler's neck and looked askance at her.

A breath of dejection escaped her. The buffalo cart ground on for a long time till they saw some carts parked in a row by the side of the country road. Several oxen were tethered nearby. The 'Demon of Gangevell' stopped near a cluster of tents. She got down and ran to receive her baby. As the cart left, she stood there, trying to get her stiffened limbs moving.

"Who's there?" a stentorian voice cut through the cold darkness.

She pressed her sleeping toddler closer, and turned in the direction of the voice. "A passenger," she said. "Please take me to the owner of this caravan."

A puny man looking like a shorn sheep drew nearer. He raised his lamp at her face as Ann strained her eyes to see his. "I am the owner, lady," he said. "Where do you wish to go?"

"To Muenduru City," she said, taken by surprise that a man of his stature commanded such a booming voice.

"We aren't going there, lady. We are going to Chendur Village."

Tears flowed out of Ann's tired eyes. Chendur was the last place on earth she had wanted to go, but in that wilderness, she did not have any choice.

16 SUMÉRIAN WOMAN IN MELUHHA

Chendur Village and Magan were two places which had been steep waterfalls in the course of Ann's voyage in the river called Life. Had it been possible to raze both of them to dust, she would have done it long ago. Born a Sumérian named Anlil, she had landed in Meluhha by a tragic turn of events.

Orphaned when she was still a toddler, Anlil was raised by her father's sister, a woman who drew appreciative glances when she went out to buy meat and vegetable in Urim. She recalled that her aunt often told her uncle, "Anlil is fast growing up in her mother's mould. I confess that I envied my late sister-in-law's beauty."

Anlil remembered Uncle Gazkir as a hard working man, oblivious to ways of the world. He cut hair for a living and taught her the trade as she grew up. When she was fifteen, her aunt fell sick and died. Her uncle remarried a thin woman who lost no time in introducing the simpleton to the realm of nagging.

Anlil silently bore the brunt of her step-aunt's malice, hoping that she would meet a handsome young man, marry him and leave her uncle's house for ever. The silver lining dimmed as years dragged on, and she realized that no bachelor in Urim wanted to marry an orphaned girl whose guardian could just make the ends meet.

One day she met a kind looking dowager, who said in her masculine voice, "You could live a queen's life, Anlil, if you settle in Meluhha. Young Meluhhan merchants run mad after beautiful Sumérian girls."

The very thought of deserting her kind uncle repelled Anlil. In order to marry a rich Meluhhan, she had to deal with unknown people. No, she would not risk taking the chance. It could as well land her from the frying pan into the fire.

The dowager kept on meeting her regularly. Gradually, Anlil started sharing her woes with the woman. Once, after being bruised in body and psyche by her step-aunt's outrage, Anlil took an impulsive step. She left home and ran to the busy port of Urim.

There she was met by the dowager who introduced her to a woman whose eyes, Anlil noticed with a little anxiety, roved constantly. "She is my close friend," said the dowager. "She will escort you on the ship sailing to Meluhha, and introduce you to a very handsome and rich merchant there."

A bright young lady, having the same spark of hope in her eyes as Anlil, joined them at the port of Magan.

Anlil avoided drinking the water which had been brought aboard at Magan. She did not want to accept anything from a place where, as her late aunt had told her, her parents and brother Sammu aged six had been massacred by raiders from the desert.

During several days' sailing, the escort made them learn a lot of Meluhhan words saying tongue-in-cheek, "You'll need them all to quarrel with the men you marry." It made the girls pinch each other and giggle.

They disembarked at a small port named Sutantoru-on-Sea, and travelled on a narrow path along which wooden poles were planted apparently without any reason. They passed through a high gate in a gigantic stone wall and reached an inn where the escort transferred the girls' custody to a Meluhhan hag. She possessed such a cold attitude that neither girl wanted to talk with her.

They were joined by several armed men. They boarded a small caravan on a tedious journey which lasted a few weeks. Once Anlil whispered to her companion from Magan, "I wonder why they all look upon us as captives rather than the future brides of their masters."

"Oh, Anlil," cried the girl from Magan thrusting her tongue through her lips. "What will happen to us in a land where we can't even speak their language?"

Every night, both the girls slept holding each other' hands, and shivered despite a warm weather.

Ultimately they crossed ominous looking ravines of a river,

which to Anlil appeared broader than the Purattu. Reaching Chendur, the carts stopped before a high brick wall that screened everything behind it. In it was a big gate, entering which they saw the only two-storey building in the village. Built of bricks, it had a spacious compound, and belonged to a man whom people knew as Agent Jittan.

Jittan climbed the stairs so leisurely while leading them to a room on the first floor that the girls exchanged glances and restrained their urge to snigger. Although impressed by Jittan's prosperity, Anlil could not but discount his ability to earn by straight means.

Soon the girls discovered with trepidation that everybody who had accompanied them from Sutantoru-on-Sea had left. That night, a drunken Jittan raped his two timid wards from Sumér.

Both the girls resigned to their fate that they were destined to live as Agent Jittan's concubines. At least, they had each other's company and they hoped that together they would bring a change for the better in the wayward Meluhhan's life.

In the morning, the girls heard a commotion in the compound below. From the only window in their room, they saw a crowd of raucous men gathered there. One of them caught them peeping, inserted thumb and a finger in his mouth, and blew a sharp whistle. The girls withdrew quickly, but not before some more men spotted them and started waving. That was when they fully grasped the meaning of the word 'agent' in their host's name. They sat on the large cot, tightly holding each other's trembling bodies.

Not long thereafter, Jittan came accompanied by a hefty guard sporting a bristly moustache and a wild beard. He raised a spear and herded the girls downstairs.

They were displayed as in a cattle market. The prospective buyers pressed and poked them lewdly, and haggled with Agent Jittan. Anlil noticed that many had joined the crowd even when they were not serious buyers. Finally, some men settled for her companion and the silver and the flesh changed hands.

The girl from Magan clung to Anlil and wailed. Her new masters pulled her away by her hair, chatting among themselves that they had struck a good bargain. Anlil stood still, looking at her departing friend through swollen eyes. She had lost the only contact from her homeland.

That evening, Anlil heard voices in the adjoining room. Jittan seemed to be pacifying somebody possessing a husky voice. It did not escape her that the other person sounded very different from how the Meluhhans spoke.

All of a sudden, the mysterious voice exploded, "*Mulla Xul*!" Anlil recognised the Sumérian exclamation. While she could not understand much of what that man spoke in the Meluhhan language, she could make out bits and pieces, which meant, "I haven't met a bigger jackass than you, Jittan." She heard Jittan pleading.

Anlil's tear-stained face was overwhelmed by a smile. She wanted to see the Sumérian who had brought the villain to his knees. Undoubtedly, her countryman would help her. She was about to shout for help when she heard the commanding voice again. "Sell her fast and deliver the silver to Siwa Saqra. I want you to pay Siwa by the weekend."

Anlil sank to the floor. "They're talking about me," she spoke loud enough to hear herself over her heartbeats. "And the Sumérian is as much involved in trafficking as Agent Jittan." She stuck to the wall like a lizard, but could not make out anything else which transpired between the two men.

'So someone called Siwa Saqra is the third and the biggest enemy of Sumérian women,' thought Anlil. 'Siwa Saqra ought to be the organizer of this entire network of trafficking.' Her eyes burnt in rage as she realized how the greed of one man was pushing countless young women into prostitution.

Now that a horrible future stared her in the face, it occurred to her that nothing but death could save her. 'If Death is the only way out,' she thought, 'why should I be afraid to strike back at the three men responsible for my misery?'

Agent Jittan was but a small *pulasa* fish, and she could deal with him later. She had to concentrate on the two crocodiles of women's trafficking – the Meluhhan named Siwa Saqra, and the Sumérian who talked about him. She had seen neither, and in order to identify them, first she had to escape from Agent Jittan.

When darkness fell on Chendur Village, she coyly conveyed through a passing servant, "I have to answer the call of nature."

Cursing her bowels, Agent Jittan pulled out hair from his nose and ordered the woman servant to go with her. As the stocky woman led her along a rough terrain overgrown with weeds, Anlil heard heavy footsteps following them. Looking behind, she saw

Jittan's scary guard coming after them waving his spear.

As they neared the woods, a steady chirping of crickets got louder. The servant asked the guard to wait, and accompanied Anlil behind a thick growth of bushes. Anlil squatted on the ground and looked at the woman servant as if asking, "Won't you too?"

With the stern expression of a guardian who does not like getting too close to her wards, the woman walked a little away and lowered herself. That was just the moment for which Anlil was waiting. She grabbed a rock and aimed hard at the woman's head. Her tense countenance eased as she watched the woman toppling over with a gasp which was quelled by the sound of crickets all around.

So far, Anlil's anger for the traitorous dowager, the dishonest escort, the rapist Jittan, the Sumérian trafficker and the villain named Siwa Saqra had gathered like steam in a tightly closed vessel. It sought an explosion through breaking the unconscious servant's skull. With a great effort, she reigned in her instinct and rushed into the denser portion of the forest.

At another time, she would have hesitated to venture into the pitch black darkness, but that evening it did not bother her. The mere instinct of escaping from an equally dark future made her face the fear as well as the obstacles.

Thorns and sharp pebbles pierced her soles, but her mind was occupied by only one thought 'I'll have to reach far enough before the guard suspects anything awry.' So despite sensing the warmth of the trickling blood, it turned numb to pain.

Anlil lost count of how many times she fell. Every time she got up and started running again. Although fatigue slowed her down, it could not stop her. Anlil herself wondered at the extraordinary energy that was driving her.

Then in the darkness, several dim lights looking like fireflies caught her attention. She halted and stared. Pressing each step, she drew closer. The smell of manure in the air raised her hopes that it was probably a caravan that had broken the journey for the night. "Thank you, *Sîn* the patron deity of Urim," she said with relief as she looked up at the moonless sky. "I've reached a place where some people might help me."

Amber light emanated from various places on the ground. She saw that the entire place was encircled by carts and tethered animals. She could distinguish two sprawling tents, and a much smaller one nestling between them. Anlil heard a baby crying, and then spotted several women sitting before wood fire. A whiff of fresh barley bread and raw onions sailed to her nose, and suddenly she was aware of gnawing hunger. With tears in her eyes, she stood silently watching them.

A modestly dressed woman, who was guiding a couple of young women in cooking, spotted her first. Anlil saw her getting up and drawing near. Several grey strands in her well groomed black hair shone in the faltering light. Her countenance and her behaviour made Anlil assume that she commanded authority.

The lady put a hand on Anlil's shoulder and said, "You look very tired, daughter. Who are you?"

Although it was rather dark to see the lady's face clearly, her voice sounded compassionate. All of a sudden, Anlil's emotions flowed over like boiling milk. Both her hands rose to her eyes as she broke into uncontrollable sobs.

She heard the lady's consoling voice and felt her hand moving on her back. Several voices joined the lady's as others left cooking and gathered around her. One of them brought a jar of cool water.

No sooner had she regained composure, Anlil started telling her tale in broken Meluhhan, but it seemed that her Sumérian intonation confused everybody. "I'll take you to my Man," the lady said, and led her to the central tent.

The lady's husband, the owner of the caravan, was a short sinewy man in his late fifties. His grey curly hair was thinning by the sides of the temple. The warmth on his face and the concern in his voice reassured Anlil, and she quickly apprised him about her misfortune. He looked at his wife and said, "Send in Yali."

A little later, a brawny young man appeared at the entrance, bent low, and entered the tent. His features looked strikingly similar to those of the elder man. "Yes, Brother?" he said. Then he saw her, and it seemed that he forgot what he wanted to speak thereafter.

"Yali," said the caravan owner. "This brave girl has escaped from the clutches of a trafficker. Get her to the next village right away." Anlil's eyes oozed with gratitude. "Take along some fresh bread and warm milk for her, and request the headman to hide her among their womenfolk."

"I will, Brother," said Yali, turning to leave.

Soon she heard the sounds of hooves and clucking outside the tent. Yali had returned with another man, both riding sturdy donkeys, and leading one more. He helped Anlil to mount the animal. His warm breath slightly blew her hair and she recoiled like a tortoise withdrawing inside its shell.

Immediately setting out, the three animals trotted throughout the night. At dawn, they reached a shallow river. They had hardly rested for some time when Yali got up and prodded the animals.

"Let's rest a little longer," Anlil said, stifling a yawn. "I've been running since last evening."

"No, fair lady," said Yali in a firm voice. "You haven't yet got out of the muck. Traffickers don't give up easily. I bet my donkey that they would reach here by daybreak."

The animals laboriously waded through the waters to the opposite bank and they continued the journey. Long after putting the river behind, they reached a group of round thatched huts. Each possessed a compound fenced with thick long branches, from where bleats and clucks emanated regularly. They stopped at a bigger hut located in the centre, from the roof of which a cockerel had just started crowing.

A scraggy elderly man came out of it, and Yali sought his help. The headman summoned his wife, a woman with thick lips and white hair. She smiled so disarmingly at Anlil that she could not believe she was meeting so many friendly people within such a short time.

"Our caravan will pass through this place," Yali told Anlil, "and pick you up in a day or two as soon as the crisis blows over."

Anlil wished that he stayed, but he turned and left the hut, accompanied by the headman.

The women of the hamlet stopped drawing water and milking goats, and gathered around her. The sheer incredulity in their eyes, as they studied her fair face and limbs, made Anlil giggle. It also made her wonder when it was that she had smiled before.

The women murmured among themselves. Their tone implied that the matter was pretty serious. From signs of their hands and a few words which she understood, she gathered that they were worried that her face could be seen clearly from afar even in dim light.

A girl ran out of the hut and brought a bowl full of henna paste. The women asked her to strip, and her Sumérian gown was thrown into fire. Two women quickly applied the dark paste all over her body, and two more fanned her till it dried. They helped her to wrap a *varati* around her darkened body.

Just as Tall Yali had warned, Agent Jittan's henchmen visited the hamlet in the morning. Looking suspiciously at every woman they spotted, first they asked some children if they had seen a 'discoloured' woman. Then they enquired with several adults, and finally they met the headman. Failing to get any clue, they hurried in the direction of another hamlet.

A day later, the caravan arrived. Finding her name unfamiliar, the womenfolk in the caravan started calling her 'Ann', which meant 'courage' in the Meluhhan language. Anlil adopted her new name whole-heartedly.

Few weeks later, the caravan reached the delta created by several branches of River Saraswathi. It halted at a small port where all its goods were loaded on a ship. They too boarded it and reached an island, Laketown Dholavira.

Ann started her life anew, determined to strive, earn and save enough to undertake the long journey back to Sumér. The caravan owner's wife, Tall Yali's sister-in-law, took a liking for her. Ann felt so secure in Dholavira that she stopped the laborious process of dyeing her skin.

That raised an issue she had not foreseen, and she confided about it to the caravan owner's wife. The lady talked to her brother-in-law Tall Yali, who accompanied Ann several times when she went out, and that ended the menace of loafing loudmouths.

Several lunar periods later when she fell very sick, Yali's sister-in-law looked after her with the care that Ann had missed since her aunt's death. While her fever subsided after a few days, there was no relief from frequent vomiting.

One evening when the men had gone out to drink, Yali's sister-in-law put a hand around her. "I'm afraid there's some bad news for you, Ann."

Ann's face did not show any expression. Could anything be worse than what she had suffered before she met the helpful family?

"It's the news which gives immense joy to a woman who is married," said Yali's sister-in-law, "and misery to one who isn't."

17 NIGHTMARE IN MUENDURU CEMETERY

Just as Sam gathered his sacks, he became aware of a shadow fluttering nearby under the light of the torches. A man wearing a slipshod yellow *vesti* stood very close to him. Pulling out hair from his nostrils, he asked Sam in a dull voice, "Are you looking for a cheap inn with clean rooms?"

Sam's caravan had reached the centre of Muenduru City a little while ago. The local cart drivers' calls for fare and the parting din raised by its passengers had awoken sleeping children who had then added to the chaos. Sam wanted to get away from it all quickly, and go to bed. "Yes," he said, relieved by the ready solution that the stranger offered.

"Come with me, *Kavintu*," said the man, looking as if he had suddenly started feeling ten years younger. "I'll take you to a decent place nearby. It has very reasonable rates." He lifted Sam's luggage and hurried ahead.

As Sam followed, it struck him that the stranger's movements lacked the knack of a skilled porter. 'Perhaps circumstances have forced him into such labour,' he thought, and resolved to pay a little extra to the unfortunate man.

They had just entered a narrow by-lane when the man dropped the sacks and scurried away into the darkness. Before Sam could grasp what was happening, he felt a powerful impact on his tired legs. He staggered and fell down.

Two hands blindfolded and gagged him. His brush with the dacoits of the Nal Forest sprang to his memory. He resigned to the fact that he was about to lose even the other half of Mad Kutti's treasure, the packet full of gold pellets.

Two more hands, comparably coarser than the first pair, tied his wrists behind his back. But what surprised him was the metallic jingle of anklets as the man moved. While he had seen wealthy women wearing ringing anklets, never had he met any man sporting them. Was his attackers' purpose something other than robbery?

Sam was pulled up from the ground and jostled on to a cart. The air smelt stuffy, and he guessed that it ought to be a hooded cart. He heard the two men climbing in after him. "Why have you captured me?" he said.

"Because you are a male foreigner," said a cheerful voice. It belonged to the shoddy man who had carried his luggage. "We were searching for one since noon."

Sam wondered if he had been selected for an occult ceremony. Would his ear be ripped or a finger hacked? Or would it be a painful castration? "Why?" he asked.

Instead of replying, the man himself raised a question. "Guru, will I be cured of my urinal torture at last?"

The little bells tinkled as someone moved, perhaps to face the first man. "Yes, of course," said a second voice. Sam's head jerked towards it. Hadn't he heard it somewhere before? The voice continued, "Give me a gold bead for guiding you successfully in your search."

The person possessing it seemed to be a holy man – a greedy one – and the other, a rich follower. Were the two after a more sinister purpose than maiming?

"The more I stay in your blessed company, Guru, the more I'm convinced about your divine powers," said the disciple in a voice which ended in a choke.

"And you, stupid boy Jittan," said the Guru in the true fashion of a strict teacher, "wanted to bring a Humérian woman from a local hook shop." Sam listened carefully. The Guru sounded as if he was pretending to be someone else. His attempt at changing his voice was too obvious. "Ask the cart man to hurry, otherwise the auspicious time for the ceremony would pass."

A shiver raced through Sam's spine. It was the same voice and the same style as that of the sham mendicant. The 'Demon of Gangevell' had caught up with him again. It seemed that under the guise of a shaman, the Demon had convinced someone named Jittan to offer Sam as a sacrifice to a deity.

Returning to his tent on the night the drunkard beat his wife, Sam had seen some pieces of their dinner near a dead dog. He had suspected it as another of the Demon's attempts to kill him, but soon afterwards another matter had demanded all his attention. Ann was missing. He did not care that the *Harsag Zalazalag* too was gone. Concerned about the safety of the mother and the child, he had begged the caravan owner to stay put for two days till they scoured several nearby villages. No one had seen any woman with a toddler. Reluctantly he had joined the caravan on its onward journey, fearing to face Tall Yali if they met again.

A sudden jerk shook Sam out of his reverie. By then, even an occasional rumble of a passing cart ceased, and he guessed that they had left the city behind and were travelling on a country road. When the cart stopped at last, the man who was 'Guru' to Jittan and the 'Demon of Gangevell' to Sam, gave a command.

Two men guided Sam to get down from the cart. The only sounds he heard around were the chirping of crickets, occasionally accompanied by jackals' howls. The ground was firm till his foot fell on soft moist earth. He was immediately tugged back on solid terrain.

Sam's *vesti* was pulled off and four strong hands forced him to sit on the ground. Cold water was poured over him, and guttural sounds of '*hu-hu-hu*' escaped his lips. He was dried with a rough piece of cloth, and somebody wound a *vesti* around his waist. His skin brushed against its crispness, and his nose twitched with the smell of dye which it emitted. A gritty powder was sprayed all over his body. A garland was put around his neck. Their fragrance made him cringe, for he recognized *ketakai* pine flowers which were commonly used in Meluhha during a ceremony, either religious or occult.

The shaman started chattering mumbo-jumbo. The drivel continued on and on and although Sam tried hard to think of a way of escaping, he could not find any. So he decided to obstruct the ceremony and delay it as much as he could, with a hope that the 'auspicious time' which the shaman had mentioned would pass.

At last the chant ended. He heard the sound of anklets approaching him in calculated steps. He surmised that the Demon of Gangevell under a shaman's guise was about to perform the final ritual on him.

Sam waited till the peal of anklets sounded about an arm's length away. Then he shot out a leg. With a brute force, his foot banged a soft part on the shaman's body. It triggered a sharp howl which was followed by a crying groan that slowly sank to the ground. An exclamation dripping with pure joy escaped Sam. He knew that he had succeeded in hitting the shaman's most sensitive organ.

Both the other men pounced on him. As he bore their savage thrashing, he heard the shaman's weak voice from near his feet. "Stop beating the sacred sacrifice, idiots. Just tie up his legs."

Again the shaman started burbling, but it seemed that he had withdrawn to a safe distance and was guiding Jittan to perform the rites. Sam's bladder called for his immediate attention. It was a sudden sensation which was similar to what he had felt on seeing the black wild bull on that Full Moon night in Babili. Unlike Babili, no one was going to entertain his request in Muenduru cemetery. Then, in that utter physical discomfort, Sam detected a ray of hope.

When Jittan drew closer, a spattering sound came from the ground. A couple of expletives dropped from Jittan's mouth as he cried, "Guru, the Humérian has polluted himself." Then he thundered, "Give me the knife, I'm going to chop off his spout."

A hand briskly pulled off Sam's wet *vesti* and got hold of his penis. With a throbbing heart, he awaited a sharp pain shooting from that part of his body when he heard the shaman's voice. "Hold it, Jittan, you ass-head. Blood flows only during the ceremony, not before it."

"But every time you complete the hymns, Guru, he would piss."

"That won't occur again. See he's trembling. This sort of thing happens when a person is very scared."

"We can't take any chance, Guru. I suspect he did it with a purpose."

There was a pause, and it seemed that the shaman was mulling over Jittan's misgiving. Sam awaited his decision with bated breath. Finally, the wise man offered a solution, "Block his spout. Bind it."

As soon Sam was bathed again, a long piece of twine was wound over his penis as if it were a bobbin. His cries initiated howling of dogs. The pain was so acute that he just about fainted.

Then he was clad in a fresh piece of cloth. Again, the garland was put in his neck and the gritty powder, which he assumed was vermillion, was sprinkled on him. The shaman rattled through his hocus-pocus a third time, and sounded as if he was tiring out. Sam tried to pull apart his bound wrists and wished that fate had provided him one chance to strike back before an inevitable end. "I'd have preferred to die fighting a python, or even a wild bull."

Sam's thoughts were disturbed with an abrupt break in the shaman's jabber. For a moment, complete silence descended all around. Then he heard it. A distant eerie sound drifted from his left. Another joined it from his right. Just when both seemed to have reached resonance, a third – the most sinister of them – arose from the direction that he faced. Starting from a low note like a jackal's howl, all three rose to a crescendo of cold-blooded shrieks.

Jittan's jittery voice indicated that he had beheld an alarming sight. Sam had always roared with laughter whenever Ann had talked of ghosts in a low trembling voice. For the first time in his life, he considered the possibility that spirits did exist.

He heard Jittan and his man scampering away in the direction behind him, which had remained silent so far. The unearthly sounds drew closer. Sam heard the shaman squeal, and he thought the voice resembled that of his friend Qwoco. The thought occurred and passed away in a flash. Sam visualized the shaman running for his life. He tried to free himself in a last ditch effort, but failed. There was no alternative but to get ready to be devoured by ghosts of the Muenduru cemetery.

Soon he heard the creepy sounds, accompanied with the stamping of feet, rushing past him. It was strange that these spirits were running instead of flying despite being in an obvious hurry to grab the three humans before they escaped from their territory. From the receding yelps of the shaman and his gang, Sam assumed that the ghosts were throwing some sort of missiles at them.

As the noise receded, the screeching of bats, the howls of jackals and the barks of dogs took over. For quite some time, he could not hear anything else. Perhaps the ghosts had caught up with the shaman and his disciples and were already crunching them with glee. In utter helplessness he waited for them to return and feast on him.

Sam's chattering teeth had had some respite when, instead of the eerie sounds which he had feared, he heard plain hilarity approaching him. He hoped that if the spirits were so happy relishing the shaman and others, they might forget that one more prey was still available, tied up at the place of the ceremony. He prayed to Marduk to get them spare him.

The laughter drew closer. It sounded not only human but also boyish. Warm hands untied his limbs and pulled off the blindfold. In the light of torches, Sam made out three youngsters, about the age of fifteen. They looked identical with cropped hair and trace of a moustache, except that their heights were vastly different. He hurriedly removed the painful piece of twine from his body and threw it in the fire left dying by his perpetrators.

Looking around, he saw graves everywhere. There was an open pit nearby. Had his young saviours not arrived just in time, he might have occupied it by then. Sam fell on his knees to thank Marduk for His grace.

"Foreigner, how did you get into the clutches of a shaman?" asked the tallest of the boys. Sam narrated how he had been abducted, and enquired if they lived nearby.

"No, we don't."

"Then what made you come here so late at night?"

"Our friend here works at an inn," said the tallest boy putting a hand on the shoulders of the shortest among them. "The man who was getting this ceremony performed visits Muenduru regularly and stays at his inn. The other man who was pretending to be a shaman beckoned our friend this morning."

The shortest boy picked up the thread. "He asked me, 'Would you like to earn a pumpkin simply for getting two men together?' Who wouldn't? So he pointed out our regular patron to me. 'Tell that man, '*Kavintu*, I know an expert shaman who can cure any disease. I will take you to him if you wish." Then he made me repeat it several times, and led me to the river bank to show the place where the shaman would be sitting."

The tallest boy said, "As we ate the pumpkin, he told us that the shaman was none other than the man who had given him the pumpkin. We considered that was rather fishy, and ran to the river bank. By then, the shaman had left."

Sam showed no sign of surprise because he had started understanding how the Demon of Gangevell worked. "How did you find them again?" he asked.

The youngest said, "I had overheard the fake shaman talking about sacrificing a human being to cure our patron's malady. So we waited for them at the cemetery where occult ceremonies are normally performed."

"How did the fake shaman look?"

"He had plaited hair and a flowing beard. He wore a headgear fixed with a pair of ram-horns. A long ox tail was –"

Sam hastened to cut him short. "I meant the man who pretended to be the shaman."

The two taller boys looked at the shortest, who said with pride, "He looked ugly with a big black mole under his nose."

"Qwoco!" cried Sam. The man he had considered a friend had attempted to kill him all this while. As he contemplated, he saw the boys blankly looking at each other. He smiled and said, "So when you saw them bringing me here, you decided to save me."

"No, we were very scared at the outset," said the tallest boy. "I noticed that the shaman looked over his shoulder whenever an owl hooted. I told my friends, 'That man is a coward.' We agreed that it might be possible to send all of them home if we could scare their leader."

Sam joined the boys in their glee, not wanting to admit that he too would have made good his escape had he not been bound.

18 MYSTERY OF THE FISH-HOOK

Looking forward to meeting his sweetheart under the pretext of delivering a message to her father, Sam followed a road winding up to a ridge on which Muenduru City lay. Keeping to the inn-keeper's directions, he reached a high brick wall with a gate, and entered within. Inside, it looked very much like the central locality of Laketown Dholavira, and they called it the Citadel.

Enquiring about Siwa Saqra's residence, he was guided to a street at the corner of which was a pottery workshop. Reaching the place and glancing inside, Sam met the owner's eyes. Even before Sam opened his mouth, the hunched potter leered at him, mumbling, "Another Humérian, come to meet Hiwa." Not only was Sam taken aback by the man's words, but he was also perplexed by his crafty smile. The potter winked. "If you need any clay document to be baked, I'd understand."

Shrill voices drew Sam's attention down the street where four small boys were arguing, pointing to several marbles on the ground. Two colts stood under a nearby tree, tenderly rubbing their muzzles.

"That's Captain Paravar's foal," Sam cried, and ran towards them.

He heard the potter calling out, "I've helped your countryman earlier." He did not understand what the potter was talking about, and did not bother either. All his thoughts concentrated on the foal which had bonded with him during the short time they had spent together.

The baby had grown into a pretty young mare. She neighed and licked him. Seeing her welcoming the stranger, the other colt – a brown male – turned friendly too. One of the boys darted up to Sam, and his friends followed, throwing their differences to the wind.

"Aren't they sweet?" asked the boy. Sam looked down at him and could not move his eyes away. It occurred to him how his beloved would have appeared as a child aged about seven. "Both are ours," the boy added, touching his chest.

"They are the most beautiful ponies I've ever seen," Sam said, now in no doubt that the boy was the sibling of the damsel he had met in Sutantoru-on-Sea. "What's your name?"

"I'm Muruku –" said the boy. Sweeping a hand to indicate his friends, he added, "They call me 'Red Muruku'"

Not waiting for Sam to ask 'why', another boy grabbed Red Muruku's wrists and said, "Just see his palms. Aren't they the reddest amongst us all?"

Red Muruku proudly displayed them. Sam looked with interest, tapped him on the shoulder and asked, "What are the names of your ponies, Red Muruku?"

"This is Gani," the boy said patting the brown colt, "And that's Humi. My father purchased Gani in Gandhara."

"And I guess he bought Sumi in Sumér?" Sam said with a glint of mischief in his eyes. How he craved to get his beloved maiden mentioned in the conversation.

"No, my sister rescued the poor thing from a fat bald sailor and a dumb Humérian."

"Ugh?" Sam looked as if a carpenter bee had hit him between the eyes. "Ah – Ahem, does Siwa Saqra live here?"

"He's my father," said Red Muruku, running to the only teak wood door in the street, and knocking it vigorously. "Velli, Velli."

Only half a *mu-eš* earlier, Sam would have been delighted to have discovered her name. It did not matter any more.

An annoyed voice shot out from the other side. Sam thought 'How bitter', when the door threw open. The Girl from Sutantoru emerged, chiding the boy. She stopped in mid-sentence when she saw Sam. Although her eyes had widened, she behaved as if she did not remember him.

"He wants to meet Father," said Red Muruku, and took off.

Velli gave a brisk nod, turned and started walking. Sam followed her like a new-born calf follows its mother, through a courtyard in the centre of which stood a majestic neem tree. She raised a hand to the low thatched roof of the foyer and pulled out one of the rolled reed mats which were tucked in it. She threw it to the floor and spread it out with a flick of her foot. "Father will join you soon," she said in a voice devoid of inflection.

Sam squatted on the mat, wondering what had made him lose his heart to a woman so swollen with conceit.

From the foyer, two doors led inside the house. White cotton curtains hung across both of them. The scent of sandalwood from smouldering incense sticks permeated the air.

Velli went back to a knee-high wooden pilon where a gangly girl was waiting for her. He heard Velli speak in a low voice. The other girl giggled.

'I can very well guess what she might have told her friend,' thought Sam. Had he started disliking the girl for whom he had travelled over a hundred *da-na* from Port Lothal? Sam was not sure.

Despite the constant thumping noise and the lanky girl's rattling, his ears could pick up the tinkle of Velli's bangles. He imagined her lissom body moving in rhythm as she pounded grain in the pilon, and wanted to watch her. With a great effort, he kept looking away lest the host consider it rude of him ogling at his daughter.

Sam recollected that Ann had purchased several sets of bangles in Gangevell. "All these are from Kalibangan, which is famous for its bangles," she had told him. "Every Meluhhan woman wants to possess them." Feeling grateful to her for reminding about a gift which had not occurred to him, he too had bought a few sets of Kalibangan bangles for the girl from Sutantoru. He wondered how they would sound on Velli's wrists if he presented them to her; but did the bad-mannered girl deserve his gift at all?

The pounding stopped. The lanky chatterbox left and Velli hurried inside the house through one of the white curtains. A man aged about forty had emerged from behind the other.

Sam sprang to his feet and bowed to Siwa Saqra, who serenely joined his hands in the typical Meluhhan greeting. With it arose a part of the cloth which flowed up from his waist to his left shoulder and then down his back. Sam thought that its design of big red trefoils matched well with the golden bands on Siwa's arms. The golden diadem that he wore was inlaid with a big piece of steatite. Sam wondered whether a diamond would not have been more appropriate instead.

"Are you coming from Suméru, young man?" Siwa asked, as he sat down on the floor, his hands encircling his knees.

"Yes, *Kavintu*," Sam said, following the same pose. "I am Samasin from Babili." He halted as he heard a ringing sound drawing near. Velli came and placed before them two big beakers containing a reddish drink. "Your man had handed me a fish-hook to give to you," he continued, "but I lost it somewhere on the way."

As he spoke, Sam sensed a short break in the retreating jingle. Did she hesitate? Or was it simply his imagination?

"A fish-hook for me? Why?"

Sam had expected Siwa to ask about the metal of the fish-hook. Since similar miniature fish-hooks of gold, silver and copper had been found on the dead man's body, he had inferred that each was meant to convey a specific mutually agreed message to its receiver.

"I don't know," said Sam. From the corner of his eye he perceived some movement in the adjoining room. It seemed Velli was listening behind the curtain.

Sam narrated the incident in Babili. He said how the dying Kayl had requested him to meet 'Hiwa Haqra'. As he spoke, he closely watched Siwa and received an impression that a screen of mistrust concealed the man's thoughts. "As Kayl hit the ground, I saw a gold necklace falling out of his turban," Sam said, pausing awhile. "It was just like the one the lady wears," he added, nodding towards the room where Velli had gone.

Siwa's blank face turned curious. "What happened to it?"

"Another villain named Biggie, who arrived later, stole it."

Siwa lifted his flask and took a sip. "Did Kayl tell you anything?"

"Yes," said Sam. "He spoke what sounded like *'Amma nacciyar aru perum'*."

"That's all?"

"He died before he could finish. I think he tried to say a word starting with the syllables 'ha' followed by 'ra', but couldn't complete it."

"Harax–" Siwa said, as if prompting him. "Haraxwaithi?"

"Maybe, but – Wait." Sam put down the flask that he had taken up to his lips, and from its aroma, assumed that it was the juice of rhododendron flowers. "Could it be 'sara' and not 'hara'?" he asked. His jaw dropped open by an unexpected flash of logic. "Just as many people pronounce 'Sindhu' as 'Hindhu' and 'Saqra' as 'Haqra'?"

For the first time during their meeting, a smile surfaced on Siwa's face. He chanted with deliberation, "'*Amma-perum nacciyar-perum aru-perum Saraswathi*'". It means, "The Saraswathi is like a mother to the masses. She is extremely sacred as her waters are the clearest among all rivers."

Sam scratched behind his ear. "He didn't speak all that."

"Wasn't his time running out? He spoke the repetitive words only once, but that's what he meant – our secret code," said Siwa getting up. Perplexed that the host wanted him to leave so soon, Sam too got to his feet. The Meluhhan drew closer and embraced the Sumérian. "I believe you, young man. Had you not come to Muenduru all the way from Babili, I would never have come to know the truth about Kayl's death."

"Were you aware that he had died?"

"Yes, I was. A man – I forgot his name – came here to return Kayl's purse to me."

"Was it the same black leather purse that I told you was snatched away by the murderer?"

"Yes."

"When did he –" Sam started coughing as some juice he had gulped went down his throat the wrong way.

Siwa looked as if he knew Sam would choke by his answer. "He came here six lunar periods ago," he said. "Posing as a trader, he told me Kayl had died of sickness in Babili. He turned out to be a labourer who had been bribed by a Sumérian into delivering the purse and assuring me that Kayl had completed all his tasks in Sumér."

"That Sumérian ought to be Biggie, who stole the gold necklace," said Sam. "I presume that Kayl's assignment was to deliver it to Chief Bel of Babili?"

Siwa concurred and narrated that he had visited Sumér two years ago when Chief Bel had placed an order for three gold necklaces on him. "Eight or nine lunar periods after I returned from Babili, Chief Bel's son-in-law came here –"

"Nergal?"

"Yes, Nergal brought a missive in which Chief Bel wrote that the weddings of both his younger daughters had been finalized," said Siwa. "He desired that I should hand over the necklaces to his son-in-law. So I gave him two which were ready."

It took a while before Sam could speak. "*Kavintu*," he said at last, "I'm afraid that those two gold necklaces didn't reach Chief Bel."

"What do you mean?" cried Siwa, jerking upright.

"Chief Bel's eldest daughter came to meet me in jail –"

"El – Lady Ella?"

"Yes, Lady Ella – a very kind hearted lady," Sam said. "When I described the necklace I had seen inside Kayl's turban, she told me it was one of those which her father had ordered on a merchant of Meluhha. I remember that she said, 'Maybe all aren't made yet, although it's about a couple of years after ordering.'"

"That means Nergal would have lied to Chief Bel that I hadn't been able to address Bel's request."

"Yes, if we assume that it was indeed Chief Bel's missive that the Fo– I mean Nergal – presented to you," said Sam, breaking a second piece of unpleasant news as lightly as he could. "I doubt its veracity because Lady Ella was divorced from Nergal long before he called on you."

"'Divorced'?" Siwa echoed. "What's that?"

Sam was perplexed. Siwa's query meant that such a social arrangement was unknown in the Meluhhan culture. "It means retracting the matrimonial oath."

Siwa looked as if he had heard Sam saying that the earth was round and it moved around the sun. "Can a married couple break up in your culture, Sumérian?"

"Yes, *Kavintu*, it can," Sam said, "provided that the lady has very convincing reasons for seeking divorce."

Siwa's hand rose to his chin and held it lightly. He asked, "Had Nergal ceased being Chief Bel's relative when I gave him the ornaments?"

"Yes, he had."

"Now I see the whole picture," said Siwa, slapping his thigh. "Kayl was killed to prevent him from meeting Chief Bel and finding out that my client had not received the two necklaces which I had sent earlier with Nergal." He lowered his voice. "Only one man would pay someone to assure me that my commitment to Chief Bel was executed completely."

A cotton curtain screening the adjoining room gently blew aside, but Sam was too deep in thought to peep inside. What Siwa's inference meant was unbelievable. Was it Nergal the Fox who had been behind all the attempts to eliminate him before he met Siwa? Did Qwoco, the 'Demon of Gangevell', belong to a gang that carried out the Fox's orders?

"I can't wash my hands of Chief Bel's order," Siwa murmured, more to himself than to Sam. "I am deeply concerned that my client has not yet received the jewellery for which he paid me long ago." He put a hand on Sam's shoulder. "Young man, I request you not to leave Muenduru till I get three new necklaces made by my goldsmith. I want you to deliver them personally to Chief Bel with my apology for the delay."

Sam nodded vigorously. It was like the physician prescribing a diet that included the patient's favourite dish. He wanted to hang around in Muenduru City despite Velli's snub, because he hoped that she would relent one day; and here was her father begging him not to go away.

Bowing and taking his leave, Sam walked down the street, troubled by the mystery of the fish-hook. Why did Kayl request him to give it to Siwa when he very well knew that Siwa was ignorant about it? Was the message implied through the fish-hook intended for someone close to Siwa? Was it about some matter which neither the sender nor the receiver wanted Siwa to know?

Sam heard a shrill voice calling out 'Big White Friend,' and saw Red Muruku running towards him. He perceived grief in the boy's voice. "I heard Uncle Kayl's dead?"

"Yes, Red Muruku."

"He'd sent a toy fish-hook for me?"

"I suppose so, but I'm so sorry I lost it."

"It's all right," said the child waving a hand. "Was it golden?"

"No."

"Silver?"

Sam wondered why the boy was asking questions which he had expected from his father. "Not silver either," he said, turning his head to glance behind.

He caught a glimpse of Velli's lovely face hastily withdrawing behind the teak wood door.

19 VELLI GETS WILD

"Do you like Meluhhan girls, foreigner?" asked one of the youngsters instead of replying to Sam's query about why barricades were being raised along the main road. Sam smiled. The youth winked and added, "Then don't miss the buffalo fight tomorrow. If you do well, all the beauties in Muenduru would like to know you better."

"I want just one to take notice," Sam said, raising a hand to thank them and continuing on his way.

What could be a better opportunity to impress Velli than one that revealed his physical skills and prowess? Once she got over the erroneous bias against him, he would get down on one knee and declare his deep feelings for her.

The following evening, as Sam approached the venue of the buffalo fight, long drawn hoots of conches floated to his ears. The entire space behind the barricades teemed with young ladies dressed in colourful *varati*s. Among them he searched for a familiar face, but could not find it. Assuming that she was present somewhere, he ran to join hundreds of young men who were raring to face the buffalo barehanded. Like them, he too rubbed his palms in the dust and jogged around.

The sound of conches reached a crescendo, and the spectators craned their necks towards the place where the road was blocked for raising a temporary pen. A roar went up in the air as the water buffalo was led forth.

Sam had never seen a buffalo that stood higher than humans. It possessed a head bigger than a lion's. Its curved horns, painted red, drew his attention so much that he missed seeing the award of the challenge – a small purse said to be containing gold, hanging between them. His thoughts materialized in a voice carrying a quiver: "Ominous."

It was insane to face such a massive adversary without any weapon. Common sense advised him to quietly withdraw from the suicidal event. Charged with excitement, the atmosphere nudged him to take part.

Nearby, the participants jeered and the spectators giggled. Everybody was looking at a handsome youngster who had climbed the barricade and jumped over to the other side. Girls over there were busy forcing some bangles up his wrists. 'Poor man,' thought Sam, 'he has just earned the moniker 'coward' for the rest of his life.'

He concluded that the risk was higher in withdrawing from the contest than getting hurt in it. So he turned his attention to the buffalo, whose black hide gleamed rather unnaturally in the sun. "The brute's well oiled," said a young man standing nearby, "to prevent us from getting a firm hold on him."

As the gate of the pen was thrown open, Sam heard screams among the women spectators. The buffalo, frothing at mouth, glared at the contestants with absolute resentment. Flinging his tail in the air, he bellowed as if declaring a firm intention. The next moment flew out an enraged beast which seemed determined to punish the entire clan of his puny masters.

The youngsters dispersed, turned back and ran along the sides of the road narrowed by the barricades. They hoped to move by the flanks of the beast and get a hold on his collar. Their shouts added fuel to the fire, driving the brute berserk. He flung one man high up in the air, and trampled upon several others. Cries of unbearable pain cut through the noise, arousing anger in Sam's mind. He wanted to kill the beast but recognized that it was an unequal fight.

Sam found himself standing isolated, and saw the monster heading straight at him, trapping him against the barricade. His teeth chattered when he saw the buffalo, with ears spread out like wings, coming to a halt and ogling at him. Sam tried to gauge how to avoid those horns and hooves. The buffalo's nostrils quivered, and he snorted and dug his hooves into the ground sending up a small cloud of dust.

The girls clapped and chanted in chorus, "Foreigner, foreigner." The attention which Sam had garnered seemed to make a couple of moustachioed men envious of him. They came up from behind and grasped the buffalo's tail. Momentarily distracted, the beast turned and knocked down both of them.

In the meanwhile, Sam scampered out of the corner and dived to get both his arms around his adversary's broad neck. The brute turned again. There was a massive impact and Sam became aware of a powerful force lifting him off his feet. For a moment he got a bird's eye view of the gathering which rapidly started spinning. The next moment he saw the sky, then a huge pile of red clay pots behind the spectators, and then the sky again. His descent ended with a loud crash. He lay dazed, screaming in anguish, amidst the debris of broken pottery. Intense pain shot through his back and the right leg, and everything seemed swimming around him.

Some volunteers came running, and carried him to a large open tent like structure where several injured participants lay groaning on the floor. All the city's barbers, who were required to learn muscle and bone related remedies besides their profession, were trying hard to cope up with the increasing number of injured participants.

One wearing long hair like a hill atop his head, a style which Sam thought the man might have innovated recently, came to examine him. "Foreigner, you're lucky that the pottery broke your fall," said the innovative barber, as he plastered Sam's leg with black swamp mud. "You've escaped with a minor fracture and a sprained muscle." He placed palm leaves over the thick layer of mud, arranged narrow strips of bamboo over the leaves and wound twine over the entire casing.

Later in the evening as the last stretchers were brought in, Sam came to know that about a hundred participants were injured, and two had lost their lives.

A steady stream of visitors called on his fellow casualties. Among them he spotted Velli's friend, the lanky chatterbox. Sam was elated that he was injured. Mentally, he started constructing the account of how he had narrowly missed snatching the small purse tied between the buffalo's horns; because he imagined his sweetheart, with deep lines of concern etched on her face, visiting him soon.

It was not long before he wished otherwise.

Little past noon, Sam heard the voice of a child outside his room. Then a firm knock sounded on the door. On opening it, he exclaimed "Velli?" Without acknowledging, she marched in with a leaf-package in one hand and a wide-mouthed clay pot held upon her hip by another. Red Muruku trailed behind, holding the leash of a brown mongrel.

"My friend informed my father that you were injured," said Velli. "He told me to send you the meals till the time you're able to walk again."

"You shouldn't have taken the trouble," Sam said, a twinkle in his eye giving away what was actually on his mind.

"I wouldn't have bothered," she retorted, "had Muru seen the way to the inn." She strode to a deep wide niche in the wall, and dumped the package and the pot inside.

Sam was dumbfounded, but he recovered promptly. Flashing a big smile, he asked, "Did you enjoy the buffalo fight yesterday?"

"I don't attend such absurd events," she said, throwing a scornful glance at his plastered leg. "There are better ways to prove gallantry than meddling with beasts."

Sam gaped at her. He had broken a limb in an effort to please her, and there she was doubting his wisdom. He wanted Velli to change her low opinion of him, but she was check-mating his every move.

Then he recalled the bangles he had bought for her. "Wait a moment," he raised a forefinger and tilted his head. He rose with a hand pressed to the injured leg. Despite trying hard to suppress any sign of pain, a groan escaped him. He limped to his possessions, opened one of the sacks and frantically searched inside. The mongrel wagged its tail and ran to him. Cursing the ugly little pest under his breath, Sam raised a smiling face at it.

At last he fished out a cotton clad package and held it out to Velli.

"What do I tell Father?" she asked, receiving it.

"It's for you," Sam said, "They're Kalibangan bangles – I had bought them in Rocky Gangevell."

Velli's stern face seemed to mellow. Did he detect a trace of smile on it?

While Sam had smartly tackled odd situations time and again, he was lost for words in the matter of the heart. Although he had carefully prepared what he would say when gifting the bangles to her, he could not recall anything when the time came. In a desperate attempt to convey that his act was spontaneous, he gave vent to what came out of his drying throat. "Someone talked me into buying them. I thought you could use them."

There came a loud metallic sound from the floor. Velli had dropped the package as if it were a lump of smouldering charcoal. Her lips pouted. Before Sam could recover, she had picked up the clay pot and poured all the buttermilk over him. Red Muruku started clapping. The dog jumped and barked excitedly, and its tail wagged as if the appendage had slipped out of the body's control.

"All Sumérians are the same," her voice came along with the crashing sound of the pot. "Jackals."

Velli pulled Red Muruku by his arm and the next moment she had gone.

As the barks receded, several questions sprang out of Sam's soaked head. How many Sumérians besides him did Velli know? Had she come in contact with Nergal the Fox when he visited Muenduru City? Was Kayl's bronze fish-hook meant to reveal any vital information about the Fox?

20 OUTRAGEOUS PROPOSAL

As the first rays of the sun permeated through the tall trees, Sam trudged over red and white coral jasmine which carpeted the narrow jungle path. He was going to a hermitage, hoping to meet Velli and smooth her ruffled feathers.

Sam had befriended Red Muruku when the boy came to deliver meals during his long period of recuperation. He had discovered that on the first day of every fortnight, Velli used to visit a hermitage in the forest located on the outskirts of Muenduru City.

Inhaling the fragrance of jasmine, he whistled in response to a cuckoo and soon heard a rejoinder from her. The bird and the man were whistling back and forth when sudden screeching and chattering overhead made him stop. On the path ahead, a dog was barking. Then a series of screams broke out and sounded drawing closer.

Under the light and the shadows created by the thick foliage, Sam caught sight of a middle aged woman running down the path towards him. Her bright scarlet *varati* had slid down her chest, and Sam stood captivated by the wobbling of her small breasts.

As the person drew near, Sam realized that it was not a woman but a podgy man whose fluttering *vesti* gave an impression that he rode a flame.

Another figure followed close on the man's heels. It was a slim feminine form with hair so dishevelled that it impeded her movement. 'She's mad at him –' thought Sam. 'It seems the boor has molested her.' He jumped, spreading apart his legs and hands.

The man started screaming even more shrilly.

Sam's feet picked up ominous vibrations on the ground. An enraged snort hit his ears. Behind the woman, he saw a huge rhinoceros charging with its head down and horn ready to rip. He leapt sideways and the plump man passed by squealing.

The rhino was closing in fast upon the woman. She neared the place where he stood pegged to the earth. Instinct made him turn around and run in the same direction as the woman. He motioned to her wildly, "Left, left, go left."

The woman seemed too scared to comprehend. As she came neck to neck with him, Sam collided with her, imparting to her a forceful shove into the bushes. A cyclonic gust of wind passed behind him, and he heard the rhino grunt as if it were surprised.

The stomping sound receded down the pathway culminating in a nasal scream. Sam rose from the ground and strained to listen, but complete silence prevailed. Then the parrots and the monkeys picked up their routine.

Sam looked at the young woman who was lying face down and breathing heavily. He dropped on his knees, turned her on her back and combed away the dense strands from her face.

"Velli," he cried in utter surprise.

There was a warm and wet sensation on his elbow. Velli's ugly pet had appeared like a spirit, and was now licking her cheeks. Fuming at the animal's behaviour, Sam tried to 'shoo' it away, but it stood its ground growling at him.

"Get up, Velli," he said, shaking her like a sieve. Her eyelids fluttered open and for a moment, she kept staring at him. Then she pushed away his hand from her face and sat up. Her hands furiously sought the loose end of her *varati*, which she promptly flung over her bosom. "Sumérsin?"

"Yes, it's I – Samasin," he said with such delight which he had rarely experienced earlier. "Be quick, Velli. Let's get away before the beast returns." As he hastily led her towards the river, he could not believe that his cold sweetheart was co-operating.

There was a downward tug on his hand as Velli slumped at the foot of one of the bael trees. "You – you saved my life," she gasped. "Scary – terribly scary – to think what would've happened if you weren't there."

"Thank Marduk," he said, scratching his head and tightly pressing his lips. Since the incident of the buttermilk pot, he had decided to keep mum if he couldn't think of anything sensible to speak.

"What shall we do now?" she asked, "The rhino would be blocking our way."

"Isn't there another route?"

"Perhaps there's one a little downstream – from the bank to the Hermitage, and then to the city."

"Then let's go – fast," he said, grabbing her wrist. "Let's sound a warning about the rhino lest it kill an unsuspecting person."

They hurried in the direction of the river and reached a place where it had formed a lagoon. Sam was awestruck by the innumerable pink lilies covering its surface. They walked along the lagoon, each lost in one's thoughts.

Suddenly she said, "Was Kayl's fish-hook copper or bronze?"

Sam was about to answer, when it occurred to him that it was an apt moment to resolve the mystery of the fish-hook which had been bothering him since he had met Siwa.

"Velli," he said trying to sound casual, "I'll tell if you share with me what message it conveyed."

She walked on without a word for quite some time. Then she stopped and faced him. "Samasin, can I trust you?"

"I could have informed your father about three more fish-hooks which were found on Kayl's body, but I didn't. So you decide whether I'm trustworthy or not."

He perceived gratitude in her eyes. "Was it copper?"

"No, bronze."

Velli looked shocked. After a moment of silence, she said, "Samasin, I'm afraid that Father is unknowingly involved in a shady pursuit."

"Like what?"

"I can't say anything definite," said Velli, meeting his eyes. He perceived deep concern in them, and wanted to do all he could to address it. "Father purchases 'Stone dye' from a Gandharan trader. He's the one who ran ahead of me blocking my way."

"The man in the red *vesti*?"

"Yes."

"What was he doing in the jungle?"

"Stalking for a fourth wife, I suppose," she said. "I wish the rhino ran him over."

Sam grinned at the mere thought of the happy prospect, and

she too joined the mirth.

Velli briefly recounted how Siwa paid the Gandharan trader from the silver he regularly received from a man called Jittan. Sam remembered that he had recently heard that name in the Muenduru cemetery. 'It's a common name in Meluhha,' he thought, and concentrated on what Velli was saying.

"Father sends the 'Stone dye' to Merchant Zibigi of Urim, who told him that it was required for a temple which was being built in Ngirsu.

"Sounds like normal trade transactions," said Sam, again hearing another familiar name and applying the same logic that 'Zibigi' was not an uncommon name in Sumér.

"Except that they don't use any such material at the Temple of Ngirsu."

Sam's torso jerked slightly backwards. "That was Kayl's message, was it?" he cried. He was in no doubt that Merchant Zibigi of Urim was none other than Biggie the villain. All his confusion about why Biggie, whom he did not know, was bent upon getting him executed in Babili seemed to be cleared. "Is it likely that Merchant Zibigi of Urim got Kayl murdered when he came to know that Kayl had discovered the truth about the so-called 'Stone dye'?"

Velli nodded. "I think Father is being used as a link in an illegal trade, and he doesn't know it."

"Have you talked to him on the matter?"

Velli did not reply.

Once Sam had suspected that the fish-hook was meant for Velli, he had wondered why Kayl carried four of them. During the ample time he had had while his wounds healed, he had reached an inference that Kayl was supposed to answer two specific questions. Two fish-hooks meant 'Yes-Yes' and 'No-No' respectively, and the other two meant 'Yes-No' and 'No-Yes' respectively.

"What was your second query to Kayl?" he asked.

Velli looked at him with an open mouth. Despite the seriousness of their conversation, he could not help grinning.

Tears welled up in her eyes and her bosom heaved.

"I regret having hurt you, Velli," he said. Plucking some heart-shaped leaves of a *pipal* tree, he ran to the bank as he crafted a bowl out of them. He spotted a shoal of small fish dispersing helter-skelter as he dipped it into the water. He hastened back and she drank it, trying hard to smile. He stood before her like a naughty boy before his teacher expecting a reprimand.

Finally, she spoke: "I want to tell you about an incident that I wish had never occurred." Sam's eyes questioned hers. "I – I fell in love with Nergal," she whispered, "and I trusted him." His eyes gawked. "He forced himself on me. I resisted, but in vain."

Sam kicked a rotting *bael* fruit out of the way. "Didn't you know that Nergal was married, and father of a child?"

"I did, but polygamy isn't uncommon in Meluhha," Velli said. Then she added, speaking to self rather than to him. "I breached Father's trust and Nergal breached mine – perhaps 'twas natural justice."

Sam blamed his fate that the Fox's manipulations invariably spoiled anything that was going well for him. He heard Velli's voice choking.

"Even when Nergal had spurned me, I couldn't forget him," she said. "So I asked Kayl to request Nergal to come again to Meluhha and marry me." Sam's head shook in disgust. Velli continued, "We agreed that if Nergal acquiesced, Kayl would send either gold or silver fish-hook, otherwise one of the others."

The tense lines on Sam's face relaxed. "Kayl sent the bronze one so you knew Nergal had refused," he quipped with utmost relief. The irony of the fish-hook did not escape him. Was the choice of a fish-hook incidental, or did it symbolize Velli's feeling about the Fox's treatment to her?

Sam plucked one more *pipal* leaf, pressed it to his chest, and thrust it at her. "Velli.." The sound reverberated from deep inside his throat and he could not believe it was his own voice. She locked her hands, expressing her unwillingness to accept the heart-shaped leaf.

Sam looked into her eyes and said, "I love you, Velli." He lifted both her hands in his, and felt their softness and warmth. "Will you marry me?"

Velli pulled them back. "Would you –" she hesitated. "Would you love me if – if –"

"If what?"

"If I were not unblemished as you believe?"

Had he heard her right? "What do you mean?" he asked.

"I had had a baby girl by Nergal." Velli wrung her hands. "I had to spend some time away from home, so that Father wouldn't know."

Sam saw the trees slipping by, and reached for a low branch. "No wonder, they call him 'the Fox' in Babili," he said, and regretted it the moment the words left his lips, as Velli's earlier aloofness returned to her face. He tried to make up, asking her in an anxious voice, "What happened to your baby?"

"My aunt – the lady you saw with me in Sutantoru – forced me to part with the poor little thing." Velli sighed. "She gave her away to a childless couple."

They walked on silently for quite some time before Sam reached for her wrist and halted her. "I'd rather think it was a bad dream. I still love you, Velli."

She scratched the loose earth under her feet with her toes. He waited patiently, looking at her with hope. At last, she spoke: "How much?"

"For you, Velli, I would dive to the bottom of the Sindhu Sea, climb the Himala–"

She raised a hand. "In short, you love me like –"

"Like no man has ever loved a woman."

"Then do me a favour Samasin," she cooed. "Marry me, ra–"

"Of course, of –"

"I haven't completed yet. Rather pretend to marry, not marry in reality." He stared at her speechless. "Take me to Suméru," she said. "I want to face Nergal and ask him myself."

"But Velli, I'd be your husband wouldn't I?"

"No, you'll play the role so that Father doesn't mind sending me to Suméru." She touched his arm which had suddenly gone limp. "Samasin, only you can help me."

By that time, they had come out of the forest and were walking on the road leading to the city. Sam saw an overloaded cart approaching them, and his eyes glued on the ox laboriously pulling it. A strange affinity seemed to bind him with the animal. He imagined himself as an ox which was requested by a vixen to kneel down so that she could chew its ear.

"A while ago, you felt sorry for betraying your father," he said, perplexed about the strange logic of the woman walking by his side.

"I still do."

"Velli, you don't," said Sam, stopping and staring at her. No more did he give two hoots about sounding unpleasant. "Aren't you aware how Nergal deceived your father, took away the gold necklaces from him but didn't deliver them to their rightful owner? And don't you know why your father thinks Kayl was murdered?"

She sat down on a wayside rock, tears flowing down her cheeks. "I still love Nergal despite his weaknesses," she said, shaking with each sob. "I can't be happy with any other man."

"After what he told Kayl, do you expect the Fox to marry you?"

"Who?" There was anger in Velli's voice.

"You know who." Sam looked her in the eye and spoke each word separately, "Nergal - the - Fox."

Seeing Velli looking stunned by his affront, Sam's chest inflated. He was prepared for a showdown. However, Velli recovered quickly. Meeting his glare, she said, "Replying to your question, yes, I still hope that Nergal would marry me. As soon as he agrees, I'd seek divorce from you just as you explained to Father the other day."

"And if the Fox says 'no'?" said Sam, feeling lost about how to convince 'Siwa's spoilt offspring'.

"Then you and I would consummate our marriage."

"Brilliant. Didn't you say that you couldn't be happy with anyone else?"

"I promise that if Nergal refuses – which I pray he doesn't – then I'll be totally devoted to you, Samasin."

"In going along with your suggestion, I'd lose your father's esteem."

"And you'd get me if Nergal doesn't agree."

"The reward is imaginary whereas my loss is certain. You want me to breach a simple man's trust just as you did. What do I gain for my sacrifice?"

"Isn't love all about sacrifice?" Velli asked, throwing back her head on one side. Then she hailed a passing donkey-cart and clambering upon it, called out, "I look forward to hearing your 'yes', Samasin."

21 BONDAGE OF DESIRE

The anxiety of running into Agent Jittan forced Ann to get off the caravan just outside Chendur Village when she saw a hut in the centre of a lush green field. The bleating of a goat drew her attention a little farther down where a woman in her fifties was labouring to split firewood. Tying the baby on her back, Ann thought, 'Her hut would be a safe place to hide from Agent Jittan till I'm able to leave Chendur.'

The woman saw Ann and beamed as if she had known her for years.

"I am on my way to Muenduru City. Could I stay with you for a few days?" Ann bent down and yelled in the woman's ear after she failed twice to get her message across. A hen took to flight clucking.

"You're welcome," the woman shouted as she panted. She picked up a long thick staff and rose slowly with its support. "Just help me in my daily chores."

Her one leg was shorter than the other. 'Probably weaker too,' thought Ann, 'as a result of a sickness that some people suffered in childhood.' She handed her the baby and stooped to pick up the axe. She found it quite heavy. "You should have waited for your husband to do this task," she said, thinking what a wonderful man he ought to be to keep such a severely handicapped spouse in high spirits.

"He left me long ago to marry a younger woman," said her host, without any emotion on her face. "Could you get me some provisions from the weekly market?"

So, while the woman took care of the infant, Ann nervously trudged to the village. Although she had intended to return as soon as she could, the hustle and bustle in the air was so refreshing after nine days on the country road that she merrily haggled with the vendors.

While trying to get the best bargain on fish, twice she caught the vendor looking beyond her shoulder. She turned and saw a stout woman walking away. "Was she Agent Jittan's servant?" Ann wondered with a start. "Did she recognize me despite my henna-painted skin?"

Ann immediately left for home. Several times on the way, she looked behind but did not spot anybody following her. She thought it might be her fear of Jittan that had made her imagine things.

That afternoon, wringing a load of washed clothes at the river, Ann heard a wailing sound, accompanied by the tapping of a staff on hard ground. The sight of her host without the baby increased her heart-beats.

The woman trembled uncontrollably as she gasped, "The villain Jittan – Jittan, a bad man –"

"I know. What has he done?" Ann shrieked.

"His servant kidnapped the baby." The host sobbed. Ann clutched her arms. "I was massaging it when that buffalo of a woman hurtled into my hut and snatched him from me." She sniffed as she showed red rashes all over her arms. "When I held on to the howling tot, she beat me mercilessly."

Ann sank to the ground. "My poor baby would die screaming for me," she said. She heard a long sigh, and her host sat down beside her. "Jittan won't return it to me. The villain would rather capture and sell me."

"Don't lose heart, dear," the woman said putting an arm around her waist. "It isn't impossible to handle a sewer hog like Jittan."

Ann looked up with tearful eyes. How could this woman always shut out negative thoughts from her mind?

"Besides devouring slime, Ann, what's a hog's only other pursuit in life?"

It seemed to Ann that her brain had ceased working. She looked blankly at her host.

"Just dangle this before Jittan," said the woman, curving her first two fingers against each other at their tips. "He would follow you like a drooling dog, even if you were to lead him into a potter's hearth."

Hope sparked in Ann's eyes. "You've hit the peg on the head," she cried, shooting erect and hugging her host. "Immediately I'll get dressed to kill."

Escaping again from a trafficker was well nigh impossible. The two flask-shaped vials which she had prepared for Siwa Saqra could be handy in the sudden crisis. She scratched the wax on one of them and dipped several bone hairpins in it one after another. She laid them to dry in air as she combed her hair.

Although she was no more the meek Anlil of two years ago, Ann decided to play the role. She tied her hair into a style requiring several long hairpins. Upon it she put on a tiara of purple crown flowers. In the bronze mirror, she spotted her host weaving hurriedly, but her mind was too tense to ask.

As she was leaving, her host handed her a long garland made of white *champaca* flowers, and winked. "This might come handy."

Ann noticed that the flowers were held together not with cotton thread but with twine which was normally used for trapping small animals in the woods. She smiled. Tying it like a belt on her red *varati*, she presented herself at Agent Jittan's gate.

There she was accosted by an apparition that despite being clad in a *varati*, walked like a man, and carried a spear. Two vertical creases appeared on its forehead upon seeing her. "Nobody can escape from Agent Jittan, stupid woman," said a manly voice. Bangles chinked as the apparition struck both its hairy hands in a resounding clap. "See what your getaway cost me."

Recognizing the voice of Jittan's scary guard, Ann's jaw dropped as she stared at his clean shaven face. Little silver rings quivered from his nostrils and earlobes, suggesting that he had been initiated in the community of eunuchs. A sigh escaped her as she looked piteously at the man who had been deprived of virility for failing in his duty. If anybody deserved such a harsh punishment, it was Agent Jittan himself.

"Be quick, go upstairs," said the guard, picking up the spear and thumping it on the ground. "I'd be delighted if Master Jittan ordered me to scald your pink bottom."

Reaching the first floor, Ann passed the room in which the villain had raped her on her earlier stay. It was unoccupied. 'Awaiting the next batch of innocent girls from Sumér,' thought

Ann. She reached the second room from which she had heard the voice of the mysterious Sumérian. There, Agent Jittan lay sprawled on a thick mattress upon a broad wooden cot, looking flabbier since she last met him. He got up sluggishly when he saw her at the door.

He deeply inhaled the fragrance she had brought along, and bellowed in broken Sumérian. "Anlil – the tastiest trout which flipped away from my hook, tanned under the Meluhhan sun but, ravishing as ever."

"Give me my child, *Belum*," she requested, speaking in the same language.

"I own you, and I own my little bastard," he said, motioning her to sit on his lap. "I intend to recover the big loss that I suffered by your escape."

"Let me keep him, *Belum*, and I'll submit to your wish," she said, extending both arms at him.

He roared with laughter. "Revenge is sweet, but it is sweeter when prolonged. I won't give him, and yet you will yield to me." Tugging at his nasal hair, he chuckled. "Thereafter, you will join any cathouse that I choose."

Ann's lips pressed together. It was not as if she had not expected that, but his words gave it a frightful air of finality. She shivered when she thought of what the villain could do to her baby. He had already expressed his intention about her future, and that ruled out her entire plan of avenging the unknown Sumérian trafficker as well as Siwa Saqra.

Siwa Saqra? A thought flashed in Ann's mind. Could she exploit to her advantage the little that she knew about Jittan's criminal connections?

She stood before him at her full height. "You won't, Agent Jittan," she said, switching over to Meluhhan language. "I'm married in a powerful family which knows I am in Chendur Village." She was reassured when she perceived confusion on his face. "My in-laws' large circle of friends and associates throughout Meluhha would recognize me anywhere."

Jittan shifted uncomfortably, but grinned. "You're talking rubbish, woman."

"Harm us, and the authorities will come down with all its force, not only on you," she paused before adding, "but also on Siwa Saqra."

"Hiwa?" he cried, nearly getting up from the cot. "How d'you know Hiwa Haqra?"

"Just give back my child, and I'll return your favour. Let's enjoy each other's company and part as friends." Her brows danced in mischief. "I confess that you're more virile than – than –" She paused, and then with a wave of a hand, said, "Oh! Forget it."

Agent Jittan thought awhile. Then he surveyed his chest and arms approvingly. His face lit up in sheer delight, and he clapped twice. A servant appeared at the door. Ann recognized her as the escort she had almost killed with a rock on the night of her escape. The woman turned so pale on seeing her that Ann wondered if she had recently gone through a miscarriage.

"Get the tot," said the master. The servant hurried away and soon returned with the infant.

As Ann showered her sleeping toddler with kisses, she heard the servant muttering, "Shall I, *Kavintu*?" From the corner of her eye she perceived Agent Jittan shaking his head in the negative.

"There are some flasks of Sumérian red wine in the cellar," he told the servant.

"The ones Zibigi gifted to you, *Kavintu*?"

'Zibigi' was a Sumérian name. Ann wondered if it was the name of the hoarse voiced Sumérian who had reprimanded Agent Jittan for not selling her quickly.

While Jittan's attention shifted to replying the woman, Ann removed a flask-shaped vial from her *varati* with a flick. She slipped it inside the folds of the baby's mattress. As she stooped to put him on the floor, Agent Jittan clicked his tongue and pointed at the far end of the room. She obeyed, regretting that the simpler of her two ruses to get back at the villain had run into trouble.

The servant returned with two crane-necked flasks and a bowl brimming with black dates. She quickly started arranging them on a wooden stool.

Agent Jittan coughed. The servant nodded, walked to Ann, and searched her. Then she asked her to remove all the pins from her hair. Disappointment came over Ann's face as she handed them over. Her second ploy had also gone.

"I don't want anybody to come upstairs," Jittan said in a firm voice. Even before the servant had crossed the door, he turned to Ann and winked. She winked too. From his jovial chuckle, she knew that he had noticed just the flutter of her eyelids, not the blaze behind them. It was an apt moment to recover the lost ground.

"Jittu, could I hold my baby just for a little while again?" she implored. He waved, and she ran to the sleeping infant. While kissing him over and over again, she retrieved the flask-shaped vial. The baby neither woke up nor protested in sleep. The woman servant had probably administered opium to her little one. Ann had an intense urge to run downstairs and wring her neck. She quickly recovered, for she needed all her energy to 'wring' Agent Jittan's frog-like neck.

Ann walked towards him, undoing her hair and letting it flow down her bare shoulder. With a flick, she released the *champaca* belt. Her red *varati* slid like a snake down her voluptuous body to the ground. As she ambled towards him, he ogled at the huge blotch of white skin between the dark brown face, shoulders and limbs. The sight of such a deviant feminine form would have repulsed any man – but not Agent Jittan. So much did he seem to marshal his thoughts on the essence that Ann knew he had even missed noticing what else she held in her hand besides the belt of *champaca* flowers.

Drawing nearer, she had to hold her hand from pressing her nostrils. She told herself that she would have to numb all the senses if she wanted to ensure her infant's safety. She held a date between her teeth and pressed her lips on his.

A few words which dropped from Agent Jittan's lips amply expressed the thrill of her warm intimacy. His paws started exploring her body. Curbing a strong impulse to push him away, she poured wine in a goblet and held it to him. As he sipped it, his poetic flair boiled over. Sounding like an ass in heat, he brayed:

"Humérian red wine, Humérian dates and a Humérian woman,

"Enjoying all the three together, I ask,

"If this isn't the Paradise, what is?"

Dropping a couple of dates in his open mouth, Ann snuggled closer. "Jittu, I'd love to play 'Bondage of Desire' with you," she sighed.

"What's that?"

"A Sumérian game," she whispered, hiding her face against his chest. "But I'm scared to play it with you."

Her cheek sensed his chest heaving with pride. "Why?" he asked as he guzzled the wine.

"Because Meluhhan men get offended by the game," she said refilling the goblet. "My husband did."

"Dull bastard. I'm different."

"'Bondage of Desire' – It's nothing short of womanly affront," she said. "He slapped. You'd strangle me."

"Promise I won't. Tell me, how do we play it?"

"How can I if you go on staring at me?" she asked lowering her eyes. Feeling the warmth of blood rushing to her cheeks, she knew she was playing her role well.

Jittan shut his eyes tightly. "Now tell me."

Ann scratched away the wax seal off the vial saying, "In the 'Bondage of Desire,' the lady binds her lover's hands with a garland of flowers."

She paused. With eyes still closed, he asked, "Then?"

"Oh you're so naïve, Jittu," she said lightly slapping him on his shoulder. As she spoke, she emptied the vial into his wine. "Does a man need to be told everything?"

"I'm all for it!" he gasped, quivering with ecstasy, and holding out both his hands.

She picked up her flower belt and commenced tying his wrists gently. Suspending the act for a while, she raised the goblet to his lips. He downed it in one gulp. Then he frowned: "The damned wine tasted different."

"Have some dates," suggested Ann and fed him a few. She continued tying knots, kissing his fingers and palms; and he relaxed, with sheer delight radiating from his face.

The extract of rosary peas did not take long to take effect. Agent Jittan started panting. It seemed he wanted to press his stomach, but the twine in the garland restricted his movements. His eyes flared with rage.

"Dates, dear," she cooed, smiling at him in triumph. Grabbing a fistful, she shoved them into his mouth, which had gaped in a struggle to call for help. "That's for wrecking my life, you son of a bitch."

Jittan's legs beat around like those of an overturned beetle. A beastly noise emanated from his throat. His eyeballs exploded out of the sockets. Blood spluttered from his nose.

With utter glee, Ann watched him struggling to get free. It was an apt revenge for her own struggle under his heavy frame when he had robbed her of her virginity.

Rushing to the baby, she picked it up and drew it close to her bosom. A moment later, she happened to throw a glance behind. Jittan was motionless, sprawling bare and gawking at the ceiling.

As Ann looked at him again, thoughts rapidly passed through her mind. 'Oh, *Sîn*, what have I done? I've taken a human life. I'm a murderer! Why, oh why did I do it?' She was overwhelmed by a deep sob and she tried to stifle a series of moans which followed. She sank to the floor and wept – for a sin forced upon her by fate.

By the time she composed herself, the sunlight outside had dimmed. All the while, she kept telling herself that she had to get used to such bloodshed. Her major enemies, Siwa Saqra and the Sumérian with a peculiar voice, both were yet to be eliminated.

At last recovering from the shock, she sprinkled on her body the little wine which had remained in the flask, and removed the blood spots. Then she wrapped on her *varati*, picked up the infant and silently closed the door.

She would have to head straight to the river port of Chendur, from where as her host had told her, a small vessel sailed for Muenduru port every evening. "There's a hermitage in the jungle just outside Muenduru City, Ann," the kind woman had said, "where you and your baby would be safe from wolves like Jittan."

As Ann descended the stairs, her feet halted abruptly when she caught the woman servant's words –"before selling her."

Ann wondered whether they were talking about her.

"My previous master," the eunuch's masculine voice followed, "whom Jittan has succeeded, never harassed the girls."

"They say he was murdered in Sutantoru."

"Yes, by Zibigi," said the eunuch. Ann was now sure that they were talking about the hoarse voiced Sumérian."The hand was Zibigi's; the brain, his master Nergal's."

"Nergal?"

"Yes, Nergal; and Master Jittan has not even seen him. He's a tall handsome man with naughty eyes and deep laughter. I bet Sumérian women would be swarming around him like bees."

Ann stared at the steps. So there was a big crocodile, one who led both the small ones – Siwa Saqra and Zibigi. Her revenge would remain incomplete unless she liquidated all three of them. She had heard the name 'Nergal' earlier, but was too tense to recollect.

"Doesn't Master Jittan know his ultimate master?" The woman

servant's voice sounded unconvinced.

"He does, after I apprised him. Zibigi didn't tell him. The villain double-crossed my previous master."

"Who did, Zibigi?"

"Yes, Zibigi talked my earlier master into a partnership. They were about to launch a rival operation when Zibigi realized that Nergal had smelt a rat. Being familiar with the man's style of functioning, Zibigi informed him that the Meluhhan agent, that's my previous master, was about to usurp –"

Ann wondered what had made him halt in mid-sentence.

The eunuch said, "Do you smell wine?"

Her presence had been detected. She descended the remaining steps and casually walked into the open compound. They looked at her ruffled hair and wrinkled *varati* with unusual interest. As she passed them, the eunuch held open a palm and the woman servant brought hers down upon it. The clap was followed by a snigger.

Ann turned around and, seeing them laughing, screamed, "I'm going to wake up Jittu." She started walking towards the staircase. "I'll tell you're making fun of him."

"No, please," begged the woman, rushing to hold Ann. Dropping the spear, the eunuch fell on his knees and touched his brow to Ann's toes.

She let them plead for some time before saying, "I'm going home to leave the baby while Jittu is resting."

"Yes, mistress," they both chorused.

It made Ann smile to herself. "Don't you disturb your master till I return," she said, pointing a finger at the eunuch's face. "He wants me, and only me, to wake him up."

22 ATTACK ON SIWA

Ann's tired feet scampered to the nearest mango tree and scaled it – like a monkey that had been trapped, and had pretended to be dead until its bonds were removed. She had heard a tiger's roar. Her hand went to her back where the baby was securely bound, and she was thankful that her dash had not disturbed it into howling.

At last she had reached Muenduru to avenge Siwa Saqra, and was heading for the hermitage about which her host in Chendur Village had told her. Ann had decided to bide her time there, study Siwa's daily routine, and then plan an attack on him in such a way that she could escape safely with her baby.

As a second roar came over the air, another sound which she heard along with it made her exclaim. A deep voice was approaching from the same direction. Rather than expressing panic, it sounded like singing. Intermingled with it, she also heard some giggles.

Moving aside the thick foliage, she peered below in the direction of the sounds. The winding forest path, abundantly strewn with flowers of the coral jasmine bushes on both its sides, looked like a brook of milk from her high perch. A couple of squirrels came scurrying upon it.

Then she saw them, a brawny white man and a shapely dark woman. Neither seemed concerned about the tiger. The man was trying to croon a lovelorn damsel's song in a feminine voice. It expressed the girl's resolve that she would not speak with her lover until he brought her jasper and carnelian jewellery from Port Lothal and black bangles from Kalibangan.

'He's making an ass of himself,' thought Ann. 'No wonder that his companion can't stop chuckling.'

Then she recognized the man's voice and almost lost her balance. Although taken by surprise, her first reaction was, "Thank *Sîn*, 'the Demon of Gangevell' hasn't harmed Sam."

There he came, virtually prancing down the path. A slim girl, looking like a carving in ebony come to life, trudged with him. Ann recollected that Sam too had bought many Kalibangan bangles when they went on a shopping spree in Rocky Gangevell to celebrate the discovery of Mad Kutti's treasure. "Do you have a girl friend in Meluhha?" she had asked, and Sam had simply laughed it off.

"I don't see any Kalibangan bangles on her wrists," Ann murmured. "Moreover, from the distance she is keeping on the narrow path, I guess that woman is hardly in love with Sam."

She had a deep urge to climb down the tree quietly and jump in their way. She could imagine both of them scream – Sam in surprise, and the girl in fright. However, she considered it apt not to let them know of her presence just then, and struggled to hold herself from making any noise.

She watched them passing under the tree as the tiger roared again. Amidst the wild thumping of her heart, she wondered why they seemed the least bothered about the beast. She remained glued to the branch for quite some time before she heard the sound of tapping coming from the direction in which the couple had gone. Her eyes popped out and she shrieked. A woman, her silver hair fluttering in the breeze, was limping her way with a walking stick in one hand. With another, she was tugging a thick dead branch.

Ann made the sound "Sh.." The woman stopped and squinted upwards. Her nose and chin seemed to be growing to meet each other. "There's a tiger nearby," said Ann in a low voice as she climbed down precariously, and offered her a hand. "Quick. Come up here."

Instead of a suppressed squeal that she had expected, she heard a strident cackle. "Don't be scared, girl," called out the old woman. "That tiger is as harmless as a kitten when he comes to our hermitage. My husband is known as the Horned Hermit, and wild animals have a strange affinity for him."

Upon descending to the ground, Ann untied the sleeping baby from her back and handed it to the hermit's wife. Then she lifted the firewood and placed it on her own head. "It's quite heavy, isn't it?" she said, detecting a whizzing sound in the old woman's breathing. Briefly telling her that she was running from a flesh trader in Chendur, she said, "Could I hide in your Hermitage for some days, *Amma*?"

"Daughter, you may stay as long as you wish," said the hermit's wife, exposing her gums in a smile. She pressed Ann's baby to her bosom. "Consider the Hermitage as your parents' home."

When they reached there, Ann saw a skeletal old man, wearing a hood which carried buffalo horns, sitting cross-legged in the midst of several animals. His bare torso was adorned with long necklaces and his arms were covered with shell bangles.

A tiger rested with its head upon its front paws at the meditating hermit's feet. A mammoth elephant stood nearby, fanning his ears as if trying to keep the Horned Hermit comfortable in the warm afternoon. A wild water buffalo sat munching under a *bael* tree. A little away, a huge cow rhinoceros grazed, followed closely by her baby whose tiny legs struggled to bear its weight. Ann assumed that the cuddly little animal was just a few days old.

She felt that the Horned Hermit was as much a part of the forest as were the trees, the animals, the birds, the flowers and the butterflies. For quite some time she stood there taking in the scene.

The hermit's wife led Ann to what she thought was a conical stack of hay. Built from river mud and thatched with dry reeds, the hut seemed too flimsy to protect her little one from the cold. Carefully laying the toddler down on the dung-plastered floor, the old woman went to stoke the fire near its entrance. "I'll boil some milk so it cools by the time your baby wakes up."

Ann mumbled her gratitude as she lowered the dead branch and placed it on a nearby pile of firewood. Anxious to know more about Sam, she said, "A little while before we met, *Amma*, I saw a young couple passing by. Did it meet you on the way?"

"Yes," smiled the hermit's wife. Holding a piece of cloth in both hands, she lifted the clay bowl from the wood fire and put it down near Ann. "Hamasin and Velli had come to the Hermitage to tell me that they were getting married."

Ann hoped that Sam did not discover her presence in the

Hermitage before she had dealt with Siwa Saqra. "Who are they?" she asked, looking as casual as she could.

"Hamasin is a brave Humérian who saved Velli from an irritated mother rhino – the one you saw outside; and she is the daughter of a merchant named Hiwa Haqra." Ann's jaw dropped. She was peeved that Sam was already sold to the enemy camp. The hermit's wife continued, "If Hamasin hadn't been there, Velli's fate would've been similar to her suitor from Gandhara."

"Why? What happened to Velli's suitor?"

"That day, Velli's aunt from Sutantoru was going to the river to wash clothes," said the hermit's wife, sitting down beside her and folding one leg over another. "In the woods, she saw a gigantic lump of clay blocking the path. As she tiptoed towards it, she heard a wail up in the sky."

Ann's hands rose to her chest and her fingers clenched. "Wail in the sky?"

The hermit's wife was unable to control her toothless cackle. "Throwing down the load of clothes, Velli's aunt ran for her life. She told me, she turned to see what it was. A man with a big paunch was suspending by a scarlet *vesti* from the branch of a tree. She said that he reminded her of a skinned hog at the butcher's shop."

Ann joined in the mirth. "And what was it that lay in her path, *Amma*?"

The hermit's wife reached inside the folds of her *varati*, brought out a few pieces of areca nut, popped two in her mouth and offered the rest to Ann. "The cow rhino that you saw had chased him, taken him upon her horn and tossed him up in the air," she said grinning. "His *vesti* got entangled in the long pin-like thorns of the bael tree, and saved him from falling at the rhino's feet. Then, we believe, the beast ate something which induces sleep, and she collapsed on the forest path."

"Velli's aunt must have helped the poor man to get down," said Ann conclusively.

"No, she didn't," said the hermit's wife. "She told me she would be the last person to do it. She said the insatiable wretch already had three wives, and yet he had his eye on her young niece." Ann made 'tch, tch' sounds, and the lady continued. "How long can a silk *vesti* bear a heavy load such as his? She watched him crashing down to the ground naked, applauded his performance, and hurried back home."

Ann saw that her toddler had sat up and was looking around with curiosity. Upon seeing her, he hurried to her on all the fours. Dipping a finger in the bowl of milk, she drew him to her lap. "When are Velli and Samasin getting married, *Amma*?"

"The day after tomorrow," said the hermit's wife, picking up a basket and walking to the door. "I'll serve some fruit to my husband."

Ann was lost in thought. There was not much time to caution Sam against marrying a trafficker's daughter. Not only was it difficult to contact Sam, but she was not even sure how he would take her advice. His first query could be, 'Ann, you were aware that I was searching for Siwa Saqra. Why didn't you tell me earlier what you knew about him?'

She could not disclose to Sam that for quite some time, she had suspected that he was connected with Siwa's trafficking work. Even if she tried to meet him, it might forewarn Siwa, who in all probability would strike before she could.

Moving her fingers through the baby's hair, Ann concluded that there was no alternative but to kill Siwa on his daughter's wedding day. That way she could get the ceremony postponed indefinitely, and might earn some respite during which she could warn Sam.

Sound of approaching feet brought Ann to the present. It was the hermit's wife, and she spoke as if she had never left the hut. "I told the happy couple that we hermits avoid revelry," she said, sitting down beside Ann, "but I might send somebody." She pondered for a while and said, "Why don't you attend it on my behalf, Ann?"

Ann smiled. In the old lady's offer she saw a rare chance to get very close to her enemy Siwa Saqra without raising any suspicion.

Ann was not unaware of the risk involved in attacking a wolf clad in a sheep's garb. However, she was afraid that if she missed the current opportunity, another might take long to come her way. 'Now, I'll settle the score with Siwa,' she thought. 'Thereafter, I'll go to Sumér to avenge his associates Nergal and Zibigi.'

She had already prepared a bone hairpin for use on Siwa Saqra, having dipped it in the extract of bamboo shoots which were found in abundance in the forest. It was a perfect way of poisoning a person in a crowded place, and escape unnoticed.

However, having attended several Meluhhan weddings at Dholavira, Ann was aware that it was not easy to get within a 'scratching' distance of the bride's father. Relatives and friends crowded around him like ants around their queen. She would have to disperse them and clear her way to reach Siwa.

So on the morning of the wedding day, Ann put on a head-dress like a fan connected on either side with a cup. As she filled the cup-like spaces with finely ground pepper, she murmured, "Such an outrageous head-dress is bound to attract undue attention, but I can't do without it."

She wanted to pick up her sleeping toddler and press it to her bosom yet once again, but the pepper prevented her from bending. Near the door, a bronze mirror on the wall reflected her image. "Don't worry, Ann," she addressed it. "If the trafficker's men kill you, *Amma* would raise him like her own son." Her voice broke as she spoke.

She threw a glance at her child, touched her lips and sent a kiss flying in its direction. Then wiping her eyes, she hurried out of the hut. Lest her concern for the baby break her resolve, she kept running till she had crossed the woods and was well on her way to Muenduru City.

Ann had found out the place where Sam lived in the Lower Town. She reached a spot where the streets crossed near his house and waited. The sound of drums told her that the wedding procession was about to start.

Soon the beats grew louder. She craned her neck and saw two men emerging from a lane. They were leaping in air, and madly beating the folk drums which hung from their neck. Several youngsters danced with abandon to the throbbing beats. The more vigorously they danced, both the men seemed more determined to tear their drums apart.

An elephant, painted in red and white stripes, turned the corner. Ann perceived mischief in the animal's eyes. They seemed to convey that in a short while, the young man it carried would descend from his high perch to toil for a woman all his life. Ann could not hold back a giggle as she watched Sam sitting astride majestically, vainly trying to see the procession through a veil of jasmine which hung from his crown of orchids. A group of women followed the elephant, singing in chorus, and bringing all other movement on the narrow street to a standstill.

No sooner did the procession draw near, Ann joined the women and started singing too. They passed through the streets of Muenduru producing a cacophony that, she thought, would never have been permitted in Sumér. When they reached Siwa's street, they were greeted by a group of richly dressed women who broke into a song which joked about the 'outlandish' groom and his 'ragtag' entourage.

As they jostled through the door of Siwa Saqra's house, Ann looked out for its owner. A tall bearded man wearing a diadem, standing amidst a crowd in the courtyard, seemed to be Siwa. Perceiving a twinkle in his eyes and a smile on his face, her lips quivered. "Trafficker, all your happiness is watered by the tears of innumerable Sumérian women like me. I'm determined to rub that smile off your face."

Loud shouts diverted her attention to a spurt of activity. Two sturdy men pulled a buffalo calf towards a sacrificial altar that seemed to have been freshly raised under a *neem* tree. Decorated with scarlet posies of saraca flowers, the animal seemed to have sensed what was in store, and dug its hooves into the ground. Several men ran to push it. The priest, a dark man possessing a belly that looked like eight lunar periods into pregnancy, lifted a huge axe over his head and came down heavily on the calf's neck. A crack of the vertebra was heard and the poor animal collapsed on its knees with an almost human wail.

Ann eyed the blood splattered axe in the priest's hand and thought, 'Similarly, my dreams were butchered by another of Siwa's henchmen.'

Women rose on their toes to look beyond the host and his 'welcome team'. Velli, with her eyes cast down, was making her way through the crowd holding a garland of yellowish medaller flowers. To Ann, she appeared to be dragging her feet.

A push in the crowd forced Ann off her balance. She tilted and a little pepper powder flew out of her headgear. The next moment, those nearest to her started sneezing.

All eyes, which till then were fixed on the bride, turned to Ann. Her wildly throbbing heart told her that she had to get away before people inferred that she was there to create trouble. The crowd was so thick that slipping out was well nigh impossible. Once she was caught, she would have to abandon her plan of assassinating Siwa

Saqra. She had to think and act quickly.

She did.

In one leap, Ann was standing like a spectre before the 'pregnant' priest. He saw her wide reddish eyes, and his belly started trembling. She snatched his axe, and shoving a couple of women who stood in her way, she reached Siwa.

Her free hand rose to the cup-like portion of her head-dress, drew out a fistful of pepper powder, and threw it at him. His hands flew to his eyes and he started sneezing violently. She lunged at him with the axe, but just before she expected to hear the cracking of a skull, a creeping sensation inside her nose forced her to inhale deeply and sneeze.

Before she could recover, a sudden impact loosened her grip on the axe. Two powerful arms grasped her from behind, restricting all movements of her hands. The whiff of jasmine which enveloped her, told that they belonged to the bridegroom.

A middle aged woman overly bedecked in finery, led several others into pulling Ann's hair and scratching her with their sharp nails. Intense pain made Ann cry out '*Ga-ti, ga-ti*'. She was taken aback by the words which escaped her lips.

"Stop it, ladies, stop it," said a firm masculine voice nearby. It ought to be Siwa's, she thought. "She speaks Sumérian. Let me talk to her."

The women drew back, and Ann rose from their midst wondering how she would justify her violent action.

"Ann?" exclaimed Sam, and she knew she had better find an excuse that seemed credible to him too.

"Do you know her?" Siwa's voice sounded incredulous.

"Let me explain," said Ann, thinking out a convincing reason. "I lied to Sam in order to reach you. Siwa Saqra, your men murdered my husband."

"Ann, have you gone crazy?" cried Sam.

"Lady," Siwa said to Ann, "why do you think that your husband was killed on my orders?"

"He had discovered about your role in Sumér's slave trade with Meluhha, and you didn't wish that he went around exposing you."

"What's the slave trade to do with Siwa Saqra?" asked Sam, glaring at her.

"Don't you know that Siwa is the King of Sumérian slavery in Meluhha?"

She saw Sam raising a hand, and before she could duck, her left cheek sensed a strong impact which was followed by burning warmth. She staggered. Siwa held Sam before he could deliver another whack.

Several guests shouted angrily, "Hand her over to the guards."

"Let's try to understand her," said Siwa, raising both hands to pacify them. "Any woman here might not have behaved differently under the trauma she seems to have undergone." A murmur passed through the gathering. As the hostility eased, Ann was a little unsure of herself. "We'll talk after the wedding is over," Siwa told her. "Till then, I'd prefer to lock you up." He beckoned to the woman clad in fine clothes, the instigator of women's attack on Ann.

"Ann has a baby," said Sam. "Father, please arrange to get it here to be with her."

"No, no, no," a firm retort came from the woman. "If the bitch really cared about her child, Hamasin, she wouldn't have attempted a murder."

Ann looked at her. Instead of the rage that her strident voice suggested, the woman's lips were pursed into an unmistakeable expression of sagacity, looking like (–).

However, Siwa did not care for her wisdom. "Let her go home," he said, and turned to Ann. "I'll speak with you tomorrow evening, Lady. Right here."

All night, Ann murmured the lies that she would tell Siwa Saqra and Sam. The following morning, as she trudged through the forest carrying her babbling baby on her back, she wondered whether the man she had attacked was the same Siwa Saqra who was mentioned by the hoarse-voiced Sumérian whom she had overheard talking to Agent Jittan. Siwa had impressed her as a gentle person. Could he ever be a trafficker?

On the way she was met by a donkey cart on which she saw Velli and the woman who had advised Siwa. The cart was loaded with heavy luggage, which indicated that the woman was going on a long voyage. Ann flashed a smile at them, but neither passenger responded.

When she reached Siwa's house, the teak wood door was wide open and both the men were sitting on a cot under the *neem* tree.

The father-in-law was noting expenses, and the son-in-law was regaling some boys by flexing his biceps. Putting aside the piece of bark, the crucible of dye, and the peacock feather, Siwa pulled up a wooden stool for her. And the boys carried away her toddler to play.

Sam commenced with a question which she had anticipated. "Why did you lie about your race, Ann?"

"Had I divulged my real identity," she said, placing both her hands on her lap, "you'd have raised questions about my past, which I didn't wish to rake up."

"From which part of Sumér do you hail, Ann?"

"Urim."

"Urim," muttered Siwa. "By the way, have you heard of Merchant Zibigi?"

Ann could not respond immediately. Siwa was probably talking about the person whose name she had discovered from the conversation between Jittan's guard and servant. Most likely, Merchant Zibigi was the man with the hoarse voice, who wanted Agent Jittan to pay Siwa Saqra without delay. Mentally, she countered, 'If indeed Siwa was a trafficker, why would he unravel the name of an associate in crime?'

She shook her head. "No, I haven't."

Sam seemed upset as he looked from Siwa to her and back to Siwa.

She heard Siwa's voice again, "Ann, I can't make out how you connected me to the slave trade."

"A young Meluhhan came to Sumér for trade and got to know my uncle," Ann said as if she were speaking a dialogue in a play. "During the time he stayed in Urim, he often came for dinner at our house. We fell in love, got married and sailed for Sutantoru-on-Sea. On our voyage, we heard some sailors talking about a flourishing trade of Sumérian slaves in Meluhha. The name 'Siwa Saqra' came up then."

Ann was pleased with herself for giving a twist to how she had overheard Siwa's name from an unseen Sumérian in Village Chendur.

"There ought to be another man with the same name as mine," said Siwa. "A coincidence couldn't be more damaging."

"It upset my husband very much," Ann continued. "He often told me, 'Men without scruples – slave traders like Siwa Saqra –

ought to be in jail, Ann.'"

She saw Sam nodding as he addressed Siwa. "My friend Tall Yali of Dholavira, who intends to marry Ann, did mention once that Sutantoru was notorious for slavery."

Even the little unsteadiness in Ann's voice disappeared. She could even bring forth a tear as she spoke again. "Later my husband might have vented his feelings to his friends. One night several men attacked our home and beat him up fatally."

She buried her face in her hands, and her body shook. Siwa sighed. "That explains everything, Ann, and I feel extremely sorry for you and your little one."

Ann knew that Sam would not be convinced so easily, and was not surprised when she heard him speaking. However, his query was directed to Siwa instead of her. "By the way, Father, who's Merchant Zibigi?"

"He is my saviour," said Siwa, sounding as if he were relieved at being diverted from the distressing matter. "Merchant Zibigi helped me prosper when I was struggling to get up after losing everything in a partnership."

"How?"

"He regularly buys a large quantity of Stone dye from me although he could procure it directly from Gandhara." Ann looked up and studied Siwa's face.

"I presume that he sends you products like woollen textiles in barter?" said Sam.

"No, he pays me silver through a local agent who works out of Village Chendur."

Ann winced. Indeed, Siwa was talking about Agent Jittan. Therefore, Merchant Zibigi was none other than the villain with the gruff voice who had reprimanded Jittan for not selling her fast. Obviously, some of the silver earned from trafficking was used to pay Siwa Saqra for despatching Stone dye to Sumér.

"You said Merchant Zibigi could directly get Stone dye from Gandhara," said Sam. "Why doesn't he do it?"

Ann was glad that the son-in-law was so inquisitive about Siwa's dealings.

"You see, we work just like long-distance messengers. They relay messages, we pass on the Stone dye," said Siwa. "The supplier, a Gandharan merchant, brings the Stone dye upto Muenduru, and I ensure its regular delivery to Urim through one of the several Meluhhan ports."

"Your supplier is the man who was tossed by the cow rhino, isn't he?"

"Yes," said Siwa, breaking into laughter. "The poor man must be so embarrassed that he went away without meeting me."

"And without delivering his package of Stone dye," Sam added.

"He could have sent it with somebody," said Siwa, turning serious.

"I guess all his Stone dye dropped to the ground as he swung from the *bael* tree, and the cow rhino ate it," said Sam. Ann thought that Sam was looking into Siwa's eyes as if trying to gauge his reaction. Siwa dismissed the suggestion with wave of a hand.

Ann inferred that Sam too suspected something wrong in Siwa's dealings just as she did. Siwa obviously seemed to be clueless that the Gandharan supplier, the client Zibigi, and the agent Jittan were using his services for carrying out an illegal activity.

Ann looked at Sam, who seemed preoccupied in thoughts. Should she caution Siwa? If she did, he would want to know the reason behind her warning. That would entail uncovering the real face of Jittan, which would negate most things about her past that she had had them believe.

She decided to keep quiet on the matter. If Siwa was blind to what was as clear as day, it was his problem. No wonder a trading partner had cheated him.

She considered changing the subject, and what could be better than broaching what was on Sam's mind? "After you left the tent on that night, Sam," she said, " 'the real demon of Gangevell' came and threatened to kill my baby unless I gave him the *Harsag Zalazalag*."

"Demon of Gangevell?" Siwa looked perplexed. "*Harsag Zalazalag*?"

Sam recounted how an unknown foe had shadowed him from Lothal to Muenduru creating trouble, and how he and Ann had discovered Mad Kutti's treasure.

"The Demon of Gangevell is very different from the two avatars in which he met us," said Ann. "He's aged –"

"About thirty," Sam interjected, "and he carries an ugly mole under his left nostril."

Ann looked at him in disbelief. When did Sam see the real man behind the Demon of Gangevell? Before she could ask, Siwa cried,

"That's the man who came here to deliver Kayl's purse!"

Ann wondered why Sam's smile was suddenly wiped off by a dropping jaw. "That man wasn't just a port labourer as he confessed, Father. He's a sailor named Qwoco, who works with Captain Paravar." After a pause, he added, "I guess that Qwoco also serves another master – Nergal."

Ann's hand rose in a hurry to press her mouth which had very nearly screamed "Nergal?" She was relieved to see that neither man had noticed her reaction. Both seemed to be preoccupied in the thoughts of not only Nergal, but also of the mysterious villain called Qwoco.

Siwa scratched his beard. "Nergal had to do all that just to hide that he had stolen three gold necklaces."

Ann looked from Siwa to Sam and back at Siwa. He was on the wrong scent. The issue of gold necklaces was insignificant when compared with Nergal's role in trafficking. She also guessed why the Demon of Gangevell or Sailor Qwoco knew her and was familiar with her background.

Sam seemed to think that she needed some explanation, and said, "It relates to a rich man named Nergal for whom I worked in Babili." Ann's back stiffened. She was about to get some more information on the ringleader of the traffickers. Sam continued, "Once I had told you about a murder in Babili, and that the murderers wanted to kill me because I was the only witness. Kayl, the victim, was sent to Babili by Father. It now transpires that behind that bloody act was my employer, Nergal."

"He ought to be a horrible person," said Ann, trembling perceptibly. "I would be scared of him."

"If you mean his looks, Nergal is one of the most fine-looking young men in Babili, isn't he, Father?"

Ann did not bother to look at Siwa's reaction. It was confirmed that the Nergal they were discussing was the same man who was the master of 'Merchant' Zibigi and Agent Jittan. It occurred to her that she could share with Sam and Siwa what she had already discovered about Nergal in Village Chendur. The next moment she reminded herself that in doing so, she would expose all the lies she had told them so far.

"I suggest," said Sam looking at Siwa, "that everything we've found out about Qwoco, and – and Nergal, shouldn't be discussed with anybody else; not even with Velli."

Siwa chuckled. "Are you afraid that she would slap Qwoco if she meets him?"

"I wouldn't mind her doing that," Sam said, laughing. "What I'm concerned about is that it might alert Qwoco. That would wash out my plan of bringing Nergal to justice."

Ann was glad that Sam too wanted to punish Nergal. It was of utmost necessity that she went to Sumér with him. Unfortunately, that was likely to raise Sam's eyebrows, as he had assumed that she would be returning to Dholavira to get married to Tall Yali.

"That reminds me, Sam," said Siwa. "I expect to receive new gold necklaces for Chief Bel in a fortnight."

"We'll leave for Sumér immediately afterwards, Father," said Sam, rubbing his palms together. "If we delay, we might miss the last ship of the season, and wouldn't be able to sail for four lunar periods."

Ann sighed. "I wonder when I'd be able to go to Sumér after marrying Yali."

"Why don't you go with us now?" Sam asked enthusiastically.

Ann looked away. She had exhausted all her silver. She would have to return to Dholavira for several hectic years of hair dressing before she could save enough to undertake a long sea voyage.

Sam excused himself and got up, and Ann was relieved. She hoped that he would forget his question when he returned. Sam came back, smiling broadly. "Here, Ann," he said, offering her a leather packet which she recognized immediately. "Mad Kutti's gold."

"I lost the *Harsag Zalazalag*, Sam," she said, not moving her hands from her lap. "I don't have a claim on that gold any more."

"The *Harsag Zalazalag* isn't lost, Ann," Sam said with confidence. "Now that I know who robbed it from you, I will get it back."

Ann extended her hand. Her fingers clutched the leather packet, and as they ran over its familiar rough surface, there was a glint in her eyes. She had moved one step closer to punishing her two Sumérian tormentors.

23 EVENTS FALL INTO PLACE

As the river craft sailed into the port of Alatinam, a dark sturdy form resting faraway on the sea drew Sam's attention. He broke away from Velli and Ann, and ran to the stern. Despite looking vague in the morning mist, the shape was too familiar to get the blood rushing through his veins because it conveyed that Captain Paravar was present in Alatinam.

Sam had an intense urge to swim to the ship, as he had done in Urim, and share with the Captain everything he had found out about Nergal the Fox. A voice within enquired, "Can you do it without cautioning the Captain of Velli's sensitivities about the Fox?" That was bound to lead to explaining about his arrangement with her, and as a result, suffering the embarrassing roar of the Captain's hearty laughter. Undoubtedly, the impression that the Captain had formed about him would tarnish. Sam knew that he had no option but to pretend that he and Velli were happily married.

Deep in thought, he walked back to the ladies, only to be brought to reality by Velli's shrieks of wonder and excitement. Sam realized that the vastness of the sea, its apparent meeting with the sky on the horizon, the waves, and the salty smell, everything together was a novel experience for her. Probably he too might have gone through similar feelings in Urim had his mind not been preoccupied with the fear of Biggie's gang.

No sooner were they permitted to land, Sam filled his lungs with the pervading odour of fish, and ran to hire a cart. As he reached it, his nostrils twitched. A strong stench of mustard oil overwhelmed that of the fish. Even before turning around, he knew he was going to meet the man who worshipped Qwoco.

"Cock-eye?" said Sam. The next moment, he realized that it was a nick-name that he had invented for private conversation. "Is Captain Paravar here?" he hastened to ask despite having inferred it already. The grin on the sailor's countenance did not wane, and Sam was relieved about his unseemly utterance.

"Yes, and Qwoco too," said Cock-eye.

"Is Qwoco here?" Sam cried. He did not expect to meet Qwoco again. What he had told Ann was just to make her comfortable in accepting Mad Kutti's gold, which she needed more than he did. Why was Qwoco still working after robbing Ann of the costly diamond? Had he lost it? Or was there a more pressing issue that he needed to settle before he enjoyed the stolen wealth?

"Qwoco had been on land yesterday, so today he's on duty –" Cock-eye chortled, "in the kitchen." Sam echoed his chuckle, but deep within, he was worried. He did not want Qwoco to know that Ann had already apprised him about the real identity of the Demon of Gangevell. He was jolted out of his thoughts by what Cock-eye spoke next. "Who's that Sumérian lady who followed you down the ramp?"

The subject of women, especially young women, was a popular topic in the sailors' idle talk. Cock-eye was sure to tell Qwoco about Ann if he were not put off her scent.

"You mean that tall virago?" Sam said with disdain, and spat. "She is neither a Sumérian nor a lady, and I don't know her."

"I saw you kissing her kid."

"Did you see me kissing her?" Sam saw Cock-eye recoiling, and realized that his voice had risen. Putting a hand on the sailor's shoulder, he winked and asked, "Would you like to marry her?"

Cock-eye was not one who gave up easily. "You carried her sacks," he mumbled.

"You're a keen observer despite certain limitations," Sam said with a snort. "Now get this straight. She was travelling alone with that sweet baby, and I gave a helping hand. I'm sure you too would have extended such a gesture if you were in my place."

Cock-eye smiled approvingly. Looking totally flattered, and a somewhat satisfied, he left. Sam waited till he had turned the corner, and then hired a donkey cart. As it rambled through narrow streets, with Ann's toddler having determined to howl all the way, Sam wondered whether Ann should board Captain Paravar's ship at all. Qwoco had to be kept in the dark about the fact that Sam had surmised who had stolen the *Harsag Zalazalag*, and who had tried to kill him under various guises.

By the time the cart halted, Sam had decided that Ann should follow them in another ship. He would have to inform her when alone, and think of a convincing reason to tell Velli why Ann could not accompany them.

"Whose house is this, Sam?" asked Velli.

"My friend Tall Yali's sister's," Sam said as he knocked on the door. He looked at Ann. "I suppose you've met her earlier?"

She shook her head from side to side.

There was a noise of the latch, and the door threw open. Sam saw Captain Paravar, slightly leaner than when he had seen him last in Port Lothal.

"Samorist," cried the Captain, stepping forth with both his arms wide open. The two friends embraced as Velli and Ann looked on happily.

Tall Yali's sister, both her hands soiled with dough, rushed out hearing the commotion at the door. She squealed like a little girl. "Ann, I presume?" she asked. "Yali has talked so much about you that I'd recognize you even in my dream."

Ann looked pleased as she continued her efforts to pacify the baby.

"She's Velli," Sam told Captain Paravar. "My wife," he muttered as an afterthought.

The Captain rubbed his eyes before asking Velli, "Aren't you the heartless lady who refused to employ a keeper for my poor foal?"

Velli smiled rather uneasily.

"You've a sharp memory, Captain," said Sam.

"Memory, my foot – I just happen to remember that lovely ornament around her neck."

Tall Yali's sister looked at it, and drew closer to Velli. Sam could not miss noticing the change of expression on her face as she stared at Velli's necklace. He wondered if it was jealousy. Then he recollected what the Captain had told him long ago, about how the lady had been cheated of all her ornaments by one Nergal of Nibru.

"Sister," he said, intending to divert her mind from the necklace, "could you send a flask of beer for the two of us while we catch up with each other's work?"

"Of course, I will," said Tall Yali's sister, regaining her composure. "Velli, Ann, let's go inside."

After the ladies retreated, Sam nudged the Captain to a nearby Flame of the Forest tree which was in full bloom. "Our host's reaction upon seeing Velli's necklace sparked a thought in my mind, Captain," he said, "a thought which had not occurred to me so far. Nergal of Nibru, the man who duped Tall Yali's sister of all her jewellery, could be none other than Nergal of Babili – the Fox – for whom I worked."

Sam narrated how the Fox had swindled his father-in-law Siwa Saqra, arranged to kill his man in Babili, and used Qwoco's services to convey a false message to Siwa. "Qwoco even tried to kill me not once, but four times before I could reach Siwa," he concluded.

The Captain was speechless. "I knew that Qwoco wasn't upright," he said when he found his voice, "but I never thought he possessed such a murderous mindset."

"Ann and I were lucky in discovering a diamond as big as this," said Sam, picking up a stone roughly the size of the Harsag Zalazalag. "Qwoco threatened to strangle Ann's child, and robbed her of the diamond."

"I can't employ the villain on my ship any longer," said the Captain, flinging off a piece of straw that he was using as a tooth-pick. "I'll force the son-of-a-bitch to return Ann's diamond, and then dis–"

"Don't," Sam hastened to cut him short. "He's one person whose alibi could get the Fox behind the bars."

"There's Ann," Captain Paravar said, his countenance shedding all the anger. She was slowly coming towards them, precariously carrying a couple of long-necked flasks and goblets.

"Velli's necklace," she said, putting them down on the ground. The two men looked at each other and then at her. "It has ruined our host's happiness. A couple of similar necklaces were used by a crook to gain her trust and relieve her of all her jewellery."

"That villain is none other than Nergal of Babili," Sam said in a monotonous voice.

"She said it was one Nergal, hailing from Nibru," said Ann, "but I suspected it must be the same person who cheated Siwa of two necklaces."

"By the way, Ann," said Sam, "Qwoco is on Captain Paravar's ship."

Ann's face wilted.

Noticing her reaction, the Captain said, "Don't you worry, Ann. Another ship would be calling at Alatinam within a fortnight."

Sam emptied his goblet in one gulp. "Velli is bound to ask why Ann can't come with us."

There was a pause. Then the Captain spoke. "Leave that to me. I'll announce during the dinner: 'My reed ship is loaded with timber, and it can carry only two more passengers now. You make your choice about who will go with me.' "

"Excellent excuse," Ann said, brightening up. "It would look natural, and very sensible, when I volunteer to stay back."

The Captain looked at Sam. "Had there been three necklaces instead of two, I'd have thought that Nergal of Babili had disposed them off to a merchant who later sold them to my friend in Lagaš."

The swig of beer which was still in Sam's mouth, sprayed out and he started coughing. Captain Paravar and Ann looked at him eagerly. "There were indeed three necklaces that Chief Bel had ordered on my father-in-law," Sam cried. "Siwa had sent the third with Kayl who had been your passenger, Captain."

"Kayl?"

"Do you remember the owlish man wearing blue headgear, about whom Velli had enquired in Sutantoru?" asked Sam. "He was murdered in Babili and the third necklace that he carried was stolen."

Captain Paravar pressed his hairless crown. "Then I suspect my friend, King Gudea's Minister, is duped too," he said, letting out a long sigh. Sam saw that his eyes had turned red at the edges. "The villain you call 'the Fox' deserves to be thrown to the sharks, Samorist."

Sam smiled. "We'll request the Council of Elders in Babili to grant us that privilege, Captain," he said, "but before that, we'll have to prove everything for which we suspect the Fox."

"Yes, we'll need witnesses."

"Yes, Ann," Sam said, and drew Siwa's symbol IIOII on earth. "Captain, my father-in-law told me that the terminal beads of all three necklaces carried this mark. If the Minister's necklaces have it, our hunch would be confirmed."

"I will check with the Minister," said the Captain. "The first matter I'll discuss upon reaching Lagaš would not deal with the timber I'm carrying for the Temple of Ngirsu."

"No, Captain, you will discuss the Temple of Ngirsu first," said Sam. "Not for the timber, but for the so-called Stone dye from Meluhha."

Both the Captain as well as Ann looked perplexed. Sam told them about Velli's apprehension of Siwa's role in the transactions between the Gandharan trader, Agent Jittan and Merchant Zibigi or Biggie.

Sam thought it strange that Ann appeared to be losing her head over what he was saying. No sooner had he finished, she said, "I believe Siwa Saqra could be the most effective witness against the Fox and Biggie."

"Of course he would, Ann," said Sam, his face flushed with excitement. The Captain nodded in agreement.

"Captain, I think the next ship to Sumér won't be here before ten days," said Ann. Seeing him nod, she added, "I'd use that period to travel back to Muenduru and apprise Siwa about the events falling into place."

Spontaneous smile on the men's faces indicated that her suggestion was well received. Sam turned serious the next moment. "Is it necessary to disclose about our decision either to Tall Yali's sister or to anyone else?"

"Not at all," said the Captain shaking his head vigorously. "The lesser we talk about it, the better. Sam, I'd advise you not to discuss it even with your beloved wife."

Sam heaved a sigh of relief.

24 PLOT ON THE SHIP

Sam heard a cheerful voice as four rough hands pulled him up the deck. "Welcome to Captain Paravar's ship, Hamasin."

It belonged to Qwoco whose face wore a smile, but his eyes stared. The other two hands belonged to the head sailor, whose blank face did not convey anything and yet a twinkle in his eyes said a lot.

Sam smiled, more to himself than to Qwoco, as he imagined how they could use the sailor to corner Nergal the Fox. However, it was quite a challenge, behaving in a friendly manner towards a villain who had attempted to kill him. Sam's arms stretched out, intent to tear off that silly bun from Qwoco's head. Instead, they encircled and embraced him. "Qwoco, my bosom friend."

He was aware that they both were pretending. As Qwoco's hand patted his back, he was concerned that perhaps his acting was not as convincing as Qwoco's.

"Samorist," the Captain's irritated voice came from below. "Will you stop socializing, and help your wife?"

Sam hastened to give a hand to Velli, mentally thanking the Captain.

Sacks of vegetables and dried fish lay helter-skelter all over the deck. Carefully stepping over them, the Captain led Sam and Velli to his cabin. As he opened its door, a whiff of fragrance greeted them. Never before had Sam seen the place so spic and span; but what shocked him was that its bamboo walls were decorated with bunches of fresh crown flowers. The Captain's cot could not be seen under a thick blanket of coral jasmine and *champaca* flowers.

"This cabin is just for the two of you," Captain Paravar announced. "During this voyage, I'll sleep under the open sky with my boys."

He turned and left before Sam could say anything.

Seeing a blush on Velli's cheeks, he whispered, "I wished to tell the Captain that his magnanimity was futile."

She fixed him with such a glare that he too hastened out of the cabin.

Later that night, Sam got up to answer the call of nature. A few days had passed after the Full Moon and the sea reflected the moonlight in all its abundance, turning the clear night as bright as a cloudy day.

While half the deck bathed in the moonlight, another half was darkened under the shadow of the sail. Through that darkness, Sam groped at the ropes, and staggered to one of the two *zooly* toilets on the stern.

A little later, a sound – like a few exhausted messengers arriving together – woke him up fully. "Dirty sailors," he mumbled as he washed himself.

He threw open the door, preparing to take the culprits to task. Nobody was there. The sounds came over the sea. Silhouetted against the silver reflection of the moon upon the water, he perceived several fins gliding along with the ship.

"They're dolphins," he cried as he watched them streaking to and fro under water, creating a weird glow. "I'll wake up the woman I love," he told himself, and hurried towards the cabin.

As he emerged in the moonlit portion of the deck, he thought a shadow was closing upon him like an eagle on its prey. He perceived a lightning movement behind him, and intuitively ducked. An object hit his head very hard. His hands flew up to suppress the acute pain. A thought passed through his mind: How could he be so careless when killer Qwoco was around? Then everything blacked out.

The next thing that Sam remembered was that he heard low voices nearby. He lay with eyes closed, trying to make sense of what it all meant. A cold soft hand lay limp on his forehead. 'Something seems terribly wrong,' he thought. His eyes opened with some effort, and he made out the tense faces of Velli and the Captain peering at him.

Velli gently pressed his temple. "How do you feel, Sam?"

"What happened to –" A yelp escaped him before he could finish. He became aware of an acute headache.

"You were clobbered," said the Captain, taking Sam's hand in his. Sam followed his gaze as it settled on Velli.

"Last night, I sensed an eerie silence," she said. "I missed your snores and didn't find you in the cabin. I came out, just in time to see one dark form trying to heave another into the sea. The sight scared me so much that I shrieked."

The Captain picked up the thread. "We all woke up. The attacker dropped you and vanished." He bent down to pick up an object, and held it up to Sam. It was a stone mace-head stained with clotted blood. "Fortunately, this didn't work as well as your assailant wanted."

Sam looked at Captain Paravar, whose eyelids fluttered.

"Who was he, Velli?" Sam asked despite having already inferred it from the Captain's response.

"A sailor named Qwoco," she said.

"Never in my ten years of seamanship has a crime of such magnitude occurred on my vessel," the Captain said, putting a hand on Sam's shoulder and pressing it lightly. He got up and went out of the cabin. A little later, Velli too left to assist the cook.

Sam closed his eyes. The skin on his forehead crumpled. "I could understand why Qwoco was intent upon killing me before I met Siwa, but why would he want to harm me now?" he wondered. "Has Qwoco got wind of what we've in store for the Fox?"

Two matters kept Sam awake at nights. One was the worry that Cock-eye's report about 'a fair woman accompanying Sam' had possibly cautioned Qwoco; and the other was Velli's acute nausea. Although after a few days, she joined him and Captain Paravar at mealtime, he knew from the way she nibbled that she had not fully recovered.

As the ship glided into the port of Magan, Captain Paravar pointed to a towering edifice faraway on the port side. "That's a watch tower built to keep a lookout for marauders," he informed. "Magan is rather helpless against desert raiders. Nobody can tell when they would strike, so I advise passengers not to land here."

"Nothing has changed in all these years, Captain," Sam said

with a sigh. "The outlaws murdered my parents and a younger sister here." He reflected that when he was a child, every night he had dreamt of taking revenge. As he grew, he had come to terms with destiny.

"That notoriety comes in the way of Magan's prosperity," said the Captain. "Otherwise, its location is ideal for the trade between Meluhha and Tawi, the land of the step less ziggurats."

Sam noticed that theirs was the only ship in the port, and the hub-bub evident in other ports was missing altogether. No sooner was some cargo unloaded, the vessel left Magan. Seeing the watch tower on the starboard side, he asked, "Captain, are we heading towards Meluhha?"

"Good observation, Samorist," the Captain said with a smile. "Our voyage from Magan to Urim exploits a wonder of the Nature. The waters of the Lower Sea flow towards the south from Urim to Dilmun to Magan, all on the western shore. From here it flows towards the north to Urim along the eastern shore, that's the coast of Elam."

"Does it mean that our ship is now riding those currents which move in a circular route?"

"It does."

They stood together at the parapet, watching the rays of the setting sun reflecting upon the calm sea like a mirror. A light breeze blew out the sails.

"*Kavintu*," a voice came from behind, and they turned to find the head sailor briskly walking towards them. "I've a request," he said with a bow. "Ever since Qwoco is chained, he hasn't had a proper bath."

"That's his problem," said the Captain, looking away.

"It's mine too," the head sailor said in a wailing voice. "He reeks like a goat, and I get a headache every time I've to go near him."

"Then bring the swine up on the deck," the Captain growled. "Soak him with sea water."

"Yes, *Kavintu*. I'd also remove the weaver bird's nest that he has grown on his head," said the head sailor. "Half his odour emanates from it."

"Do whatever you like." The Captain pressed the sides of his temple with a thumb and a finger. "Just don't mention him to me if you can avoid it."

A little later, loud protests arose from the hold. Qwoco's voice was begging not to cut his hair. Moments later the head sailor hastened towards where they sat with Velli, arranging terracotta gamesmen on a chessboard.

"*Kavintu*," he called out, as he approached. "We found this inside his bun," he said, giving a shining diamond to Captain Paravar.

"That's the *Harsag Zalazalag*!" cried Sam.

The Captain looked up from the diamond in his hand. "Wasn't it stolen from Ann?" he asked. Seeing Sam nodding, he ordered, "Get him here."

Velli sought the *Harsag Zalazalag* from the Captain and studied it without batting an eyelid. In the exclamations which followed, Sam detected a deep longing.

When Qwoco was brought to the deck, he ran and fell at the Captain's feet. "I spent my life's saving on that diamond, *Kavintu*," he said with tears in his eyes. "I hoped to sell it in Huméru with some profit."

"Stop acting," the Captain yelled. "You've stolen it."

Sam tried to catch the Captain's eye. His lips moved in a silent prayer, and he hoped that the Captain did not give away the fact that they had had been briefed by Ann.

"I swear, *Kavintu*," said Qwoco, moving two fingers across his neck, "that I bought it."

"Bought it?" repeated the Captain, staring at him.

"Yes, *Kavintu*. From a fisherwoman in Alatinam. She had found it inside a porpoise which got entangled in her nets."

"Ooh, how lucky," said Velli.

Trembling with anger, the Captain opened his mouth, "I know –"

Sam pressed the Captain's foot with his, and interjected, "Ultimately what matters, Captain, is that I've found the diamond that someone had stolen from me."

"I know, Qwoco," the Captain continued after throwing a glance at Sam, "that you robbed Ann."

Sam gaped. Why did the Captain have to disclose it?

"I also know for whom you work in Babili."

A shriek escaped Sam. "No, Captain, don't."

Velli looked at both of them in utter confusion.

"Take him away," the Captain commanded. "I want to see King Shulgi's guards using their tormenting techniques on a Meluhhan for a change."

25 ABDUCTION IN URIM

In a way, Sam was grateful to Qwoco for injuring him. With timely use of 'ow's and 'ooh's, he had succeeded in stimulating utmost sympathy in Velli's heart till the ship reached Urim.

'If I could sustain her compassion for a few more days,' he thought, deeply inhaling the aroma of Velli's sweat as she dressed his wound, 'I'd succeed in wooing her away from Nergal the Fox.'

Sam wished to get on a river barge immediately upon reaching Urim, but Velli said, "I'm sick of the sea voyage, Samasin. Let's get a proper bath and little rest before we proceed."

Telling Captain Paravar that he will collect their belongings and the Harsag Zalazalag on the following day, he and Velli landed in Urim. They went to one of the inns near the harbour. It was one among several wooden structures which stood in a row along the roadside. However, it differed from other inns in that several children played in the open space in front of its entrance. Colourful gowns fluttered from a nearby clothes line. A short senile inn keeper led them to a vacant room.

A little later, Sam accompanied Velli to public washrooms for women. Located quite a distance from the inn, they stood out from the neighbouring men's washrooms by the sheer noise they raised – sound of clothes being thrashed, howls of children, and shrill warnings of mothers.

Sam squatted under a nearby willow. He was not aware when he started doodling in earth. When he looked up after drawing about fifty ships, he found a small gathering of children intently watching him. He jumped up and found Velli looking out for him with concern. He escorted her back to the inn before proceeding to the men's washrooms.

Just as he was drying his hair in the sunlight after a warm bath, he saw the doddering inn keeper approaching him with wide eyes and open mouth. "Young man," he said, his lips getting entangled between toothless gums. "Your Meluhhan wife has been abducted."

Sam brought down his hands on the inn keeper's narrow shoulders. "Who are those bastards? Where do I find them?"

"I don't know," the inn keeper said calmly. "Whoever they are, deal with them with tact, young man."

Sam stomped several steps. "Shove your tact up your –" He broke off.

"Then you'll lose her forever," said the inn keeper crossing his arms and pressing fists under the armpits. Sam hated the old man for those words, but he recognized that they ought to have been gleaned from experience. He stopped and listened. "Forget about reporting to the authorities. Await the abductors to contact you. Then meet their demand."

Sam's fingers fidgeted with the bundle of washed *vesti* in his hands. He didn't have a pleasant experience of Urim's officialdom earlier. He recalled the hard kicks he had received from the red-faced port official. Perhaps it would be practical to follow the old inn keeper's advice.

They slowly walked back to the inn, and Sam sat down at its gate like a snubbed dog.

A little later, an urchin ran up to him. He carried two bumps on his forehead, and Sam imagined that two little horns might sprout out of them. The boy said, "I've come to take you with me."

"Where?" Sam asked. The boy was too occupied, digging his nose, to reply.

The inn keeper hissed. "Go."

Sam followed the boy, all the muscles in his limbs eager to deal with the child's nasty masters. Lightly colliding with several passers-by in the crowded market-place, he navigated a series of narrow streets before his small guide stopped in front of a windowless building. At its gate, he saw a resting camel which nearly hid a jet black horse. The boy signalled to him to enter the warehouse.

The place appeared as if it had not been swept after a severe desert storm. Sam started sneezing and could not stop. It disturbed the squalid air around, and brought down a cobweb upon his face. Brushing it away, he stared in the dark hall before him. At the far end, he caught sight of Velli sitting on the floor, with her hands and feet bound.

"Velli," he cried as his arms stretched out, and he hurried towards her. Just then a rope descended on him. It tightened around him, crashing him to the ground. Two men pounced on him. His arms were forced behind his back and tied. His wrists ached, and fingers turned cold and numb.

The men pulled him to his feet, and Sam recognised the elder one as Biggie. His cheeks carried an unmistakeable rosy tinge which had not been there earlier. Sam was not surprised to see Biggie, but he wondered how it had not struck him that Biggie could be behind Velli's abduction. "What do you want?" he demanded. The next moment a blow hit his jaw, and it made him see stars floating just below the ceiling.

"Learn to speak to your Father," snapped Biggie's apprentice, a young man of about twenty sporting unkempt stubble.

"Stable boy, you've increased my work by bringing along dhat girl," Biggie said hoarsely. "Now I'll have to cope with both of you instead of you alone."

"Biggie, your enmity is with me," Sam said. "The lady has nothing to do with it. Why don't you let her go?"

"Samasin," Velli screamed even as the villain was opening his mouth to answer. "That boor had followed you to Sutantoru. He had called on Auntie, enquiring about 'a Sumérian stable boy'."

Biggie saw his assistant looking blankly at Velli who was speaking in Meluhhan. He slapped the junior behind his head. "Why did you remove her gag?"

"She was thirsty, *Belum*." There was hint of a tremble in his voice.

"Gag her again. She knows too much, and could get us in trouble."

"How could she, Biggie?" Sam said on an impulse. "Velli can't speak our language and she's new to Urim – to Sumér." No sooner had the words left his lips, he regretted them as he saw Biggie's face lighting up.

"*Mulla Xul*! You've given me a brilliant idea, stable boy," the villain chuckled. "I could sell her. She's young and – heh–heh–

heh."

The hair on Sam's arms felt as if they had risen erect. His foolishness had invited more trouble for his beloved. Biggie was greedy. Could he be offered anything more valuable than what Velli could fetch as a slave?

"I suggest a better bargain," Sam said, battling to keep his voice as low as he could. "She's worth a diamond this big." He held his fingers and thumb in a rough circle, indicating the size of the *Harsag Zalazalag*. Biggie's eyes popped out. "There's a Meluhhan ship in the port, captained by a man named Paravar. I know he's in possession of that diamond. I have no doubt that he would exchange it against Velli."

"A smart way to seek help, isn't it?" Biggie laughed loudly.

"I'm sure you know how to keep your adversary in check, and get what you want."

Biggie moved his tongue as if removing a small seed between his teeth. Then he spat, looking askance at Sam. At last, he motioned to the apprentice. "Call the twigs."

In a short while, the man returned with two boys. One was the same boy who had guided Sam to the warehouse. The other was shorter and thinner.

Although hardly twelve years old, they had already started walking in Biggie's gait. Biggie took them a little away and talked to them in a low voice. Then he paced back. "While you wait for one diamond," he said, smirking at Sam, "watch me polishing another."

Before either captive could grasp his meaning, he moved towards Velli flashing a partly toothless grin.

Sam heard a desperate mumble emitting through her gag. Her eyes reminded him of the eyes of the sacrificial calf on their wedding day. He struggled to loosen the rope that bound him, but it did not yield.

Biggie knelt beside Velli and pulled her *varati*. Sam saw her trembling violently. The amused apprentice let out smooching sounds, and both the villains' laughter reverberated around the warehouse.

Velli looked as if she was seized by a violent convulsion. Suddenly her body retracted and her head bounced forward. Sam watched the gag fly out of her mouth, followed by a spray of greenish yellow liquid. Before Biggie could withdraw, it splashed all over his face. An obnoxious stench filled the air.

Humour left Biggie's countenance as he desperately mopped it with his robe. A rich variety of Sumérian expletives dropped over each other as they rushed out of his mouth. He distanced himself from Velli. The loyal assistant followed him, loudly complaining against women who retched when they were supposed to entertain.

The shorter of Biggie's urchins ran in to announce that the camel cart was ready and that the other boy would arrive shortly, towing along a bald Meluhhan. The apprentice immediately picked up his bow and arrows, and climbed a bamboo ladder leading to a low narrow space just above the entrance. Biggie took a position before his two hostages. A moment later, the boy with bumps on his forehead arrived, leading Captain Paravar. Sun rays permeating from spaces between the roof-tiles made the creases on the Captain's temple stand out sharply.

"Samorist," he cried, as soon as his eyes got adjusted to the scanty light. "Velli!"

"Talk to me, melon-head," Biggie's harsh voice echoed around the warehouse. "Show me the diamond."

Captain Paravar's eyes swept the man from head to foot. "How can I be sure you'll release them?"

"A cart is waiting outside for you and the girl. I'll ride along up to the market, where you give me the diamond and buzz off." The villain shook a thick finger at the Captain. "If you act smart, melon-head, your two legs won't carry you inside the docks –" He roared with a sudden surge of laughter and added, "Other eight will."

"What's your demand for my friend?"

"None. We want him." Biggie said as he spat in Sam's direction.

Hearing those words, the Captain seemed to get alert. "We?" he echoed, looking questioningly at Sam.

"He means the Fox and his gang," Sam said, and jerked his head to point out, "He's Biggie."

"Where's the diamond, melon-head?" Biggie's irritated voice asked.

Captain Paravar raised his hand high. Under the light and the shadows in the warehouse, the *Harsag Zalazalag* reflected like a star. Biggie ogled, speechless. It seemed that the mere sight of the *Harsag Zalazalag* had choked his throat. Immediately he walked to Velli and pulling out a dagger from his belt, cut her bonds. She got up with great effort, and stretched her limbs. "Go," said the villain, pushing her. Had the Captain not caught her in time, she would have fallen to the floor. Glancing angrily at Biggie, the Captain took Velli by the arm and tugged her towards the gate.

Her legs seemed to resist the pressure. "We can't leave Samasin to his fate, Captain," she sniffled, glancing behind.

"Keep calm, Velli, and leave," Sam called out, "I will join you soon." Despite his utmost effort to sound casual, his voice gave him away. He was aware about what Biggie held in store for him.

Captain Paravar looked at him and then at Biggie. "If you harm my friend, the Demon of Gangevell will eat you raw. That's my curse."

Biggie's resounding laughter disturbed some bats in a distant corner of the warehouse, and they flew in such a haphazard way that a large one brushed Velli's head, making her shriek.

Sam neither heard Biggie's laughter, nor Velli's shriek. The Captain's words made him smile. The fact that they could use Qwoco to bargain with Biggie had slipped his mind in the crisis created by Velli's abduction. He called out a second time, more confidently. "Follow the Captain, Velli. I've full faith in the Demon of Gangevell."

The Captain dragged Velli out of the gate. Both the villains followed them.

Sam looked around. If only he could untie the rope binding him. He tried hard to loosen the knots on his wrists but failed.

Little later, a faint sound of horse hooves grew louder and stopped at the gate. Biggie entered with the apprentice, grinning from ear to ear. His hand slipped from a solid bulge in his robe to his dagger. "Stable boy," he said. "Now I'll finish some work dhat is pending for long. Get ready to die."

"Biggie," said Sam, raising a hand. "Won't you grant me a last wish?"

"Go ahead. What's it?"

"I wish to know why you want me out of your way. I haven't ever harmed you."

The villain smirked. "It is risky to keep you alive, stable boy."

"Risky to you?"

"To my Master."

"Nergal the Fox?"

Biggie smiled, then kissed the blade of his dagger and raised it.

Sam looked over Biggie's shoulder. Why hadn't the Captain returned as yet?

Biggie grinned. "Invoke your Demon of Gangevell, stable boy," he said, waving the dagger above his head. "You will be meeting him soon."

"Biggie, please give me some time to say my last prayer to Marduk."

"First it was the 'last wish', and now it's the 'last prayer'," said Biggie with irritation. "Next you would want some time for your last 'phoos-phoos'."

Seeing the dagger rising, Sam closed his eyes. He cursed Captain Paravar. "The fatso can't run fast enough to save my life."

Just then, a shrill cry was heard in the street outside. Recognizing the voice of the boy with the bumps, Sam opened his eyes. Biggie appeared puzzled as he looked at his apprentice.

"He says the Meluhhan has returned."

Sam jumped out of joy. The Captain's voice was heard from afar, "Wait, Biggie, I've urgent news for you."

"Melon-head!" gasped the villain. His hand which was brandishing the dagger fell like a piece of deadwood.

Sam saw the Captain hurrying in through the gate.

"You know Qwoco, don't you?" the Captain panted. Biggie looked at him with suspicion. "He's on my ship, and I intend to hand him over to the guards in Babili."

"Babili?" exclaimed Biggie. Sam perceived fear in his eyes.

"Yes," said the Captain, grinning. "My head sailor would have already reached half way to the docks with Velli. If he doesn't see me and Sam in five *mu-eś*, he will report to the guards."

Biggie reeled off his entire vocabulary of Meluhhan expletives so that the Captain could appreciate his deepest feelings, thought Sam. The apprentice spoke in Biggie's ear. Biggie looked unimpressed. "Let the Master go to hell," he said, fondly patting the bulge in his robe. "I won't be serving him any longer with this under my belt."

Then Biggie turned to the Captain. "You wily Meluhhan," he said as if he were protesting to a friend. "Let's rush to the port and exchange our hostages."

26 DIAMOND FOR KING GUDEA

About the time when Sam and Velli sat with Ella for their first dinner in Babili, Captain Paravar left for Lagaš. He was anxious to check with King Gudea's Minister the matters of the Stone dye and the necklaces.

The Captain reached there two days later. After taking a quick bath and breakfast, he put on a Sumérian gown and rushed to the administrative centre in the city. It was built around a large water pond bordered with dressed stones. Along its periphery, ran a wide road, across which there were several low buildings interspersed with lush olives and willows.

The place was teeming with citizens, merchants, water carriers, and hawkers vending eatables. But what made the place stand out from a typical market place was the presence of script writers and their boys who stood by, ready to run with the raw clay tablets to get them baked at a nearby potter's workshop.

Captain Paravar was half way to the building where the Minister worked, when his sight fell on a few horses tethered by the roadside. His feet came to an abrupt halt when a black horse standing among them looked somewhat familiar.

The Captain went to a water carrier and offered a piece of copper, saying, "I want your headgear for a short time." The man happily parted with it. Donning it, the Captain retreated under the shade of an olive tree from where he could keep an eye on the black horse. Soon a man dressed in a silk robe and a silk turban emerged out of the building and briskly walked towards the animal.

The grin on his face looked broader than the water carrier's upon seeing the piece of copper.

The Captain's belly shook as he watched Biggie in a respectable role. "Aha, I thought you would, but not so soon," he murmured as the villain climbed upon his black steed and rode away. Returning the headgear to the water carrier, he entered the building.

Thatched with clay tiles, it was roughly square in layout. Upon entering it, one reached an open space, which was surrounded on three sides by several rooms separated by chest-high walls. A wide passage outside, linked all the rooms together. Right opposite the entrance, there was a room bigger than the rest, with its walls touching the ceiling.

Captain Paravar strode towards that room. A middle aged man sitting there on a stool beamed when he saw the Captain, and after a brief enquiry about health and family, he went inside to inform King Gudea's minister. No sooner was the Captain ushered in, he said: "I believe, Minister, that Merchant Zibigi of Urim has just sold you a magnificent diamond from Meluhha?"

If the Minister was surprised, his face did not show it. He smiled and then spoke in a complaining tone. "Paravar, you never told me that you two were friends. Anyway, I've called him tomorrow to finalize the purchase if the King's jeweller passes it."

Aged about forty, and battling against a receding hairline, the Minister impressed as an official who could be easily approached. Two big blobs of wax on his desk indicated that he habitually stayed late at the workplace.

"That man isn't my friend, Minister," said the Captain. "Hadn't I spotted him today, I would never have thought that 'Merchant Zibigi' is the same person as Biggie the villain who held hostage two of my passengers. He released one against a sailor who tried to commit a murder on my ship, and another against that diamond he gave you."

The Minister rolled up a couple of tree barks lying before him, and placed them by the side. "Do you mean that this man Biggie has dared to cheat my King Gudea?"

"Yes, and he isn't alone," the Captain said, raising two fingers. "The villain works for a rich and powerful Babilian named Nergal."

"Nergal?" The Minister sprang from his seat as if stung by a bee. "The Fox?"

"You seem to know him well, Minister."

"Somewhat. My brother is King Shulgi's head guard."

The Captain clapped his hands. "Did your brother have the privilege of hosting the Fox in his jail?"

"Not yet, but if Biggie is Nergal's man, then both will soon be my brother's guests. However, that's not the point," said the Minister waving a hand. "Tell me more about Biggie."

On the following afternoon, Captain Paravar, disguised as a water carrier, sat awaiting Biggie near the water pond. The Minister had promised that he would punish the villain and then hand him over for prosecution in Babili.

It was not long before the Captain spotted 'Merchant Zibigi' getting down from an ox cart. 'Biggie seems to have given his black steed as security against the gold 'demanded' by the Minister,' he thought. He rested against a tree trunk and closed his eyes.

Soon enough, the Captain heard Biggie's voice ordering 'to get your rump off the ground.' As he opened his eyes and yawned, he saw Biggie kneeling down with both his palms forming a cup. Then he heard the villain whisper '*Harsag Zalazalag*'. It was the code word which he and the Minister had agreed to give to Biggie 'to identify the water carrier who would accept the bribe on the Minister's behalf.'

The Captain reached out for a small crane-necked flask by his side, and poured water mixed generously with date syrup. As soon as Biggie tasted it, he withdrew his hands, looked up and smiled. He rubbed his hands indicating that he wanted to wash them.

Putting the flask down, the Captain unblocked the water-skin. As he bent to pour the water, his headgear loosened and fell upon Biggie. The villain looked up again, his face red with anger, which vanished when he recognized the Captain. His eyes widened in utter surprise.

"Melon-head?" Biggie gasped. His voice was loaded with panic.

The Captain cursed the headgear. He had mixed up badly, and could not afford to give a chance to the villain to prove himself innocent. He dropped the water-skin and leapt to hold Biggie, but by then, the villain had reached into his silk robe, drawn out a baked-clay tablet, and flung it towards the pond. A shrill 'kwee-kwee' from a couple of herons indicated that the evidence of the intended bribery was already sinking to the bottom of the pond.

Biggie pushed him and ran. The Captain gave out a wolf whistle. Some guards in plain clothes picked up the hint, and pursued the villain.

The chaos startled a donkey which was calmly grazing nearby. It threw up its head, gave vent to a mournful bray, and darted straight into Biggie's path. The villain swerved, but could not avoid colliding into the bounding animal. Receiving a powerful hind legs kick on his thigh, he crashed to the ground. The pursuers pounced upon him and bound his wrists behind his back.

Not bothering to change into his clothes, the Captain ran to inform the Minister that their attempt to catch Biggie red-handed had failed.

27 VELLI CALLS ON THE FOX

Velli thought she would never forgive Sam for taking her to the house of her lover's divorced wife. His stupidity had landed her in an awkward situation. Nevertheless, her impatience to meet Nergal strengthened her resolve to bear anything – even discomfiture.

She dressed up early in the morning, and silently closed the door behind her. The intensity of Sam's snores fell as she walked out into the garden.

She saw Lady Ella seated on a long log seat. The morning sunlight filtered through the olive trees to her curly hair and fair skin, imparting a divine look to her. She was engrossed in reading a broad baked-clay tablet that rested upon her lap. 'Perhaps she is reading some holy scripture to appease the soul of her father,' thought Velli. On the previous afternoon, when they first met Ella, she had informed them about Chief Bel's death, and Sam had lost his happy disposition for the rest of the day.

A little away, a boy aged about nine practised archery, and every now and then shouted "Look, *Ama-ugu*." After Sam had told her that Ribba was born from Ella's marriage with Nergal, she could make out a certain similarity that the boy shared with his father, especially in his dense brow. In all other respects, he looked more like his mother. Velli recollected the respect in the boy's brown eyes when to one of his queries during dinner she had affirmed that she regularly went out for horse riding.

"Lady Ella," Velli said softly, anxiety clouding her face.

Ella looked elated upon seeing her. "Oh, Velli," she said,

extending a hand to hold hers and tugging it to get her sit besides her. "Please drop the formality, and just address me as 'sister'."

Velli told herself to tread with caution. She could not trust the woman just because her eyes seemed to express compassion. She hoped that Ella remained just half as friendly after hearing what she intended to tell her. "Sister Ella," she said in a voice which was barely audible. "I need your help, but I'm embarrassed to ask you."

Ella gave her a flitting glance, and Velli lowered her eyes. There was silence for a while as Velli pressed a lip between her teeth. Ella asked, "Is it about Nergal?" Velli looked up in surprise. Ella added, "Sam confided in me about his promise to you."

All stiffness in Velli's demeanour collapsed. She was grateful to Sam for easing what she had feared was a very delicate task. "I thought I'd meet him today," she said loudly.

"I guessed it," Ella said with a wry smile, "from all your finery, topped with that beautiful gold necklace."

Velli gained the courage to express the question which she had beaten about the bush to ask. "Could you send somebody to show me his house?"

Ella nodded. She clapped her hands to draw Ribba's attention. "Tell the cart man to get ready."

Velli pinched herself. Could the ex-wife of a man be so co-operative to a woman who was about to marry him?

Several *mu-eš* later, the horse cart had transported her to Nergal's mansion. As she heard the grinding of its wheels receding, her heart started pounding. She would be seeing her handsome lover very shortly.

Velli briskly entered the gate, from where a stone path with a tinge of green led to the main door of Nergal's expansive mansion. Her foot slipped, but she quickly regained her balance. Slowing down her pace, she saw a thick growth of weed entirely covering what would have been a lawn once upon a time. She smiled condescendingly and murmured, "You need a wife to turn your house into a home, Neru."

A huge dark form emerged like a spirit and stood blocking her path. A portly woman with thick lips and extremely curly hair, looking as friendly as a cobra, stared at her.

"I – I wish to see Nergal," Velli said.

The slave emitted a grunt. "Who are you?"

"Velli from Meluhha – Muenduru City."

"Wait right here," the slave said. She turned and ambled into the building. Velli stood half-way on the path till pain hurt her feet and started creeping upwards. Once she walked towards a stool that she saw nearby, but stopped and decided to keep standing.

She heard a couple of claps and saw the slave motioning her to one of the two doors in the foyer. Velli stared at her, but seeming oblivious of her angst, the slave briskly waved a hand like a jailor ordering the prisoners to move on. "You sow," Velli murmured, "I'll deal with you once I become the mistress of this mansion."

Velli walked to the foyer and entered the door. There stood her lover, facing away from her before a small shelf jutting out of the wall. He looked busy putting a cylindrical seal on a tablet. He seemed to have put on some flab. She had a deep urge to run to him, be crushed into his sinewy arms and feel his strength seeping into her. She smiled and waited.

Nergal turned around. "Yes?"

His blank face perplexed her. "Have I changed so much, Neru?" she chuckled.

His eyes rested on her gold necklace for a while. Then a flat voice came from a face that looked like a mask. "How are you."

The smile vanished from her face. "I see something is weighing upon your mind," she said with hesitation.

"What do you want?" he enquired. She had never seen in his eyes what she beheld then, and her heart sank.

"Oh, Neru, aren't you glad to see me?"

"Be quick," said Nergal, snapping his fingers with a clicking sound. "What brings you here?"

Velli blinked. Did she hear her lover Nergal speak those words? He did not sound any politer than his slave.

In a shaky voice, she said, "Have you forgotten so soon the woods of Muenduru, the bank of the Sindhu?" He strode to a window and stared out. "Neru, Neru," she cried, clenching her hands upon her bosom. "Have you forgotten your promise?"

"Woman," Nergal spoke, facing her. His brows rose at the outer edges. "You're married to the boy who once worked in my stable, aren't you?"

Velli was stunned. How did he come to know? "No, it was just a ruse – a ploy," she said, "so that Father would permit me to come to Suméru. I wanted to see you."

"You've done it now."

She hastened to explain. "Samasin hasn't even touched me."

Nergal held his belly and laughed. "Do you expect me to swallow that, woman?"

Velli blamed herself. In her eagerness to meet Nergal, she had overlooked that rarely did any rich man in Meluhha take as his wife a woman whose past he doubted. Why had she assumed that Sumérian men were any different?

Nergal picked up two copper rods from his desk and struck them. From the corner of a moist eye, she perceived the female slave materializing at her elbow.

"Neru, please listen," Velli pleaded. Her throat choked, and her eyes filled with tears.

He turned away and made for another door which presumably led to a second room. Her sight drilled into his back and she trembled. Her lips pouted as she swiftly moved to his desk. In a flashing movement, her hand grabbed the cylinder seal and rose high.

Just when she was about to hurl the heavy seal at Nergal's head, mass of an elephant collided against her back. Her tired legs gave way, and hitting the ground she was aware of a pair of dark fleshy arms around her. Through blurred eyes, she watched Nergal disappearing inside the house. The slave pulled her up and shoved her into the foyer and down the slippery pathway. Velli trudged out of the gate in a daze, even unaware of the loud clanking sound with which it closed behind her.

The dashing man, for whose love she had deceived her father, had refused to believe her. How different Nergal was from his plain countryman Samasin, who trusted her every word.

For a moment she stood outside Nergal's gate, unable to decide which way to follow. Gradually she got her bearings and started walking in the direction from which the cart had come. She heard a horse's hooves behind, and instinctively moved towards the compound wall to make way. A horse cart went a little ahead and stopped. She recognized Lady Ella's cart in which she had come. And from it, alighted the lady herself.

Velli could not control her grief any longer. Tears rolled down her face and her frail body shook. Ella's warm arms supported her, and helped her to climb the cart. The woman she had feared to trust was the one who was there to support her. As the cart started rolling, she threw her head on Ella's shoulder, and broke down.

Velli experienced a unique affinity with Ella – a closeness which could only be shared by two women treated unjustly by the same man. Ella's hand moved over her back, and she sensed solace permeating deep inside her heart.

After a long while, Velli said, "Even a she-ass wouldn't be any dumber than I was. I lost my heart to a wrong man."

Ella sighed. "I was much older than you, Velli, when I realized that truth."

That night Velli decided that if there was any person with whom she could share her anxieties, it was Ella. "I think, Sister," she said on the following morning, "that my father is trapped in a questionable trade, and he isn't even aware of it."

Ella was all ears. "Questionable trade?" she asked.

Narrating the incongruity in Siwa's dealings of the Stone dye, Velli concluded, "Kayl had found out that they didn't use any such material at the temple in Ngirsu."

"Is Kayl the old man who was murdered here in Babili?"

"Yes, he had sent with Sam a bronze fish-hook to Father. It was meant to be a message for me."

"Why didn't you tell it to your father?"

"He would have never believed me."

"Have you seen the material which he exported to Sumér?"

"Yes, it comes in small uneven pieces – brown, rather darkish, in colour." They heard voices approaching the kitchen. "Captain Paravar is here," Velli squealed.

Sam and the Captain entered. The smile on their faces augured happy news. "Velli, Lady Ella," said Sam, "the Captain comes with a big breakthrough for our complaint against the Fox. We now have a written proof from King Gudea's minister that Biggie sold him Chief Bel's three necklaces."

Ella clapped her hands, and looked at Velli. "Biggie is the villain who abducted you, isn't he?"

"Yes."

Sam added, "You've seen him, lady. He's the man who accused me of Kayl's murder. Right now he is in the Captain's custody."

"Is he? How?"

The Captain briefly apprised them about 'Merchant Zibigi', Chief Bel's necklaces and the *Harsag Zalazalag*. Then he said to

Velli, "Your hunch was correct; King Gudea's men don't import any dye for the Temple of Ngirsu."

Velli found it difficult to keep standing. "I'm afraid Father is unwittingly engaged in an illegal trade." She pulled up a stool and sat down. "His client in Sumér is none other than Biggie."

"Biggie might be the biggest bead in the necklace of crime," Ella said, with an unmistakeable pain in her voice, "but its pendant is the Fox."

"Nergal?" Velli exclaimed.

Ella turned to Sam. "You'd seen the Fox supplying yellow sachets to some inn-keepers, hadn't you?"

"Yes, lady."

"Did you know what they contained?"

"No, lady."

"By the way, Sam, the Fox's cart man came to me to ask for some silver when you were in jail awaiting the Ordeal." Sam looked perplexed. Velli too could not understand the sudden turn in the conversation. "What did you want to buy with the silver, Sam?" Ella asked with a knowing smile.

"Opium."

"That's just what the Fox's yellow sachets contain," said Ella. "I procured several of them from different sources, and found that out."

"How does opium look?"

"Brown and powdery," Ella replied.

"Like rough pebbles," informed the Captain. "Blackish brown in colour."

Velli's hand reached for Sam's elbow. "That's how the Gandharan's Stone dye appeared too," she exclaimed as its grip tightened.

"I recall that besides the yellow sachets, I had also seen a pilon in the Fox's storehouse," said Sam.

Velli's face paled. She looked helplessly from Sam to Ella and then to the Captain.

"Samorist, now my captive could give evidence not only for selling the stolen necklaces but also for the opium trade," said the Captain. "The Fox would be fighting with his back to the wall from now on."

"And he'd be trapped in a tight corner," Velli said smiling at Sam, "when Father reaches Babili."

"Fortunately, we don't need to wait for Siwa any more," the Captain hurried to put his suggestion. "I've also obtained the Minister's written confirmation that no 'stone dye' is used in the Temple of Ngirsu. It blows up Biggie's lie."

They all agreed that with the evidence at their disposal, they could, without any delay, get Nergal the Fox summoned by the Council of Elders on two charges: that he had obtained Bel's necklaces by creating a false document, and that he traded in opium.

"King Shulgi is very concerned about how opium is ruining the Babilian youth," said Ella. "So I presume that the Council will take up our complaint on priority."

Sam and Captain Paravar left immediately for the Ziggurat to lodge it. They were gone for a while when Velli heard desperate cries drawing nearer. "Captain Meluhha, Captain Meluhha."

She looked at Ella, who too appeared confused. A dishevelled man rushed in, shouting. There was a deep wound on his forehead, and blood had clotted on it. Velli thought he might be a mad man.

"Where's Captain Meluhha?" he shouted.

"Who are you?"

"I am the caretaker at the farm house where Captain Meluhha held his captive."

"What's the matter?" Ella asked.

"The prisoner –" the man said breathing heavily. "He hit me and escaped."

"What? When? How?" Velli cried.

"This isn't the time to probe, Velli," said Ella grasping her arm. "Let's rush to the Ziggurat to stop them from submitting the request."

28 SMALLER CROCODILE GETS HIS DUE

By the time their ship reached the port of Urim, Ann had thought out a couple of approaches to obtain private audience with 'Merchant Zibigi' as well as Nergal of Babili.

Entering the estuary of River Purattu, they passed an anchored vessel which too carried the dark blue flag dyed in indigo, which eloquently announced its Meluhhan origin. Ann recognized it as Captain Paravar's ship. Siwa enquired at the port, and was informed that the Captain had gone to Lagaš.

They checked-in at an inn near the docks. It was a low structure built from logs. A few horses chewed leisurely in a stable by its side, and several camels sat with half-closed eyes in the vast open space in front. Jolly voices emanated from a nearby cabin, which Ann presumed was a tavern.

After taking bath and breakfast, Siwa told Ann, "I'm going to see a client, and will be back by the evening."

Ann was feeding apple pulp to her toddler. Her hand stopped mid-air. "Merchant Zibigi?" she asked, trying to think of an excuse to accompany Siwa and see the villain, only whose voice she had heard.

"Yes, Merchant Zibigi, the man who prospered me," Siwa said, looking pleased. His attention was drawn by Red Muruku who was tugging at his hand.

"Father, I'll go with you."

"Son, you'll enjoy yourself more playing with the baby here."

Red Muruku sulked, and after some attempt at mollifying him,

Siwa relented.

"I'm scared to stay back alone," Ann said, clutching her hands over her bosom. "I too will join you."

Siwa jerked his shoulders, and hired a camel cart to Red Muruku's delight. After a long journey under the sun, the cart stopped before one of the lanes connecting the road.

"The place where you want to go is somewhere down there," the cart man said. "The street is too narrow for me to turn."

As they got down and Siwa paid the fare, two urchins came up running. "Who are you looking for, *Belum*?" asked one whose forehead seemed to have taken two hard knocks.

"Where is Merchant Zibigi's warehouse?"

"Ah, yes, Mer-chant Zi-bi-gi," the boy said slowly, pronouncing in parts. Ann saw the shorter boy turn and disappear inside the lane. "Follow me, *Belum*," said the boy with the bumps, taking the lead. He walked at a leisurely pace, kicking at every pebble which came in his way. Ann perceived impatience on Siwa's face.

At last, they reached an old building that looked just like a couple of high walls. They entered it through a big crumbling gate. The place was not only falling apart, it also smelt of decay. Siwa looked disgusted.

As they crossed the foyer, Ann saw a muscular man hobbling towards them with a grin which looked awful without two front teeth. Both his legs were bandaged. Besides what seemed to be a permanent mark across a cheek, several fresh bruises adorned his face.

"Merchant of Meluhha," he said huskily. "What a surprise."

Ann's eyes shone. It was the same voice which she had heard talking to Agent Jittan in Village Chendur. It had been imprinted in her memory, associated with the words, "Sell her fast and deliver the silver to Siwa Saqra."

A vein on her temple started showing. Her fingers bent, tightening their hold. The baby screamed, and she controlled her reflexes. She regretted that she had held back telling Siwa Saqra about what she knew about the villain Zibigi. She was aware that the two men were conversing, and yet her brain did not register its content.

Just then, the two urchins came up, carrying several jars and goblets. Biggie poured out red wine from one, and offering it to Siwa, asked, "Who is the lady?"

Ann's mind responded, 'Your ruin!' She quickly pressed her lips together lest her tongue convey her thought in words.

"She's Ann," Siwa replied, receiving the goblet of wine with both hands. "Her husband, a Meluhhan, was killed by thugs who sold Sumérian slaves. The poor girl had to stay in Meluhha till she could save enough silver to return home." Ann did not miss noticing the look on Biggie's face. It made her shudder. Siwa continued: "It seems that someone else, who's also named Siwa Saqra, does the lowly work in Sutantoru-on-Sea."

Ann stared at Siwa. Why couldn't he keep his trap shut?

She was aware that the villain was studying her over the rim of his goblet. One expression that his eyes did not carry was belief. She followed what came to her mind at that moment. She put a hand over her eyes, and pretended to be overcome by her tragedy.

Red Muruku's soft hands touched her arm. "Why are you unhappy, Auntie? Did Father scold you?"

Ann drew him closer and hugged him. She heard some shuffling, and saw the men moving away, carrying their goblets and two of the jars. While she was grateful for the respite, she was afraid that it might not last long. Siwa had inadvertently exposed her. Zibigi looked suspicious, and she would have to deal with him before he harmed her.

She heard the words 'Stone dye' mentioned several times. As she served honey drink from the remaining jar to a nervous Red Muruku, the mention of 'Agent Jittan' made her spill it.

From the corner of her eye, she watched Biggie drinking without bothering to retain pace with his guest. 'He's one who can't see wine idling before him,' she thought. She pondered how to dissociate from Siwa; and 'meet' the villain, the one whom all these years she had prepared to punish.

A little away from where they stayed, Ann had spotted another inn. What had attracted her attention was that several small boys and girls played hide and seek nearby. 'That inn seems to be attracting families in transit,' she thought, 'unlike ours, which hosts only men.'

Upon reaching their room, they got busy packing their sacks. Ann checked out two flask-shaped vials in her luggage. One contained an extract of rosary peas, and the other that of bamboo shoots. As Siwa prepared to leave for Babili, she told him, "I am afraid, Merchant Saqra, that I won't be able to join you. I think I'd meet my old aunt in Urim before I go to Babili."

The following morning, Ann got ready to visit 'Merchant Zibigi'. She bent to pick up her sleeping infant, when there was a loud impact on the door and it flew open. She shot back erect like a tender bamboo plant. The villain Zibigi stood there, glaring at her. "Woman," he growled. "You can't get away from Biggie."

Ann's eyelids fluttered several times. "On the contrary," she said, putting up a brave front, "I was about to come and meet you, Merchant Zibigi."

Biggie spat on the floor that she had swept a little earlier. "Why?"

"For two reasons," she said, praying in her heart that she sounded convincing. "I did not want you, my countryman, to believe the lie that I had told Siwa Saqra."

Biggie waited for her to complete. Instead, she picked up a small wooden stool from a corner and put it before him silently.

"What's the second?" he asked, kicking it away. Ann did not reply. She just stood there smiling, admiring his broad chest and brawny arms. "You heard me, woman." There was irritation in Biggie's voice.

"How I hope," she said in a low voice as she brought back the stool and placed it in front of him again, "that my son grows up to be a man as imposing and powerful as you."

With those words, she had expected him to display the big gap between his teeth in a genial grin. Her heart sank when that did not happen. With a frown, he lowered his huge frame on the stool. "I know you aren't what Siwa thinks you are. Who are you, woman?"

Ann had anticipated it. "It's a long story," she said, reaching for two bronze bars and striking them together. "So let me order a drink for you." When the short senile inn keeper shuffled to her door, she gave him some silver and ordered six jars of red wine. The old man inserted a finger in his ear and shook it vigorously. "Yes, six," Ann told him, raising that many fingers. "Hurry up," she said, sitting down on the floor at Biggie's feet. "That's the least I can do for Merchant Zibigi."

Biggie looked surprised. His eyes roamed all over her body as if intent to disrobe her. She could not decide whether it was due to mistrust or admiration. As soon as the wine arrived, she served it, and he downed two goblets in quick succession as if it were the last batch of liquor left in Urim.

"I was an orphan living with my uncle and aunt," said Ann. "A handsome young Meluhhan was my uncle's friend, and he used to come to our home for meals whenever he visited Urim."

"What's his name?"

"Yali."

"I mean your uncle's."

Ann cringed. Why had that question not occurred to her? Telling 'Dilmun' or 'Magan' instead would have made answering it much simpler. If she faltered, she would give herself away. The truth dropped out of her mouth. "Gazkir," she said.

"Where did you live in Urim?"

With her heart in her throat, Ann said, "In a row house behind the Ziggurat."

Biggie took a big gulp, and closed his eyes. "There was a barber by dhat name working in dhat locality," he said after a while.

Ann's mind saw an image of a mouse trapped in a corner. The villain knew her uncle. She had to keep talking confidently, lest he start doubting her again.

"Uncle Gazkir was also a small time trader, not just a hair dresser," she said firmly, looking very offended.

Two jars of wine had already made its way inside Biggie's system, and it probably discouraged him from pursuing the matter. He waved a hand, asking her to continue.

Ann's hand rose to her heart. "As I was saying," she said hurriedly, "I fell in love with Yali, married him, and went with him to Laketown Dholavira."

"What did Yali do for a living?"

"He reared bovines of the Gir pedigree."

Biggie narrowed his eyes. "*Mulla Xul*! You just said he frequently visited Urim."

Ann visualised a mouse which was about to be swatted, and superimposed on its face was a tiny image of her own. She had to divert his thoughts, and to gain time, she started laughing.

"I've thoroughly confused you, Merchant Zibigi, haven't I?" she said, picking up a jar and offering to fill to the brim the trembling goblet that he held. "You see, Yali used to trade in knick-knacks and could earn just enough silver to make the ends meet. I told him I'd help in some really hard work which could earn us more silver.

He started working as an apprentice with a breeder of –" She paused when she saw Biggie raising a hand, and was relieved that the ploy had worked.

"How did you associate Merchant Saqra with the slave trade?"

"That was a lie I told him when I was caught while trying to kill him."

The goblet in Biggie's hand tilted and wine poured out of it on his gown. "Woman, you – you wanted to kill Siwa? Why?"

"Yali had had work relationship with several merchants in different parts of Meluhha," said Ann, hoping that her tale would evaporate the lingering suspicion in Biggie's eyes. "Siwa was one of them, and he sold our cattle in the fertile land between Muenduru City and Fort Harappa."

"Siwa also deals in cattle, does he?"

"The Meluhhan is a very greedy man, Merchant Zibigi," Ann said, shaking her head in disgust. "He dabbles in whatever that earns him a lot of silver."

"What happened dhat turned you against Siwa?" Biggie asked, flinging away the fourth empty jar.

The crashing sound made Ann glance quickly at her sleeping baby. It moaned and turned on another side. Relieved, she continued, "About two years ago, Yali left a herd of twenty Gir cows with Siwa, hoping to make a huge profit. When he returned to claim the payment, Siwa told him that all had caught a strange illness and died within a week. My husband was so shocked that he turned lunatic a few days after reaching home."

Ann paused. She had not expected any empathy from the villain, but was peeved to see him smiling. "I didn't think Siwa was so smart," Biggie observed.

At that stage in the narrative, Ann had thought of repeating her sobbing act. However, considering his response, she decided that she would rather skip that part. She said, "I vowed to take revenge on the man who had broken my family. So after the baby was old enough to bear the strain of long travel, I reached Muenduru City. I tried to break open Siwa's skull, but failed. Obviously, he wanted to know why a stranger was so keen to kill him."

In his eyes, she perceived esteem. "What happened then?" he said.

"A sailor's wife had once told me that Sumérian slaves were sold in port towns like Balakottai and Sutantoru-on-Sea. So I made up a story that my husband was killed by one Siwa Saqra's men as he spoke out against the slave trade. And that was why I wanted to kill him."

"Heh-heh-heh." Biggie's eyes closed in divine joy as he scratched away the wax sealing of the last jar of red wine. "Now I get why Siwa said there was a mix up in names. You fooled the cultured Meluhhan quite cleverly."

"Hee-hee-hee." Ann responded, in an attempt to sound like a silly neighbour back in Laketown Dholavira.

"For you, woman," Biggie said, looking anxious to help, "I'll get rid of dhat bastard Siwa."

Ann gulped. She had unknowingly created trouble for Siwa Saqra, just as he had done for her a day earlier. She had to dissuade the villain from going ahead with his decision. "No, no," she hastened to say in a pleading tone as she clasped Biggie's feet. "I don't want you to get in trouble with the guards."

Stressing the word 'you', she looked up at Biggie. The coldness in his eyes seemed to have mellowed. "Siwa deserves nothing less than a violent death," he said, stamping a foot.

"I've already thought about it, Merchant Zibigi," she said, recollecting about the 'violent death' which Sam had told her he had faced in Babili. "I'm following Siwa to Babili this evening. I'll get him in a situation where I can accuse him of raping me. The Council of Elders is likely to believe a young Sumérian widow suckling a baby rather than a foreigner sporting golden ornaments. The wild bull of Babili would do the rest."

"Heh-heh-heh. *Mulla Xul*, I like smart women," said Biggie, gulping a goblet full of red wine at one go. "We two are alike in so many ways. Why don't we get married, what's your name?"

Ann cursed the situation in which all her lies had landed her; but she had to continue with it and hope for the best. "Merchant Zibigi," she said, joining both her hands in the Meluhhan way, "I am no match for a man of your social standing."

"Rubbish," said Biggie, his red eyes ogling at her full bosom. "Let's go to the priest-physician immediately." Flinging away the last jar and the goblet, he tried to get up, faltered, and fell back on the stool.

The crash of pottery woke up the toddler, and it started crying. For once, Ann was thankful to a wailing baby, and she ran to pick it up. Amidst the baby's howls, she said, "I'll be honoured,

Merchant Zi–"

"I hate formality. Call me 'Biggie'," he said, again attempting to stand up. "Let's go and get married."

Ann noticed that the rapid intake of six jars of red wine had not only dampened his energy but also affected his throat in an unexpected way. His hoarse voice had turned into a mere squeak. Her hand rose to her hair.

At last, the sharp bone hairpin, dipped in the extract of bamboo shoots, got the opportunity to mark a long deep scratch across its intended victim's neck.

29 KING SHULGI'S LAW AND THE FOX

Sam and Velli, Siwa Saqra and Ella, and the Captain, together entered the Council hall and walked to its front. Siwa, clad in a long piece of cloth with bright blue trefoil design, attracted everybody's attention. He carried two heavy-looking baked-clay tablets in both his hands.

Captain Paravar too carried two more tablets. He was dressed in a gown instead of the usual *vesti*, and that had made Sam slip a hand around Velli's slim back and whisper, "Doesn't he look more respectable than you've ever seen him, dear?"

Velli met his eyes and smiled coyly.

A familiar sight to Sam, the platform had seven seats on it placed in half a circle. The bamboo enclosure seemed to be inviting him to occupy it once again.

A murmur arose in the back rows and Sam looked behind. The Head Guard was briskly coming down the aisle, holding his head high as if an invisible force was pulling him by his wild beard. Following him closely was Nergal the Fox, his chest thrust out and head thrown back. However, when he saw Ella and Siwa sitting right in the centre of the front row, his smile vanished. He settled down meekly in the far end of the row.

The hum ceased, and everybody stood up as the Elders filed in the hall. Sam recognized the new Chief with his facial lines hard baked in a perennially unhappy mould. The entire procession climbed up the steps of the platform with considerable effort.

The Fox smiled warmly at the Chief and bowed. Without any

change in his expression, the Chief signalled at him to enter the bamboo enclosure. "Nergal, there are two charges against you," said the Chief, holding up a bark manuscript at an arm's length and reading out slowly. "That you forged the late Chief Bel's seal to obtain two gold necklaces from Siwa Saqra, and sold them away."

The Chief paused. Sam wondered whether he really wished to drink water, or he was giving some time to everybody to fully appreciate the weighty matter on hand. The Fox pouted his lips as if he was about to spit, and then gulped.

"And the second," the Chief continued, "is that you import opium from Meluhha, and sell it in Sumér." Looking at Ella, he added, "Both your suggestions seemed sound. We've ordered a raid on Nergal's storehouse outside –"

"When?" The Fox cried. "Why?"

"We'll soon know," the Chief told him calmly. He addressed Ella again. "The inn-keepers on both the country roads are also being rounded up."

Sam caught the Fox signalling to one of his cronies. The Chief had not missed noticing either. He pointed at the Head Guard. "Ensure that no one leaves the Council hall."

Then, turning to the Fox, the Chief asked, "Have you ever visited Meluhha?"

"Yes, I have."

"Do you know Siwa Saqra?"

"Yes, I do."

"Did you meet him in Meluhha?"

"Yes, I did."

"Where?"

"In a city called Muenduru."

"For what purpose did you meet him?"

"None. It was a courtesy call on an old friend whose country I was visiting."

"And Siwa Saqra gave you some jewellery," stated the Chief, looking over the bark manuscript.

The Fox's hands rose up to his chest and his palms turned outwards. "What jewellery?"

"The necklaces which, as you told Siwa, Bel had asked you to collect from him."

"That is not true." The hurt feeling in the Fox's voice was very evident.

The Chief looked at Siwa, who stood up and handed one of his tablets to the clerk. "I request for your consent to present this evidence." His Meluhhan intonation made some men laugh. The Chief stared as if he had failed to understand, but several of his colleagues nodded. Siwa continued, "It is a message which was supposedly written by Bel, asking me to deliver the necklaces to Nergal." A buzz swept through the room. Siwa added: "The seal on it looks similar to Bel's, but isn't genuine."

All the members of the Council had a look at it. "What do you have to say about that?" they asked the Fox. He casually motioned to let him see the tablet, and the clerk of the Ziggurat carried it up to him.

Throwing a cursory glance over it, the Fox raised his voice: "It's a fake document."

"So you agree with the Complainant," the Chief observed.

"It's a fake document created by the Complainant. He has framed me under a false charge."

The Chief said, "Merchant Saqra, can you prove that this tablet was presented to you by Nergal?" Siwa looked as if he was fumbling for words. "No?" said the Chief, eying the remaining tablet in Siwa's possession "You may put up your next evidence."

Siwa handed the second tablet to the clerk. "Here is the receipt for the two necklaces which Nergal collected from me. It contains Nergal's thumb impression."

"Thumb impression?" the Fox exclaimed in a low voice as if asking himself, "Mine?" Yet, it was just loud enough for the Council members to overhear.

"Show it to the Accused," ordered the Chief.

The clerk walked to the Fox carrying the tablet. The Fox thrust forth both hands to accept it. The clerk eased his grip. In a moment of ambiguity, the tablet appeared to miss the hold of either. The clerk shrieked. The Fox appeared to be trying to retrieve the falling tablet. There was a loud crash and it lay scattered in small pieces all over the floor.

The size of the pieces suggested to Sam that the tablet might not have been fully baked. Had it been hard baked, the pieces would have been larger, and it might have been possible to reconstruct the document. His eyes shut tightly, and hands flew to hold his head. His mind travelled back to the time when searching for Siwa Saqra's house in Muenduru City, he had met the hunched potter who had told him, "If you need any clay document to be baked, I'd understand."

Just when the implication of that casual remark dawned upon Sam, he became aware of an angry voice.

"You broke it," the Fox yelled at the clerk. "It was yet another forged document. Now I won't be able to take legal action against the foreigner for tarnishing my image in the society."

The clerk's face was damp with tears as he stammered to explain, but the Council brushed him aside. Sam's eyes met Siwa's. He looked aghast. Not only they, but even Ella – the woman who had spent a decade with their adversary – seemed to be taken aback by the Fox's wile.

The Chief announced, "Now we proceed to that portion of the first charge, which is said to have taken place in Sumér; and that is, instead of delivering the necklaces to Bel – their rightful owner, you sold them off through your man Zibigi."

"That accusation is not true either," said the Fox, thrusting forth his chest like a courting pigeon. "Who's this man you call Zibigi?"

Captain Paravar came to the fore. "I seek permission to present the sworn statement of King Gudea's Minister." He passed the tablet to the clerk.

"I don't know any Minister in Lagaš," said the Fox. Then glaring at the tablet which the clerk held, he extended a hand for it. The clerk looked at the Chief, and receiving his nod, stepped forth uncertainly towards the bamboo enclosure. He kept holding it tightly while the Fox moved a finger across it, reading and re-reading the contents. Then he looked up and asked: "The Complainant accuses me for not delivering two gold necklaces to Bel, is it so?"

The Council members turned to Siwa Saqra. He nodded concurrence.

"And I gave those two necklaces to someone named Zibigi who then sold them to King Gudea's Minister, right?"

"That's right," said Siwa.

Sam wondered what was on the Fox's mind.

"I request the honourable Council to read the Minister's statement carefully," said the Fox, as he imparted a gentle push to the clerk towards the seven seats of justice.

Sam watched blankly as the Chief peered over the document

and then passed it to other members. After everybody had examined it, they consulted among themselves. Then the Chief looked down at Siwa, who seemed to tremble when he met the elderly man's steady gaze.

"The Minister's statement mentions three necklaces," said the Chief, "whereas, you accuse Nergal of stealing two. There is an obvious anomaly, and hence the Council refuses outright to accept this document as evidence."

Sam heard a chuckle emanating from the bamboo enclosure.

Siwa leapt to his feet. "The late Chief Bel had ordered me to supply three necklaces," he said, adjusting the top portion of his dress over his shoulder. "I had given two necklaces to Nergal when he visited Muenduru City, trusting the tablet which carried Bel's seal. I had sent the third necklace with my man Kayl who was murdered in Babili. Nergal's deputy named Zibigi had pilfered it from Kayl's corpse, and sold it to King Gudea's Minister who had earlier bought the two necklaces from him in good faith."

"What proof do you have," said the Chief, "that Zibigi had pilfered a necklace from a corpse?"

"My son-in-law Samasin was witness to it, and he had talked about it before the august Council in the case where Zibigi had accused him of murdering Kayl."

"Is the witness your son-in-law?"

"Yes, Chief."

A loud snigger was heard from Nergal the Fox.

"Then, Merchant Saqra, even if you were to hide the truth, your son-in-law might not contradict you," said the Chief. "Do you have anything further to support your argument?"

"Only one, Honourable Council," said Siwa, looking into the Chief's eye. "That the complainant wasn't my son-in-law at the time of Kayl's death."

The Chief shook his head, as if in doubt. He did not even consult the other Elders.

"Merchant Siwa Saqra's first complaint against Nergal is dismissed," he announced with an air of finality.

A spontaneous cheer resounded in the hall. Its sheer intensity made Sam gasp. The Fox's cronies occupied almost the entire Council hall.

The Fox surveyed them with a broad smile, raised both hands, and shook them as if he had lifted someone and was about to throw him down. Sam gnashed his teeth.

He saw Siwa looking at Ella for succour. She was biting her nails.

The Chief asked Nergal to take his seat, and then turned to Siwa. "Yes, Merchant Saqra, what do you wish to tell the Council about your second complaint?"

Siwa strode to the bamboo enclosure, and bowed to the Elders. "On my earlier visit to Suméru a few years ago, I came in contact with Zibigi of Urim. Posing as a respectable merchant, Zibigi told me that King Gudea of Lagaš was constructing a temple in Ngirsu, which required a huge amount of 'Stone dye'. He gave me the name of a supplier in Gandhara. Zibigi sought my help to procure the 'Stone dye' from the Gandharan supplier and send it to Suméru. Recently I came to know that no 'Stone dye' was ever used in the Temple of Ngirsu."

The Captain got up. "I, Captain Paravar, supply timber for the temple, and therefore regularly meet King Gudea's minister who is in its charge. I seek your permission to present the minister's written confirmation that no dye or colour used in the temple originated in Meluhha," he said, giving one of his tablets to the clerk

After the Council members had carefully studied the Minister's statement, Siwa picked up the thread. "Captain Paravar also found that the person I knew as Merchant Zibigi is actually a criminal popularly known as 'Biggie' who works out of Urim and reports to Nergal. He is the same Zibigi who stole the third necklace from my man Kayl's corpse."

"Lies, lies, lies," shouted the Fox. "I don't know anybody with that name."

"Sh...sh..." The Chief raised a finger to his nose. "We will listen to you too, Nergal. Just keep quiet now."

Siwa continued. "I have reasons to believe that the brown pieces, which I thought were 'Stone dye', are actually opium."

The Fox stood up and looked at his cronies. They jumped up on their feet and started abusing Siwa.

"Nergal," the Chief said, "I warn you that the Council would be compelled to take strict action if the sanctity of the Council hall is not upheld."

Unfazed, the Fox stared at the Chief. The Chief stared back. The Fox gradually lowered himself in his seat. As if taking the cue, his supporters too calmed down.

"Merchant Saqra," said the Chief, "why do you believe that the material that you sent to Zibigi was opium and nothing else?"

"For two reasons, Honourable Council – a rhinoceros that accidentally ate it lost its senses, and, Lady Ella could procure opium from several inns and taverns on the country road. In all likelihood, it came from Nergal's storehouse."

Ella got up opening her leather purse, and picked out from it three or four yellow sachets. She passed them to the clerk. The Council members smelt and felt the contents, and one even took a pinch and put it on his tongue.

"Assuming that the material in this sachet is opium, how can you blame Nergal for it?" The Chief asked Ella.

"Honourable Council, we have information that such yellow sachets are used only in Nergal's storehouse."

Sam saw the Fox desperately waving his hands to attract the Chief's attention. The Chief looked at him. "Yes, Nergal?"

"The Meluhhan merchant as well as the woman are lying, Honourable Council," Nergal said, wailing like a dog beaten with a staff. "Both of them, along with my stable-boy and the Meluhhan captain, have plotted against me."

"The Council takes a note of your contention, Nergal," the Chief said in a reassuring tone. "We would also hear the guards and the innkeepers tomorrow before we pass the judgement."

On the following day, the Head Guard presented a roll of bark to the Chief. "This is the list of material which we found upon searching Nergal's storehouse."

Five witnesses were filed in before the Elders. Sam recognized two men clad in silk gowns as the owners of the apple and the pomegranate orchards which flanked Nergal's storehouse. Two men dressed in decent cotton gowns, were introduced as traders who were returning from the port to the town and had consented to be witnesses. The fifth was a scared little man who said that he had opened a new tavern in the town, and had been to the storehouse in search of opium which many of his young customers demanded.

The Head Guard and his assistants climbed the platform to display before the Elders a sack full of sewn yellow sachets, and a wooden pilon. However, what the Chief and other members keenly studied was a torn piece of jute cloth with the seal of the port of Alatinam, and bearing the words 'Merchant Zibigi, Urim'.

"That is my writing," cried Siwa Saqra. He wrote the three words on a piece of bark, and the Council unanimously agreed that the handwriting on the seized jute cloth was his.

The Fox shouted hoarsely, "I deny the charge, Chief. All those objects have been planted in my storehouse. There's a massive conspiracy against me."

"Honourable Council," the Head Guard said, bowing low. "Nergal keeps one man on duty during the day as well as the night to guard the storehouse. How could anyone either remove or place anything there?"

"I have no doubt, Honourable Council," said the Fox, "that my employees have been heavily bribed by my enemies to enable them put all that material in the storehouse."

"Nergal," the Chief said serenely, "either produce the evidence to prove your point, or keep quiet." Ignoring the Fox's grumble, he looked at the Head Guard.

On the Head Guard's signal, eight men – everyone of them carrying a protruding belly – were led in. Among them Sam recognized the sleepy owner of the tavern where Kayl was murdered. The Chief summoned Sam, and he pointed out four inn-keepers who he had seen buying the yellow sachets from Nergal's storehouse. Ella identified the heavy-eyed tavern owner, and one more inn-keeper who had sold her the yellow sachets. The Chief ordered to release the remaining two, and seeing them running out, the Council hall was filled with spontaneous laughter.

All the six confessed that they sold powdered opium packed in yellow sachets, and that they procured it from Nergal's storehouse.

Just at that time, Sam noticed several youngsters craning their necks towards the back of the hall. Following their gaze, he saw a tall fair lady clad in a *varati* about to take a seat in the last row. "Ann," he gasped under breath. Siwa had informed that she was not expected in Babili for another week as she had decided to spend some time in Urim.

As the Elders huddled together for consultation, peoples' murmurs gradually rose in intensity. Ultimately, the noise became so loud that one council member broke away from the rest and raised both his arms at the public. With his fingers, he conveyed that they needed a little more time to announce the verdict.

At last, the Chief came to the fore, and the hall instantly turned silent. "Considering all the evidence provided to us, the Council of Elders holds Nergal guilty of impor–"

Cutting the elderly man's speech mid-way, came a sharp noise that sounded like a cane being struck on a wooden surface. Everybody turned in that direction, and saw the Fox standing with both hands on the waist. He spoke in a raucous voice, "The Council should examine some documents before it sits in judgement over me."

As he climbed the steps of the platform, he nodded at one of his men. Soon a porter hurried into the hall, carrying a huge sack on his back and placed it carefully before the Elders. The Fox fished out several hard baked clay tablets from the sack and passed them on to the Council members. "Respected Elders," he said with a smirk, "these documents prove that each of you has given permission to send helpless women to Meluhha."

The Chief looked up from the clay tablet in his hands. "Certainly we have – to enable them to marry Meluhhan gentlemen and settle down over there. What's wrong in that?"

"Absolutely nothing," the Fox said tongue in cheek. "Since none of you holds either ethics or conscience."

"Nergal," the Chief spoke sternly, "you are attacking the dignity of the Council."

The Fox glowered. "I accuse you all, the so-called 'Elders', of lining your mansions with gold by selling young Babilian women to Meluhhan brothels." Two Council members rose up to protest. "Aren't these documents proof enough of your black deeds?" the Fox raised several clay tablets in his hands. A murmur passed through the group like a draught of chilly wind.

"Nergal," said the Chief, and Sam discerned incredulity on his face. "We signed in good faith upon your request as a trustee of the destitute women's home."

"If I requested you to jump into a well, Chief, would you do it in good faith?" said the Fox grinning. "I might as well be hung for a sheep as a lamb. However, if I just reveal this information outside the Council hall, the Babilians would throw your entire lot into the Purattu."

The Fox's cronies, who had filled the Ziggurat allowing hardly any space for other citizens, raised a hue and a cry. To a person unaware about their affiliation, it would have appeared that the public opinion in Babili had veered against the Elders. The Fox sneered. "Therefore, if you gentlemen wish to save your skin, announce your withdrawal from the Council of Elders right away."

Sam saw Siwa Saqra's head shaking in dismay, and the Captain's lips fluttering.

It seemed that several Council members wanted to declare the Fox not guilty in Siwa's complaint, and drop the curtain over the matter of Babilian women in Meluhha. On the other hand, the Chief and some others seemed to be arguing that they should not give in to Nergal's blackmail, and ought to put all the facts before the people of Babili. Their discussion turned into an argument and pandemonium broke out in the Council hall. The Fox watched the happenings merrily.

That was when a firm feminine voice pierced the din: "Excuse me, Chief."

Sam, who was watching the Fox, was perplexed by a sudden change in his countenance. It reminded him of a cat which had landed on a batch of pottery just out of the furnace. Sam turned to look behind, and saw Ann coming to the fore.

"I am Anlil, a woman gravely affected by the subject of these proceedings, and I request the Elders' Council to permit me to speak," Ann announced, walking to the centre.

"Anlil!" Sam murmured.

Ann continued: "The trade in opium is just half the story, Chief. From where did Nergal obtain the funds to finance it?"

The Fox protested. "Intruders shouldn't be permitted to waste the precious time of Babili's honourable Council." He made brisk movement of his hands at the guards, saying, "Don't keep standing; act."

Not a single guard moved. They glanced at the Head Guard, who remained standing at attention. Several of the Fox's cohorts took upon themselves the guards' duty, and closed in on Ann.

"Nergal," bellowed the Chief, getting up from his seat with a vigour that raised the brows of even his colleagues. "Don't take the law in your hands."

The Head Guard swiftly pulled out his dagger, and held it against the Fox's throat. "Arrest the rabble," he commanded. Immediately the guards rounded up the villains threatening Ann and marched them out of the Council hall.

"Yes, lady," said the Chief, turning to Ann. "What do you know about the funding of Nergal's opium trade?"

"Thank you," said Ann, and bowed. "Ironically, Nergal himself is neck-deep in the flesh trade for which he accuses the Honourable Council." She narrated how she had been lured into going to Meluhha, how a companion from Magan had been sold to a brothel, and how she had overheard a voice instructing Agent Jittan. She swore that she recognized the voice as that of Zibigi alias Biggie when she met him in Urim a few days ago.

Siwa confirmed to the Council that the payment for what he thought was 'Stone dye', was regularly made to him by a man named Jittan who hailed from Village Chendur. He said that Jittan had been introduced to him by Biggie as his agent in Meluhha.

After some deliberation with the Council members, the Chief got up. "Listen, O Babilians," he said in his whiny voice, "listen to King Shulgi's justice, imparted by the learned Council of Elders. As I announced earlier in the matter of opium trade, the Council of Elders holds Nergal guilty." He paused and drank water before continuing. "An additional matter is that Nergal's underlings lured Sumérian women to go to Meluhha, where they were sold to brothels."

A cry of 'shame, shame,' went up in the air. The Fox stood like a statue staring at the floor. The Chief went on, "In both the inhuman activities of opium trade as well as trafficking, Zibigi co-ordinated with the Meluhhans and is found guilty. He is sentenced to twenty flogs in the square of Babili as soon as he is arrested."

At that moment, Sam happened to look at Ann. He thought he saw a faint smile passing over her face like the flash of a meteor.

The Chief drank from a beaker of water again. Then looking at the public he said, "The Main Accused, Nergal, is found guilty of running narcotic as well as flesh trade. The Council of Elders unanimously considers this as the rarest of rare crimes and sentences Nergal to the Ordeal of the wild bull."

30 THE FINALE

Sam manoeuvred through the crowd that was descending the Ziggurat steps. He caught up with Ann who had hired a donkey cart, and was looking out for Ella and Velli.

"I saw both of them leaving the hall long before you did," said Sam, jumping on the cart and extending a hand to her. "Ann, which of your parents expired first?" he asked as the cart started rolling.

She looked at him incredulously, but recovered quickly. "They were killed by robbers."

"In Magan? About twenty years ago?"

"How do you know?"

"Anlil, my sister!"

"Sammu?" she shrieked. "Sammu – Sam – Samasin! Oh *Sîn*, why didn't that strike me earlier?"

The teenaged cart boy looked behind, a somewhat perplexed.

"What happened after that fateful day in Magan?" Sam asked Ann as he tapped the boy's shoulder and pointed to an approaching camel cart.

"Some people took me to Urim and handed me over to Uncle Gazkir and Auntie."

"And how did you land up in Meluhha, Ann – I mean, Anlil?"

"Auntie died and Uncle remarried. Step-aunt made me so miserable that I ran away from home. The rest, you heard at the Ziggurat."

"One misfortune following another – it summarizes your life till you found Tall Yali."

"Yes, and what happened to you after Magan, Sammu?"

"I returned to Sumér with a kind Akkadian who adopted me. Working as a camel boy, once I accompanied the Fox and his family – Ribba might be about three then. Later Lady Ella got me hired as a stable boy. You know what happened thereafter."

Ann gaped at Sam as if he had descended from the sky. "Do you really mean that first the sun and then the moon waned precisely when you were facing the wild bull?"

"I told you so long ago, didn't I?"

"I thought you were boasting," she said, with doubt still lurking in her eyes. There was a long pause during which Sam wondered about the circumstances which had brought them together.

Soon they reached Ella's house, where Velli met them at the gate. Looking at her face, their smiles waned.

"It's Sister Ella. She's troubled about Ribba," Velli said wrenching her hands. "So far, she has kept him in the dark about our complaint against the Fox. She is extremely worried that it won't be long before he comes to know about his father's sentence. She told me, 'The mere thought of how the Ordeal would traumatize my child is killing me.' "

Velli was in tears, and Ann too looked as if she would not hold back for long.

"Perhaps Lady Ella and Ribba could go out of Babili for a few months till people forget the Ordeal," Sam said. He did not sound very convinced by his own suggestion.

"She's prepared to leave Babili for even a year," said Velli. "But, Sam, one can't wish away the fact. The Babilians would remember Ribba's father by the Ordeal."

As the three entered the garden, they heard Siwa's voice behind. "What's the matter, Sam?" he asked. "Why do the girls look sad?"

Sam apprised him about Ella's dilemma as they all walked towards the nearest olive tree in the garden. Siwa was lost in thoughts for quite some time before he spoke. "I am not familiar with the laws of Babili," he said, "but we should find out if any alternate punishment is possible instead of the Ordeal of the wild bull."

"Lady Ella would surely know if there was one," Sam said. "She used to discuss, and even debate such matters with Chief Bel."

"Velli, Ann, both of you meet her and find out," Siwa said.

"We'll wait for you here."

As the ladies withdrew, Siwa informed Sam that Captain Paravar had agreed to join him on a journey to Lagaš. Siwa wanted to thank King Gudea's minister, whose statement had helped considerably in strengthening their complaint. Siwa intended to present to the Minister the three gold necklaces which the latter had handed over to the Captain upon realizing that it was stolen jewellery.

"By the way, Sam," said Siwa, shifting his position to watch the main door of the house, "you once told me that in Sumér, divorced women could marry again."

"Yes, they can," Sam said emphatically, wondering whether his father-in-law had had an eye on a Sumérian woman.

"Tell me, Sam, do you think that Lady Ella might consider remarrying?" Siwa asked.

"Probably," Sam said, raking memory. "She casually told Velli that as Ribba grew, she was finding it difficult to deal with his tantrums. She said, 'A father figure is essential for a boy entering manhood.' "

Siwa's face lit up. "She's absolutely right," he said emphatically. Then he turned serious. Sam smiled politely, having realized that Siwa was trying to hide his excitement.

This was no time for match-making. Sam expressed his reading of Ella's mental state as described by Velli. "Lady Ella is very worried about the Fox's misdeeds embarrassing the boy. She might even seek to leave Babili."

"There, the door has opened," Siwa said. "The girls are back."

Both Velli and Ann were talking amiably as they came, and Sam saw a ray of hope. Velli apprised them that the Elders held the authority to change a sentence from the Ordeal of the wild bull to either an exile or a life imprisonment.

"I am afraid," said Ann, "that a fiend like the Fox, if exiled, would re-establish his web elsewhere. Suppose he goes to Tawi, the Sumérian women would attain safety, but the Tawian women would be exposed to his wiles."

Siwa nodded. "Yes, Nergal is one of those rare men who are like a dog's tail; they can never straighten up."

"Then let's go for the only other option," Sam said. "Let the Fox spend the rest of his life in King Shulgi's prison."

"What's the procedure that we need to follow?"

"Lady Ella told us that the complainants just need to request the Council to consider one of the other punishments," said Velli. "Nine out of ten times the Elders respect such a wish."

"What are we waiting for, Sam?" Siwa got up. "Ann, please join us, for the Fox has affected your life more than ours."

Sam entered the guest room hand in hand with Velli. Siwa Saqra was arranging his diadem before a copper mirror on the wall, and they saw his image smiling. As he turned to greet them, Sam said, "Father, don't you think that a piece of steatite, however expensive, doesn't go well in a golden crown?"

Siwa looked from Sam to Velli and again at Sam. Their smiles seemed to perplex him. "Well?"

Sam reached into a pocket in his gown and brought out the *Harsag Zalazalag*. "I wish to present this to the man who gave me his daughter, who is more valuable than any diamond on the earth."

Velli giggled.

Siwa beamed. "Those words, Sam, are what every man yearns to hear from his son-in-law."

Just as he held the diamond before the steatite inlay to show them how it would look, in walked Ella, carrying a big silver plate in both her hands. "Celebrate your successful visit to our country, Merchant Saqra."

Siwa grinned. He picked up a big piece of sweetmeat and shoved it into his mouth. "Delishioush," he managed to speak with the mouthful and shot out his hand for more.

Sam was closely watching Ella, and he thought Siwa's spontaneous response elated her. As she offered the sweetmeats to them, she whispered to Velli, "Have you spoken to him?"

Siwa heard her, and answered instead. "If you mean the rehabilitation of Sumérian women living in Meluhha, she has." He produced a piece of silk cloth from the fold of his attire and wiped his lips. "Lady Ella, I'm so disturbed by my role in the nefarious activity that I haven't had sound sleep since Ann exposed the Fox. I want to make amends by putting my time and silver after the cause."

"Great," Ella exclaimed.

Sam nudged Velli.

Siwa said, "My first task would be to get the Gandharan trader detained as soon as he arrives in Muenduru City. Then I'd visit Chendur Village, and get Agent Jittan arrested with his gang. I'll collect the details about all their customers, the brothel owners. I'd like to get the entire lot hanged."

"While that is important," Ella put in, "have you given a thought to the unfortunate victims?"

"I'll track down all the Sumérian women who Agent Jittan and his predecessor sold. I'd ensure that each lady, according to her wish, is either sent back here or assisted to settle in Meluhha. But, Lady Ella –" Siwa broke off. She looked at him with wide eyes.

"That's a gigantic task, isn't it Velli?" said Sam.

"Exactly," Siwa said, throwing a grateful look at him. "I can't take up the work alone." There was a tremble in his voice. "I need someone like-minded to help me, Lady Ella."

Sam imagined that Ella shivered.

"Could you join me – to – to Meluhha?" asked Siwa.

Never had Sam heard Siwa sounding so timid. Ella fidgeted with the plate in her hands. A sharp pinch on Sam's arm made him turn to his wife and wink.

Ella's lips were parting when there was a clamour in the corridor, and she held herself. The boys burst in the room with their arms interlocked. Siwa looked irritated.

Red Muruku went straight to him and seized his wrist. "Father, can Ribo come with us?" he asked. A smile swept Siwa's face as he translated it to Ella. She turned to her son.

"Yes, *Ama-ugu*, may I go?" said Ribba. "They have a colt and a mare, so I won't miss my riding practice."

"But Ribo," Ella said, swiftly glancing at Siwa. "I'd feel very lonely if you were to leave me."

Siwa happily translated what she said to Red Muruku. The little boy grasped Ella's hand with both of his and looked up into her eyes. "Why don't you too come along with us, *Amma*? *Ama-ugu*?"

Sam doubted whether Ella understood anything except the last word, but that alone conveyed the mother-less child's deepest feelings. She dropped on her knees and drew the little boy in embrace. Siwa translated Red Muruku's words and hearing them, Ribba hopped and danced. "Yes, *Ama-ugu*, let's both go to Meluhha."

Siwa looked hopefully at Ella. She rose slowly. Her eyes were moist as she raised her face to him.

Sam and Velli hugged as they watched Siwa's broad hand slipping into Ella's, and her tender fingers gradually grasping it.

*

PLACE NAMES IN THE NARRATIVE

Alatinam* – Fictional name for Indus Valley site of Allahdino, 40 Km. east of Karachi in Pakistan. Now land-locked, Allahdino was a port during the Bronze Age.

Babili – Babylon, now Al Hillah city in Iraq

Chendur* – Fictional name for Chanhu-daro site, 10 Km. south of Nawabshah in Pakistan

Dholavira – Site 93 Km. north-west of Rapar in western India

Dilmun – Present day Bahrain as mentioned in tablets discovered on Mesopotamian sites

Elam – Persia, now Iran, as mentioned in Sumérian texts

Gandhara – Afghanistan as it is mentioned in ancient Hindu and Buddhist scriptures

Gangevell* – Fictional name for Ganweriwala site, 50 Km. south-west of Bahawalpur in Pakistan

Harappa – Site 24 Km. west of Sahiwal in Pakistan. Discovered by British archaeologists when they found ancient bricks being used by local railway contractors

Kalibangan – Site 33 Km. south-west of Hanumangarh in northern India

Kochi* – Fictional name for Kot Diji site, 25 Km. south of Khairpur in Pakistan. Archaeologists excavated a second burnt-down settlement under the top layer of the ancient site.

Lagaš – Lagash, now Tell al-Hiba site, 22 Km. east of Ash Shatrah in Iraq

Lothal – Site 85 Km. south-west of Ahmedabad in western India. Now land-locked, Lothal is the oldest port in the world excavated by archaeologists.

Lower Sea – Persian Gulf as mentioned in Mesopotamian tablets

Magan – Present day Oman as mentioned in Mesopotamian tablets

Meluhha – Indus Valley Civilization as mentioned in Mesopotamian tablets

Muenduru* – Fictional name for Mohenjo-daro site, 28 Km. south of Larkana in Pakistan

Ngirsu – Tell Telloh site in Iraq

Nibru – Nippur, now Nuffar site in Iraq

Purattu – Sumérian name for River Euphrates

Saraswathi – As the present River Ghaggar-Hakra was known in ancient Hindu Scriptures. It flowed perennially in the Bronze Age.

Sindhu – River Indus in Pakistan as it is mentioned in ancient Hindu scriptures

Sindhu Sea – Fictional name for the Arabian Sea

Sumér – Older name for Mesopotamia

Sutantoru* – Fictional name for Sutkagen Dor site near Pakistan's border with Iran

Tawi – Older name for Ancient Egypt

Urim – Ur, now Tell al-Muqqayar site which is 240 Km. from the Persian Gulf. Abraham's native place in the Holy Bible, it was a sea port according to Mesopotamian tablets.

Zimbir – Sippar, now Tell Abu Hibbah site, 30 Km. south-west of Baghdad in Iraq

*Names of Indus Valley sites as known during 3rd millennium BC have changed over time. Several of them are influenced by cultural changes in the Indian sub-continent since then. Six such names are tweaked to suit the pronunciations of major languages which have descended from Proto Dravidian viz., Kannada, Malayalam, Tamil and Telugu. That is done considering a hypothesis of one school of researchers that Proto Dravidian was spoken in Indus Valley Civilization.

GLOSSARY OF SUMÉRIAN & TAMIL WORDS

A-la-la – Exclamation, often of joy, exuberance (Sumérian)
Ama-ugu – Mother (Sumérian)
Amma – Mother (Tamil)
Belum – Lord (Sumérian)
Da-na – Unit of distance equivalent to 10.8 Kilometre (Sumérian)
Ga-ti – Let me live (Sumérian)
Harsag Zalazalag – The Peak which emits Brilliance (Sumérian)
Kavintu – Master (Tamil)
Mu-eš – Unit of time equivalent to 4 minutes (Sumérian)
Mulla Xul – The Evil Devil (Sumérian)
Šamaš – The Sun God, also the patron deity of Babylon (Sumérian)
Sîn – The Moon God, also the patron deity of Ur (Sumérian)
Tanni – Drink derived from Palm tree (Tamil)
Varati – Long piece of cloth wrapped on body by women (Tamil)
Vesti – Piece of unstitched cloth worn by men (Tamil)

Sources:

1. Sumérian Words and their English Translation. http://history-world.org/sumerianwords2.htm
2. Sumérian Dictionary. http://www.ping.de/sites/systemcoder/necro/info/sumerian.htm
3. Halloran, John A. Sumérian Lexicon. http://www.sumerian.org/sumerian.pdf
4. Tamil Lexicon. http://webapps.uni-koeln.de/tamil/
5. Freelang Tamil-English and English-Tamil online dictionary. http://www.freelang.net/online/tamil.php

ABOUT THE AUTHOR

Vasant Davé is an electrical engineer from the University of Bombay, and he has provided Industrial Market Research services to corporate clients in India, Australia, China, Germany, Hong Kong, Israel, Singapore, the UK and the USA. His work called for extensive travelling, which helped him to address a deep interest in archaeological sites.

During one of his frequent tours he happened to visit Lothal in Western India, and was awed to learn that it had been a sea-port conducting maritime trade with distant Mesopotamia during the Bronze Age. Subsequently he visited other Indus Valley archaeological sites and had had discussions with authorities on the subject.

Studying Mesopotamia, he found that 4,000 years ago women were more emancipated than their great great grand-daughters are today in what is now the Middle East. Gradually, a rough plot started emerging in his mind revolving around trade and cultural links between two of the most ancient civilizations in the world.

After retirement in 2008, Vasant took up writing *Trade winds to Meluhha* and completed it three years later. He has narrated his experience in an e-booklet, *How I wrote a Pre-Historic novel*, which might be of interest to those readers .wanting to know how a storyline evolved from cold archaeological evidence.

Vasant could be contacted on the following links:
e-mail: twtmeluhha@gmail.com
Facebook: http://www.facebook.com/BronzeAgeNovel
Twitter: https://twitter.com/Meluhha
Author website: http://vasantdave.weebly.com/index.html

10095014R00136

Printed in Great Britain
by Amazon